The Ship

The Ship

by Jabra I. Jabra

Translated and Introduced by Adnan Haydar
and Roger Allen

A THREE CONTINENTS BOOK
LYNNE RIENNER PUBLISHERS
BOULDER & LONDON

THE SHIP

© Adnan Haydar and Roger Allen, 1985

A Three Continents Book

Published in the United States of America by
Lynne Rienner Publishers, Inc.
1800 30th Street, Boulder, Colorado 80301

ISBN: 0-89410-328-8
ISBN: 0-89410-329-6 (pbk)
LC No. 82-50880

Cover design by Max Winkler
© Three Continents Press 1985

For Jabra I. Jabra:

*For those whose love
made this ship possible*

For the translators:

For Tarik, Samir, Timothy and Mariana

A Note on the Translation

We have alluded in our comments below to the deep concern which *The Ship* shows for the underlying issues behind the tragedy of the Palestinian people in recent decades. One might suggest that there is a strong link between the personae of the speakers and the creator of this novel. These features have therefore impinged upon the process of translation, and they are present in the resulting work in English.

Jabra himself has read and given his approval of this translation as being faithful to his intentions. That does not, of course, absolve the translators themselves of any responsibility. However, certain points might be mentioned at this juncture. Jabra is one of the Arab world's best known prose poets, and that fact is abundantly evident in the level of discourse to be encountered in the present work. Some sentences are of considerable length and elaboration, containing poetic devices more characteristic of the poetic mode. Such is the essence of Jabra's novelistic style, and no attempt has been made to change or remove it in this translation. The translators have also attempted to reproduce the effect of the differing voices of the narrators in this work by each translating all the chapters of one of the two narrators before giving the results to the other translator for changes and revisions. A difference in voice between the two principal narrators is the inevitable and indeed desired result.

The Ship then is not intended to be "light reading" in Arabic, nor in its English version. However, it is our belief that it gives cogent and beautiful expression to one of the world's greatest contemporary tragedies. As such, it is an important monument in world literature.

*   *   *   *   *

This translation has benefitted from the comments of a number of readers, among whom we would like to mention in particular Dr. Michael Beard and Mary Allen. They have made a series of valuable suggestions concerning both translation and style which have been incorporated into the text. In transliterating proper names in this translation, we have adopted the practice used by Jabra himself in his writings in English, namely of using the transliterations preferred by Arabs themselves wherever possible rather than a standardized system such as that of the Library of Congress. The list of major characters which now follows will serve as a guide. The names as used in this translation will be found in the left-hand column; the Library of Congress transliteration of the same names is in the right-hand column:

Isam Salman	ʻIṣām Salmān
Wadi Assaf	Waḍīʻ ʻAssāf
Emilia Farnesi	
Luma Abdul Ghani	Lumā ʻAbd al-Ghanī
Falih Haseeb	Fāliḥ Ḥasīb
Shawkat Abu Samra	Shawkat Abū Samrāʼ
Jacqueline Durand	
Fernando Gomez	
Yusuf Haddad	Yūsuf al-Ḥaddād
Mahmud Rashid	Maḥmūd al-Rāshid
Maha al-Hajj	Mahā al-Ḥājj
Fayiz Atallah	Fāyiz ʻAtallāh

Contents

Introduction

It is an irony that the Arabs, who have bequeathed to a fascinated West one of the greatest story collections of all times, *A Thousand and One Nights,* have not themselves developed a novelistic art that the West could emulate, and that instead they sought Western inspiration for the development of the Arabic novel. This is not the place to discuss this question in detail. Suffice it to say however that the relegation by Arabic critics of *A Thousand and One Nights* to the level of popular entertainment and the concomitant failure of Arab readers to appreciate its value as literature are two of the most significant factors in the reluctance of Arab novelists to tap its limitless resources.

As a result of these attitudes, it has become customary for critics of Arabic novels to attribute any development in Arabic fiction to Western prototypes, often reducing the works of a good novelist to merely derivative status. In particular, various commentaries on Jabra Ibrahim Jabra's *The Ship* invoke the specters of Faulkner, Durrell and Joyce on the technique of the multiple narrator, thus overlooking the more direct influence of these sophisticated techniques in *A Thousand and One Nights.* While we would agree with Harold Bloom that the very act of creativity may be founded on the experience of influence (merely in the act of breathing we participate in the authority of our predecessors), we nevertheless see in Jabra's works such influence transformed into a totally new identity that is typically his own.

Jabra Ibrahim Jabra is among the most versatile litterateurs writing in the Middle East today. Born in Bethlehem in 1919, he was educated in Jerusalem and Cambridge, England (where he studied English literature). He is well known as a poet, novelist, translator and literary critic, and also devotes much attention to art in a creative and critical capacity. Forced to leave his homeland in 1948, Jabra moved to Iraq where he still lives today.

To date, Jabra has published four novels: *A Cry in a Long Night* (*Surakh fi Layl Tawil*, 1955); *Hunters in a Narrow Street* (in English, 1960); *The Ship* (*Al-Safina*, 1970); and *In Search of Walid Masoud* (*Al-Bahth 'an Walid Mas'ud*, 1978). In all four the main characters belong to a fraternity of writers, professors, artists, architects, upper middle-class socialites, political activists, remnants of aristocratic families, and nouveaux riches, all of them constantly defining their positions vis-à-vis a reality they want to escape from and a new order they dream up, aim for, and suffer from, only to find out that the escape is merely illusory and the dream impossible. To paraphrase Georg Lukacs in *The Theory of the Novel*, the world of these novels has been abandoned by God. A whole order of things has fallen apart. Men and women live in frustration, indulging in the body—their only protection against their own agonies—and celebrating life to the fullest in order to still the angst of their souls. The characters may rail against the soul, but only from a painful inability to unite soul and body and achieve a sense of identity. They are therefore distinct from the Faulknerian characters who are, as André Gide observes in his essay on "The American novelist," without souls, and who lead a precarious life completely immune to rational choice. Jabra's characters are different precisely because their choices are exercised despite the inevitable suffering which always ensues and the realization that the future possibility of salvation is there, but only as a possibility. There is something pathetically human, for example, about Husain's unsuccessful attempt to rescue Samiha the prostitute (in *Hunters*) from her life in the brothel, or the naturalistic depiction in *A Cry in a Long Night* of Amin Samma's experiences during a flood when the hovels of the helpless poor are inundated and children are drowned. There is also the constant agony of intellectuals, such as Adnan in *Hunters*, Mahmud Rashid in *The Ship*, and Walid Masoud, who suffer in body as they try to resurrect in their world a dormant conscience that looks evil squarely in the eye, a soul that aims at uprooting it. "You have taught me this word 'the body,' " says Wisal addressing Walid Masoud in a monologue. "That is how you made me fall into your sin: inflaming the body and then searching for the embers in the soul." The body as a way to the soul, the soul as salvation for the body, sex and love as vitality of flesh and mind, these are some of the issues that preoccupy Jabra's characters.

The setting is in the Arab world—Baghdad, Beirut, Ramallah, Bethlehem, Jerusalem, any Arab city—portrayed in its most tragic

4

aspects against the background of the fall of Palestine. Palestine is the microcosm of the Arabs' defeat, of their failure to determine their destiny in their own lands. The fall of Palestine is not an incidental event; it is the tragic fall of the whole Arab world, a product and a result of Arab acquiescence in a reality before which they are helpless. Palestine is the land, the soul to be reclaimed, the soul that has been desecrated, and the impossible and yet ultimate dream of Wadi Assaf in *The Ship* and Walid Masoud. Only by embracing the body of Palestine, its trees and rocks (as the obsession of these two characters makes clear), will soul wed body and body soul.

The city in *A Cry in a Long Night* has no name; it is an image of any Arab city, of the reality of the Arab world, a world filled with poverty, dishonesty, remnants of defunct aristocratic glories, an equivocal world of inaction and stasis. For Jabra's heroes, however, it is not a place of boredom, but of things breaking down. Life in the city is threatened, and so the individual must pit himself against it and engage its problems despite the hatred that he may feel towards it (best reflected in Towfiq's railings in *Hunters* against the inhumanity of cities). The city as it stands is the damning justification of the tragedy of the Palestinians and all Arabs, but failure to address its problems would be tantamount to acquiescing in defeat. This means in effect that the artist's eyes are the conscience of his society, an issue which Jabra never tires of addressing.

Tradition in its confining and outmoded values lives on in the world of Jabra's novels and perpetuates its painful reality, erasing the boundaries between the past and the present. The tribalism for which Wadi Assaf admonishes his friends in *The Ship,* the corrupt aristocratic past that Inayat Hanim is trying to resurrect in *A Cry in a Long Night* (presumably to understand better the changes that have taken place), the imprisoned girl, Sulafa, the Lady of Shalott of the Tigris whose father attempts to marry her to Towfiq against her will in *Hunters* in order to preserve his own social status, the crime of honor, the murder of Azima by her brother, Yousef, and the consequent light sentence which he receives; all these things represent the constant impingement of past on present, rendering the latter helpless and outmoded.

This is indeed a pessimistic outlook on life in general, a long night of agony with only a faint and deliberately suppressed promise of a new dawn. There is the burning of the palace and the whole history of an aristocratic family in *A Cry in a Long Night,*

5

but we are still left with the impression that the life of loss and inanity continues, the social ills persist, and the people in the city are still "searching for an ending to a long night and for a beginning of a new life." Likewise, we are afforded a glimpse of hope in *Hunters* in the murder of Sulafa's father who was at once her jailer and the enemy of change and social strife, and also in the escape of the murderer, Adnan, the symbol of such strife and change. Yet here, too, the feeling is one of lingering ills that one death cannot alleviate, despite the optimistic note struck at the end:

> In all the long months that followed, while we waited, while the Adnans and the Husains and the Towfiqs impaled themselves on rows of political and social swords, the crows and the kites in squawking formations flew over the palm groves of a slowly refurbished land.

In *The Ship*, too, it is made clear that escape is useless; Luma and Isam are finally together, but their problems remain, and the tribalism that separated them in the first place has not been uprooted. Even Wadi, who finally succeeds in persuading Maha to live with him in Jerusalem, is far from resolving his own problem, since the reader of the 1970s knows quite well that Jerusalem is occupied and that Palestinians are barred from returning to their land. Even the strong suggestion that Walid Masoud has joined the freedom fighters and is involved in forays against the Zionists remains as an individual gesture which, if anything, reveals the chasm which exists between Walid and the people whom he knew, loved, and hated, the people who represent the various facets of his personality.

What Jabra the artist is doing is exposing the sufferings of the intellectual in a world that does not understand him, the plight of the poor in a world in which they are helpless, and the agony of all in a world that tramples their dreams and fashions their destiny, oblivious to the powerful protestations of soul and conscience.

* * * * *

There is in Jabra's novels a constant preoccupation with form. He is not so much concerned with the novel as reflection, as mirror, as successful story, as he is with choosing those highly charged moments in life which he then organizes to capture in one moment's epiphany, a totality that transcends the moments themselves. The story may cover a day in the life of a writer (as in

A Cry in a Long Night), a week on a cruise in the Mediterranean (*The Ship*), a year in the experience of a college professor (*Hunters*), or time enough to play a tape and measure its impact on the people who have listened to it, bringing to bear upon it half a century of important events in the life of the hero. There is nothing exciting about the circumstances themselves; it is what they reveal about their world that is ultimately important. The technique of multiple narrators and the expert use of internal monologues afford the novelist such a revelation. Amin Samma's monologues which come as digressions during conversations with friends in a coffee house take us back to the hero's childhood, to a world which invades the present and makes it pertinent and real. In *Hunters* Jameel Farran's experience of life in Baghdad, with all its contradictions and miseries among victimized people who wander about aimlessly, is made credible through the hero's experience under Zionist occupation and terror in Palestine where the innocent fall victim to human hatred and greed. Likewise the agony of Isam Salman, Wadi Assaf, Falih, Mahmud and Luma in *The Ship* becomes, through the many monologues and digressions, a replay of past agony, an inescapable destiny that only the past can articulate. Yet Jabra's concern with form is nowhere more apparent than in *In Search of Walid Masoud*. The novel starts with a mystery, and the characters and the readers are made privy to what appears to be an incoherent jumble of words recorded on a tape. The words become more and more elusive every time an attempt is made to make them yield sense. We the readers are drawn into the mystery, forced to become involved in it, as we watch the characters' responses or lack of response to the voice from the tape, or, shall we say, to the voice from their own past. The reconstruction then takes place through successive chapter-long monologues, each character revealing a fragment of the hero's life and along with it present and past prejudices, weaknesses, equivocations and agony in each individual character. Walid Masoud ultimately emerges as the sum total of the other characters, their past, present and future. Like a mystery, however, the novel ends without resolution, and the search for Walid Masoud, the Arab, the Palestinian, continues.

In *The Ship* and *A Cry in a Long Night* the plot begins at a point close to its temporal ending, as if to emphasize that time in its chronological capacity is irrelevant. Time is not on the characters' side; it will not resolve their problems or assuage their fears. What counts is the moment out of time at which the past is liberated in the present in order to usher in the possibility of the future. In *In Search of Walid Masoud* such a moment is the mysterious disappearance of Walid Masoud, who never quite leaves the stage, but whose absence gives rise to existential queries about the meaning of the lives of the other characters. After the plot unfolds, we the readers become convinced that Walid could only "define the question," as he puts it cryptically at the end of his tape, through martyrdom in his own land. The novel starts at the end with the disappearance of Walid, and it does so precisely because the end is that moment out of time which the other characters (with the possible exception of Wisal) are tragically incapable of reaching. In *Hunters* the time of the story extends over a year, but between the destitution of a Palestinian professor forced out of his land by a foreign occupying force and the drab reality of Baghdad, where the roots of the tragedy of Palestine are evident everywhere, the present becomes the justification of the past, the past the justification of the present.

* * * * *

Even though most of the events in *The Ship* take place during a cruise at sea, the overriding issue which highlights the metaphysical yearnings of the major characters is land. In Isam's case the land is an imagined enemy which drives a wedge between him and Luma and compels him to escape. His decision to sever his relationship from his land is a voluntary one. Wadi, on the other hand, has been driven from his land, and, as a result, has lost an integral part of his identity. Ostensibly the ship is moving away from both Baghdad and Palestine, and yet at the end of the cruise both Wadi and Isam are closer to their land. For there can be no escape from one's roots; as Wadi puts it admirably: "Land, land, that's the secret in your life . . . the land will drag you back to it, no matter how much you resist, no matter how far you go."

One of the most moving sections of the novel describes Wadi's childhood in Jerusalem, where the tragedy of Palestine is depicted in vivid and painful detail through the great love which unites Wadi and Fayiz and separates them through an act of even greater love, martyrdom. Jabra's intense affection for the scenes of his own childhood brings reality into fiction. The moving descriptions of his house and the environs of Jerusalem which we

8

find in an article on Jerusalem* have an uncanny resemblance to Fayiz Atallah's house as described in *The Ship;* the various districts of the city in which Jabra describes himself as living during the fighting of 1948 form the backdrop to Wadi's graphic portrayal in the novel. Reality and fiction coalesce even in the surname Atallah, Albert Atallah being one of Jabra's dear friends who was killed during the fighting in that fateful year.** For Jabra, then, no less than for Wadi, the land, Palestine, is the dream which awaits fulfillment.

If there is a single hero in *The Ship,* it is the land. The quest for land is the motivating force behind the action of the novel. All the characters are important, and they assume importance through and at the expense of each other. Isam's escape may have brought them all together, but his position is not that of the hero of a romantic novel. For, as the plot unfolds, Wadi, Luma, Falih, Emilia, and even Mahmud assume central positions. At times the characters are defined by their relationship to Wadi. Luma and Emilia play pivotal roles in the agony of Falih whose suicide then triggers a whole series of apparent resolutions, an answer to Mahmud's railings against the injustices of the world. In a sense, all the characters of *The Ship* are heroes in that each contributes one or more pieces to a complex mosaic, at the center of which is the land with all the agony, yearning and promise which it brings with it.

In all his novels, and particularly in *The Ship* and *In Search of Walid Masoud,* Jabra transcends the local issues which occupy the attention of many contemporary Arab novelists and appeals to a universal ethos which treats the angst of man wherever he may be. *The Ship* is not specifically about Palestine, but it does deal with man and land in a state of love and antagonism, about problems which man has always faced. Even *In Search of Walid Masoud,* which may be read as a specific answer to the agony of Palestine, addresses itself to problems which confront any man searching for meaning in a world plagued by loss, ignorance, and destitution.

Jabra's novels represent an open-ended process, in the sense that there is no final resolution. They are tragic in a way which is

*See Jabra Ibrahim Jabra, *Al-Rihla al-Thamina* (Beirut: Al-Maktaba al-'Asriyya, 1967), pp. 156-158.
**See Jabra Ibrahim Jabra, in the *Journal of Palestine Studies,* VIII, No. 2 (Winter 1979), 84.

different from Shakespeare's tragedies, for example, where the order of things is re-established at the end. Macduff in *Macbeth*, the Duke of Albany in *King Lear*, Fortinbras in *Hamlet*, and Octavius in *Julius Caesar*, all bring back order to the state. Jabra's novels are tragic because "the center cannot hold," because past is present and future salvation is a distant possibility.

University of Pennsylvania, 1982

10

Isam Salman

The sea is a bridge to salvation—the soft, the hoary, the compassionate sea. Today it has regained its vitality. The crash of its waves is a violent rhythm for the sap that sprays the face of heaven with flowers, large lips, and arms reaching out like alluring snares. Yes, the sea is a new salvation. Off to the West! To the agate islands! To the shore where the goddess of love emerged from the briny foam and the exhalations of the breeze!

Nor did I know that—I can hardly utter the word—Luma, poor Luma, who had spent nights crying and betrayed the trust of her parents for my sake, Luma, whose image keeps flashing in my eyes, would also be here on this ten thousand ton Greek ship that flaunts two great funnels against the horizon and plies the Mediterranean from Beirut to Alexandria, Heraklion, Piraeus, Naples, Genoa, and Marseille.

It is a dangerous game. I am here in order to escape. I am here for many reasons, but mostly because I could not make Luma my own sea, my own ship, and my own adventure. But then Luma was never meant for me, except perhaps for a few hours which I had known and lived minute by minute and kiss by kiss.

I keep remembering how dark it was in that apartment my friend had lent me for a day. I remember undoing the buttons of her blouse, one by one. I remember the details just like an old song on the radio. The taste of her lips is still on mine; sometimes I feel it with my tongue and fear that time may erase it.

The love between us cannot be expressed by words, sense, or reason. It is a kind of being and non-being. It is like saying, "I have two eyes, a nose, and a mouth, but I can't see, smell, or speak." Yet here she is, along with the sea, with Beirut, with June, with the second-class passengers—and with her husband. And since she is with her husband, what is the use of the sea, of Beirut, of June, and of all these happy passengers?

There was an Italian woman on board returning from Lebanon. She was about thirty years old. (She claimed she was twenty-four.) She said she was not escaping from anything. But when, to the sound of the siren, the ship was released from its moorings and began to turn away from the wharf, she decided that she too was an escapee. She said that her marriage had lasted a little over a year, leaving her with nothing but the memory of the lush green mountains above Beirut and the feeling that she had to escape.

"Do you understand?" she asked. "It's the memory of a landscape, not an emotion; the memory of a country, not a man. I learned English at Bologna University and spent some time in London. It's the memory of a country, not a man. My husband left me. I thought he'd come back, but he didn't. That was two years ago or more."

I offered her a cigarette, and she took it with thanks. I lit it for her. I could not help noticing her low neckline. I could not help letting my eyes wander towards her breasts, which looked restless in the confines of her bra. As I lit my own cigarette, Emilia Farnesi talked, half angry, and half delighted at being able to empty her heart.

We were leaning against the railing of the ship. It was early evening, and the ship was approaching the Greek Isles, which sprang up in every direction. Most of the passengers were still taking their afternoon siestas, but soon they would come out of their cabins like pigeons from their cotes or mice from their holes. In fact, the faces of some of them reminded me of birds. Others had wax-like hands with tapering fingers and pearly nails that reminded me of canaries. Some looked like rodents, moles or monkeys, others like vegetables. There were faces like cauliflower, like eggplant. At times, by some optical illusion, they looked like the faces of angels! Yet Emilia's face was a face from the Inferno; it reminded me of evil. There was in her blue eyes a sharp flash that emphasized the open treachery of her large lips. Her face had the roundness of a child's and left no doubt that it was not her real face. Despite her constant smile, there was a harshness and a fury in her eyes and on her lips, as though she were saying, "You can trust me, but at your peril!"

But I am jumping ahead. It is quite possible that there is some connection between Emilia Farnesi's face and Luma Abdul Ghani's. When I saw Luma and her husband, Falih Haseeb, among the passengers before the ship left Beirut, I reacted with all the suddenness of one who sees a huge stone falling from a roof-top and moves away at once to avoid being hit. It was clear that she had tricked me, by pursuing me to the one place where I thought I would be safe from her. I edged my way through the throngs of people who were leaning over the banister waving, shouting, dreaming, and fled to the other end of the ship. What is this, I asked myself. A coincidence? A plot? A chase? A tease? Had we not said and done enough before she got married? A coincidence, no doubt, a damned coincidence. I felt I must ignore the matter completely. I could no longer stand women. I wanted to be alone. I wanted no one to recognize me. I wanted to be just one face in a million, a wayfarer whom people pass by without noticing.

But in that fleeting moment Luma had seen me. A smile had danced all over that face of hers, which, in spite of its deep tan, scandalously proclaims its innermost feelings. Her eyes cannot keep a secret; they overflow with sympathy, yearning, immediacy; their black lashes make them look like the wide eyes you see on Sumerian sculptures. No, there is no deceit in her face. If only there were! If one has to have an adventure with a woman, she should have a face like Emilia Farnesi's: worldly, earthy, with the craftiness of a vixen. But Luma's face, which reveals all its secrets at a single glance, is the face of tragedy, the face which haunts you forever, like desire and sorrow.

Her face haunted me. I might forget it for days, for months, but then in a flash it would come flooding back. Feelings of stupor and inanity would leave me with a sense of drowning in sheer fury. I would feel abandoned as though in a twilight. Love returned like a vision to a prophet; a whole world full of glow, color, and pleasure, with flesh transformed into bubbles floating in a cup of wine. But I could not have been less prepared to meet her than on that day. When I saw her on the ship I wished she had not been there. I wished I could lower the ship's gangway to the wharf again and disappear into the crowds. I had run away from her, but there she was, standing before me, like a wall, like a giant, like the sea itself.

Life is full of ordeals: death, disease, disappointment of parents with children, and children with parents. There is searing sun that burns the back of your neck and cold that paralyzes your fingers. There is death and murder and betrayal of friends. But we bear all this for good or ill. So long as we cannot commit suicide, we have to put up with it all. And as we endure we feign patience

13

and claim heroic courage. But the greatest ordeal of all is to fall in love with a woman, one who is almost in your arms, and yet one whom you cannot have. You may possess a thousand women, but that one remains a thorn in your throat. The agony haunts you; it takes you by surprise each time her voluptuous face invades your dreams or shakes up the inane numbness of your life. Death is one agony, and this is another.

The ship sailed, and the tall buildings of Beirut, embraced by Mount Lebanon, receded into the horizon. Once we had grown weary of leaning against the railing and the land had disappeared from view, we abandoned ourselves to the sea. That evening, as the passengers inspected their narrow cabins, became acquainted with their cabin mates, changed their clothes, and prepared themselves for dinner, I discovered that Dr. Falih Haseeb and his wife had the cabin next to mine. Hell, I thought. They were about to go into their cabin as I was leaving mine. They stood in the doorway.

"Isam! By God, it's Isam," Falih shouted. "Luma," he went on, "it's Isam Salman!"

Luma's answer came in theatrical tones. "Who? Isam?"

My answer was theatrical too. "What a coincidence! How do you do, Doctor? How do you do, Luma?"

"What a coincidence indeed!"

We quickly shook hands all around.

"Are you going to Italy?" the doctor asked.

"No, a little farther," I replied. "To London."

"What a coincidence," Luma said. "You'll see us in London, too!"

We all laughed. I walked away and swore. Only a cabin wall will separate me from Luma, but it is a wall of iron. And the iron is reinforced by a husband. And the husband is reinforced by everything. But there is nothing to reinforce me; just another look from Luma, filled with yearning, sorrow, and disappointment.

I did my best to avoid them on the first evening, and succeeded. I saw them in the dining room, but chose a seat which enabled me to turn my back to them. When I finished dinner, I left in a hurry and went straight back to my cabin. My cabin mate was Shawkat Abu Samra, a Damascus businessman with a fascinating accent. He did not talk much, but when he did, he made you feel you knew nothing about life. He knew not only the price of everything, but how, where, and when it ought to be used. He talked about soap, perfume, and nylon, but I was only able to express in vague words my admiration for the gardens of Dummar, the

14

Umayyad Mosque, and the excellent ice-cream in Souk al-Hamidiyya. That made him laugh: he had not eaten ice-cream there since his high-school days.

No sooner had Shawkat Abu Samra slipped under his rustling sheets than he fell asleep. I too went to sleep right away, but woke up suddenly; it was as though I had not slept at all. I could hear the waves hitting against the side of the ship, rhythmical, playful. Then I heard something moving; no, actually, I felt it against my arm. There was a muted sound to it that seemed to come in through the porthole, from the lapping waves. I could not deceive myself for long: the movement was on the other side of the wall which touched my arm. The movement was Luma and her husband. How could an iron wall be so thin? So weak? God, they were making love! Luma was in there, wasting her beauty, bleeding her femininity, giving her lips and breasts to her husband on the other side of the wall. I leaped out of bed as though I had been bitten by a snake. How could I lie in my bed and hear all this? I quickly slipped into my clothes and went up to the deck. I would leave the lovers to exhaust their passions behind that wall while I eradicated the image of this woman from my mind.

There are experiences a man carries under his skin like a disease, an ulcer which neither heals nor kills. More experiences are encountered while the ulcer in his innards rages and subsides. And when it rages, he can take a palliative, which may kill the pain for a while, but not the threat of its recurrence. Pain thus becomes part of a man's constitution, living with the heart and mind, until sometimes it seems, contrary to all logic and reason, like an abiding joy! All of us are prone to this kind of masochism, but as long as we have to carry our experiences under our skin like a disease, why not resort to stratagems by turning them into a source for daydreams and those uncomposed poems that roar unexpectedly in the soul?

There were only three or four people on deck, each alone, each carrying, no doubt, his disease in his own way. I stood there cursing. My hate filled the sea in front of my eyes—the dark, friendly sea, whose waves lapped against the ship, whispering and teasing. The moon had disappeared, and the vast expanse of the sea blackened under the sheen of the huge agglomeration of stars. The monotonous rhythm of the ship's engine was clearly audible deep down in the ship. Amid this torrent of hatred Luma sprang up before me; dressed or naked, I could not tell. She had her clothes on, but I could see every part of her body: her succulent lips perfumed with lipstick, her breasts released from her blouse. She was there, right before my eyes, at a distance from me, right in front of me.

It was night. We were in my car, driving out of Baghdad. Her hand fettered me like a chain, went round my neck, dropped to my mouth, plunged into my shirt. I swung the car off the highway into an abandoned field and turned on the headlights in order to study the terrain. The car bounced up and down on the contours of the uneven earth.

"Be careful of the canals," Luma shouted. "This land is full of irrigation canals. Be careful!"

I drove on for a while longer, stopped the car, and started to kiss Luma, to chew her lips, to plant my mouth in her neck, between her breasts.

"I'm crazy!" she said. "How did I ever consent to come here? I love you. I adore you. But I'm crazy. This is the first and last time."

Suddenly, the night was rent by the sound of violent barking, and involuntarily Luma moved away from me. I turned on the ignition and the car sprang forward. We saw a man coming from a distance, his dogs around him, jumping and barking.

"Turn back, Isam. Turn back!" Luma cried.

I backed up, and the rear wheels of the car fell into a ditch. They spun furiously, churning up mud all around us. We were trapped. I pushed the accelerator all the way to the floor. The engine roared, but the wheels turned in vain.

"What a mess. What a total mess," Luma kept repeating. "What does the man want? I'm scared of dogs."

The dogs bounced ahead of their master, filling the night with their vicious barking. Finally, the man arrived and suddenly flashed a light, which glared like an obscene eye among his dogs' eyes.

Why do people expect the worst from strangers at night in open country? He could have given us hell, for sure. We were trapped, and his dogs lunged at the car like a pack of wolves. Instead he gave us a smile.

"Good evening. Are you stuck?" he asked with a gentle sympathy. He moved his flashlight away from our faces and actually looked down as soon as he realized there was a woman in the car.

"Don't worry," he said. He went back to check the wheels. "No good trying to move," he said when he returned. "I work with the railways here. Wait until I fetch a shovel." He sped off, but his dogs lagged behind him. At least they stopped barking. "What if he comes back with something other than a shovel?" Luma asked. "Shall we leave the car and make a run for it?" I asked helplessly. "The highway's close by, five minutes or so." "No, I'm scared stiff of dogs," she answered. "Let's wait, no matter what happens." The man returned with a shovel, not a dagger. I got out of the car to lend him a hand, but he insisted on digging out the tires by himself, until he had leveled the earth in front of the wheels. Then I jumped into the car and turned on the ignition. The wheels took hold, and the car moved out of the ditch. I stopped to thank our unknown rescuer and pushed some money into his hand. He tried to refuse, but I insisted.

"If you're up for a bit of fun," he said as a parting gesture, "there's an open orchard on the other side of the road. God be with you."

I stepped on the accelerator like a madman. "Fun! What fun?" asked Luma. "I almost died of fear. Hold my hand. See how it's trembling. Feel how cold it is. Fun! Damn you, Isam!" She threw herself on my shoulder as the car sped towards the city.

The sea was getting chilly, and I was almost shivering. My throat felt as dry as hay. The sea was getting a little rough, I thought. As the ship began to sway mildly, I sat in a desk chair, trying to relax and get some sleep, despite the memory of the barking dogs around that ghost in the dark.

All of a sudden I became aware of another ghost at the far end of the ship. It started edging in my direction. It stopped short of me, turned its back, and leaned over the railing. Another man who was unable to sleep? I became aware of its long hair. It must be a woman in a pant suit. Her warm perfume, mixed with the musty smell of salt water, filled the air around me. She was smoking. I lay in my chair and closed my eyes, but after a while she came and sat in a chair next to mine. I raised myself slowly and greeted her.

"We're lucky," she said in English. "The sea between Beirut and Alexandria is usually rough. How calm it is tonight!"

"Yes, we're lucky," I answered.

"I like the sea. Do you?"

"Yes, I like the sea."

"This is only my second voyage by sea."

"To Alexandria?" I inquired.

"To Genoa. And you?"

"To Marseille, then Paris and London."

"You're lucky."

"Forgive me for asking; couldn't you get to sleep?"

She laughed. "I love the sound of the waves," she said. This woman was Emilia Farnesi. We talked in this manner for an hour or so. Strangers can converse for hours without knowing anything about each other, except for a few lies, perhaps. All I knew about her and she knew of me was perhaps just that, but I did not feel the dryness in my throat any longer. I only felt the cold and an overwhelming need for sleep. As for Luma, I could not forget her for one second. I went down to my cabin, terrified that I might hear her moving and breathing on the other side of the wall. But I heard nothing.

I came across Wadi Assaf next morning. I remember him as always talking. At that moment he was talking to a woman who, I found out later, was French. Her name was Jacqueline Durand. He was also talking to a short, fat Spaniard named Fernando Gomez. Wadi would talk and laugh with gusto; and when he stopped talking, all other voices sounded like croaking noises. He was tall, and his shoulders were bent forward in eager anticipation of whatever lay ahead. His thick black hair was always perfectly combed and betrayed a sense of elegance and a care for his personal appearance. I could sense right away that he was Palestinian, and my intuition proved right when I heard his accent. He reminded me of many Palestinian students I had met in England. One thing has always surprised me about the Palestinians: their love for words, even when they speak in English.

After my hard night, I was not eager to meet anybody. Actually I was looking around, hoping in spite of myself to see Luma walking on the deck or lying in the sun in her bathing suit. But Wadi's voice attracted my attention, and I overheard part of his conversation. I think he was telling jokes; I don't know for sure. The others were laughing. There goes a happy man, I said to myself.

Later on we got acquainted and soon we were inseparable. I listened as the words poured out of his mouth like incessant rain, like a never-ending rainstorm.

"What you knew two days ago," he told me, "and what you

know today are not the same thing. Life runs, speeds on, racing people. Every day it changes you, erodes you, gnaws at your sides, enlarges the numb areas in your heart. Every day, it adds to you, blows you up, and hammers into your heart the nails of pain and joy. You're forever changing. Your childhood accompanies you, but it's no longer a part of you. It's there, far away, with those waves on the horizon, on that island you behold in the sea of your dreams. No doubt, a man like you is full of thoughts of love. At a railway station, or in a car loaded with bags and suitcases, you left behind a beautiful woman, hazel-eyed, a brunette whose voice is like night songs heard from a distance. OK, fine. Between the ages of fifteen and thirty-five you may get to know a dozen women, fifty even. Some have small breasts like unripe figs; others have thighs like marble; some have left behind a haze of visions; others keep pressing on your eyes with their sharp physical presence. You see, when it comes to love and sex, I'm a romantic. If you come with me when we get to Naples, you will understand what I mean. I'm on vacation now, a long vacation away from everything that enslaves me and monopolizes my life. In Naples—do you have enough money?—in Naples, you'll understand the meaning of the body. It's a shameful meaning. And why? Because it's the animal in you. The body is the only irrefutable truth. The thing which connects you and me with beasts. Why be supercilious and hypocritical? In Naples, we'll get four, five, six women, depending on the size of the bedroom, and there we shall behold wonders. The only truth, the ultimate boredom. Because truth is ultimately boring. I always prefer liars. Liars are aristocrats. They're rebels in their own way, and rebellion is always aristocratic. Truth is for the birds. Ha!

"This morning I said all this to Jacqueline, the Frenchwoman who wears her hair à la garçon.

" 'Do you want to know the truth?,' she asked.

" 'The truth?' I said. 'Never!'

" 'Stop joking,' she said.

" 'I don't want to hear the truth,' I replied. 'I want you to lie to me all the time. On this ship, truth is a beggar, a monk, a heretic, a despot, a son of a bitch. We don't want it. Let your words be like your haircut. You look like a boy, but your breasts tell the lie.'

"She laughed. 'Shut up!' she said in her limited English.

"Actually, anyone who claims to be telling the truth is either deluded and doesn't know it, or a liar and knows it. What is truth? My foot! We spoke the truth till our throats grew hoarse, and we

19

ended up as refugees in tents. We fancied the world community cherished the truth, and turned out to be the victims of our own naiveté. We came to realize all this both as a nation, and as individuals. This is why, as an individual, I don't care what people say any longer. The only thing that matters for me is my feelings and intuition. Long live liars, dissemblers, and imposters! At least I'm safe from their harm because I'm a master at their game. As I told you, I'm on a vacation; and I hope it'll last a year or two. If I could, I would extend it to a whole lifetime. Why not? I'm over forty—don't let my black hair deceive you—unmarried, and my family can do without me. I was forced out of my country, and yet I've managed to make money in Kuwait, I still make enough, thank God. This is my third trip to Europe, and I shall squeeze every drop out of it. At night, I'm plagued by painful memories, very painful, and painful desires too. I used to find some relief by putting my thoughts down on paper. By writing poetry. After all, all Palestinians are poets by nature. They may not actually write poetry, but they are poets all the same because they have experienced two basic things: the beauty of nature, and tragedy. Anyone who combines these two must be a poet, don't you think?

"Do you know Jerusalem? You were probably too young when the Zionist monster gobbled up the most beautiful half of the most beautiful city in the world. It is said that Jerusalem is built on seven hills. I don't know whether it really has seven hills, but I have walked up and down all its hills, among its houses built of stone—white stone, pink stone, red stone—castle-like houses, rising high and low along the roads as they go up and down. You'd think they were jewels studding the mantle of the Lord. Jewels remind me of the flowers in its valleys, of spring, of the glitter of its blue skies after spring showers. And spring in Jerusalem really was spring: when it came, you would think it was a stage set which had been changed by a producer. The barren hills in winter suddenly become green, right there before your eyes. Even your disrepaired little house at the corner of the road with the dead tree, where rocks have lain neglected since Ottoman times, feels the advent of spring. Flowers like children's eyes spring up from beneath the stones and around the barren roots of trees. This is why nights bring back to me memories of Jerusalem, and I grieve and rage and cry. I was staying in a hotel in Damascus once when such memories came back to me unexpectedly. I cried. A man I knew saw me crying and asked me what had happened. I told him I was crying for my father, my mother, and

20

my brothers and sisters, and that I had lost all shame.

"That was many years ago. Others wrote poetry instead of crying. But who can compose words that are the product of thirty years of experience in the most beautiful of God's cities? Our creative attempts are merely tranquilizers, a kind of weeping. Yet nothing in life can take the place of large flowing tears. Time, in any case, is a horrible thing. In its unabating tide it robs everything of vigor and newness. In the end, it leaves you nothing of any worth. Time has trampled down everything I see and left it faded and dull.

"If I were a painter, I'd paint it. Do you know how? One huge black smudge on a canvas. In two or three places I would spot it with red paint. Time is the enemy. Live, if you wish; stay alive as long as you can. But you'll have nothing else: a big black smudge filling the fabric of your life, with a red spot here and there; the trivia that come your way whether you want them to or not, without your ever being able to achieve that great relentless experience which is the product of choice and will.

"You know, primitive man, who lived by hunting in the wilderness, was luckier than we are. Every day of his life he had a definite choice: facing danger. He was always on the verge of disaster, and his very survival was his daily victory. But our survival? Ha! We survive in spite of ourselves. It is a kind of passive survival, something we accept but cannot control. Despite all this apparent chaos, society has come to be so organized that we can live mechanically. All we have to do is move our arms and legs. Of course, we are not endowed with free will, and so we eat—anything; we drink, and bear children, and plunge headlong towards the inevitable pit. This is progress, rather like the progress of a disease. As for me, I prefer primitive life. I believe nobody, and I cannot presume to tell the truth. I cry sometimes, but I laugh a lot too; and I love women, all kinds and colors. I won't put up with passive survival. In Naples we'll find women wholesale, and I won't compose any poems because words deflate my resolve. Did I say all Palestinians were poets? In fact, they're all merchants. They have shut poetry out of their hearts, and concentrated instead on business transactions everywhere. And I'm one of them, as you can see. I'd travel a thousand miles for money, but in the end I trample it under my foot. Money is for the birds!

"If I have any real emotion, it's religious; mystical, if you like. My emotions are stirred by church music: chants that rise wounded, agonized, from the throats of choirs, organ music that thunders in the lofty ceilings, and all those humble supplications to God, the God of gods, the Kingdom of Heaven, the Lamb of God who carries the sins of the world. All these overwhelm me, sometimes almost hysterically. For then I feel torn to pieces in joy and sorrow. Perhaps more in sorrow. Because beauty is sad. The most beautiful things in life are sad, like my homeland, like the angels who carry cups filled with blood dripping from the palms of Christ crucified; a sacred beauty, frail, supplicant, with ripe lips and large eyes, daubed with tears. In this kind of harmonic beauty, arranged for choruses like those of a Greek play, I see life. I see my life. I see my land, my country. I see everything I've achieved and failed to achieve. In the final analysis, you and I are nothing but small particles of dust floating within this great music, particles in the vast nebula of the universe, meaning nothing and meaning everything.

"In my childhood I used to feel invigorated by prayer and piety. Things got complicated when the emotions of prayer and supplication changed into the emotions of love, death, and beauty. This calm moonlit sea is unreal. So too is this blueness, this unrestrained flow of waves, this night that embraces the world like a sleepless lover. The only real thing is my memory of it, a memory that is transformed into something resembling music. Daily happenings recede into the dark tunnels of time, leaving behind waves of music in the mind. Everything is transitory except these waves, not only metaphorically, but physically as well. They are the tunes of joy and sorrow connected with God, the angels, and the saints; tunes into which merge the wild notes of love and violent hidden sensations. They contain the memory of a little pool outside the walls of Jerusalem where rain water collected. It was called the Sultan's Pool, and to me it was as big as the ocean. I used to stand there on a protruding rock and gaze at the little ripples on the green pool, stirred up by the wind. I'd get the feeling that the rock was ploughing its way through the pool just as this ship of ours is doing through the blue waters of the Mediterranean. I was fourteen then, full of yearnings for the distant and impossible. I used to turn away from our house and its numerous inhabitants and head for the Sultan's Pool to stand on the rock that sped through the oceans of the imagination. I was, no doubt, like the man who invented the flying carpet. He had to invent it because he could not get out of his crowded quarter in Cairo or Baghdad filled with poor people, garbage and stench. So he invented the magic carpet, and with it he invented the Rukh and the invisible hat, and saw white doves descend from the clouds, settle on marble fountains, shake their feathers, and become beautiful women. All is music, ballet, **dreams**, yearnings, the impossible, the genius of man whom the city tries to enslave.

"I wanted to tell Jacqueline about all this, but she knows neither English nor Arabic well enough and I'm no better at French. Besides, I don't think she would understand even if I were able to convey my thoughts to her. She laughs at the slightest word. For her, the whole trip is one great continuous joke. She eats as if she has not eaten for years, and she is not afraid of putting on weight. She'll never get fat, though, because there's a monster inside her that devours everything and is still hungry. Otherwise, how could she still have such firm, challenging breasts at the age of thirty, or such fine legs, from her buttocks right down to her feet. Music! It's all music. Music is water, and so is beauty; water that flows, then freezes into shapes lovely to the eye. And all is harmony.

"I think I know the secret. In my youth, I used to read many books: mostly translated novels that were irrelevant to my life. I had to take off into imaginary forests in pouring rain and mad hurricanes, under clear suns after rain storms. Then I would mount my horse, which, I discovered later, was akin to Rosinante, Don Quixote's horse. For, like Don Quixote, I drew my sharp sword against imaginary devils and encountered numerous ladies of surpassing beauty, with whom I fell in love at first sight.

"I was in constant contact with a beautiful veiled woman who used to meet me at the cemetery outside the walls of the City. I still honestly don't know whether I actually met this woman, whose unveiled face framed against the grey twilight is etched in my memory, or whether the whole thing was a concoction of my imagination. I used to tell the story of my encounters with her to a couple of friends who came from their village once a week. Her father was a condiment seller in the Spice Souk in the Old City. I used to see him after passing the coppersmiths, who would fill the vaulted market with the din of their hammering. He was always to be found, with his short beard and in his long *gunbaz*, standing still as a mummy among the fragrant sacks of his trade. 'That's my father,' she told me once. (I've forgotten her name; maybe she is a creation of my mind after all.) 'If he finds out that we've been meeting in the cemetery, he's sure to kill us both on the spot and save himself the cost of two burials!' She was a high school student. Her hair and eyes were black, and her Jerusalem face was like a rose after the rain. Anyway, this is how I described her to my two friends, for the faces of the women of Jerusalem are all like roses after an April shower. I don't remember exactly how it all ended. I've loved many women since that time, and each of them has a story; I can usually remember the beginning, but it's the ending which gives me problems. But for some reason I can't forget the cemetery; love within the sight of death! The power of life defying the power of Thanatos. Such thoughts came to me after I got older, of course. At any rate, the girl stopped coming without a word of warning, and the dream was over. Even so, I kept on seeing her father daily on my way to school. I'd look at him and smile. 'I've kissed your daughter a hundred times,' I'd say to myself, 'and you don't even realize it.' When a man grows older, his evil thoughts increase. Gone is the innocence of such a thought (and why shouldn't a young man kiss the daughter of an old man who is almost croaking amid his spices?) to be replaced by such a thought as: I've kissed this man's wife a hundred times, and he doesn't even know it!

"Fascinated by my fabricated stories, my two friends moved to Jerusalem with their families. Yet life is of one's own making, not of anyone else's. If my friends failed to enjoy what I enjoyed in my eager adolescence, it was no fault of mine. But perhaps they were no less happy than I, since in those days even the slightest thing made us happy: those long walks on Jaffa street or in the labyrinth of rocks and olive trees that surrounded the City. Have you ever sat down on the red earth, Isam, under an old, knotted olive tree, surrounded by thorn bushes and a few anemones that fought their way out through the strangling thorns? Or by those little yellow flowers that our farmers called *hannun?* How beautiful the olive groves were in Talibiyya, Katamon, and Musallaba! How beautiful was the valley that stretched all the way to Maliha! It was there that we left a part of our lives as a gift, as a pledge that we would return. One goes into the world and finds everywhere there are tall trees, thick forests, well ordered gardens, but none of them is equal to one crooked branch from those ancient dust-laden trees. Nothing is equal to that red rocky land that greets your feet like a lover's kiss; and when you lie down on it, it provides you with all the comfort of a bed in Paradise. To be an exile from your own land is a curse, the most painful curse of all.

"Ask the Palestinians. Ask the farmer who remembers with the greatest delight the wounds the land inflicted on his feet. As though he would say that his life, after he'd been evicted from his land, was no life at all. This blue sea sparkles, carefree, indifferent. I know, because it thinks its shores are the rallying ground of all the world's civilizations. But it also sparkles because it licks our own sparkling shores. I love the Mediterranean, and I like to sail on it because it is the sea of Palestine, of Jaffa and Haifa, of the western hills of Jerusalem and its villages. If you climb those Jerusalem hills and look to the west, you won't be able to see where land ends and sea starts, where land and sea meet with the sky. They all merge together, they're so alike. This azure is the only thing that makes my exile bearable: it enables me to communicate with my land again. It takes me back to the Sultan's Pool. I discover that it has become so vast, it has overflown into rivers and waterfalls.

"Deep inside, we're all alone. Our life resembles Chinese boxes, one box inside another, each getting smaller and smaller until we come to the smallest one in the heart of them all. And what do we find there? Not one of the precious rings of the Sultan's daughter, but a secret which is even more precious and marvelous: loneliness. Why was I uprooted and cast about under hoofs and fangs, driven into flaming deserts and screaming oil-producing cities? I know why; too well, I think. The canvas is huge; black is everywhere, and the spots of color are few and far between. The young student who stole away from her father's house in order to meet her lover for two awesome minutes among the graves has lit a spot in the heart of the black canvas. Then I revert to an agony, an agony of the cross, the tragedy that renews itself. And people talk about me. 'He's a decadent, cunning fellow,' they say, 'who contradicts himself. He worships money, and his land no longer means anything to him.' It's as if they're asking me to carry a handful of soil around in a little paper bag as a proof of my pain, whereas I carry all its blue volcanic rocks in my blood, in that smallest box inside all the other boxes, together with my loneliness. We're all lonely, you know. We all hide this gem in our hearts away from people's eyes. We hide it, together with one or perhaps two secrets. But the eyes that we love and die for are the same eyes that pierce through our hearts like x-rays, extracting our innermost secrets. In our hearts we carry love and loneliness, but we don't want our loved ones to know what we are hiding; not out of fear for us, but for them. Shall we go back to music and this sea? What secrets do they hide, I wonder? Who can pry open the secrets of harmony or the impetuosity of waves?

"Today Jacqueline compared herself with the beautiful Iraqi

woman who has become the talk of the ship. She pronounced her name 'Luna.' Fernando went into a fit of laughter. 'Luna, Luna, the moon,' he said. 'Now I know the secret of madness!' For my part, I was not interested in correcting the error, for, in fact, it wasn't an error at all. Isn't it our prerogative to confuse the beauty of lips* with the moon and with madness? It's all the work of these waves, awesome, fascinating Mediterranean waves! Do you know that the ancient Arab poets used to fall in love with place-names, and that they repeated them in their poems as frequently as they repeated the names of women they loved?

" 'Halt, my two friends, and let us weep for memory of lover and abode / In the sand dunes between Dakhul and Hawmal,' says Imru al-Qays. And don't you remember these lines by Abeed Ibn al-Abras, of whom we know nothing except that King al-Mundhir killed him because he met him on one of his unlucky days:

> Malhub is desolate, all its people gone,
> And Qutabiyyat, and Dhanub
> And Rakis and Thuaylibat
> And Dhatu Firqayn and Qalib
> And Arda, and Qafa Hibirrin

And when he could not think of any more place-names to fill the second hemistich, he said, 'No Arab soul is left of them there.' How could a poet reel off all those names if they had not been part of his blood, flesh, and bone, complete with their rocks and their sands? Part of their fascination is their power to evoke love in the heart of the hearer too. It is enough for us merely to hear the name of Baghdad and we jump with elation, despite all the killing and torture that took place there. And to utter the words 'Luma and Baghdad' is to trigger in our imagination the most fantastic poems. Isn't it so, Isam? Are you really innocent of all this, or are you simply an architect who cannot be stirred by place-names or the names of women like Luma?

"As I said, Jacqueline compared herself with Luma. 'What does Luma have that I don't have?' she asked.

" 'It's a long story, Jacqueline,' I replied. 'Do you know any Arab poets?'

" 'What do poets have to do with Luna?' she inquired.

"Fernando laughed again. 'You have to be Spanish in order to

---

*Luma, in Arabic, means "beauty of lips."

understand this,' he said. 'Do you know Lorca?'

" 'Who's Lorca?' Jacqueline asked innocently.

"Fernando's jaw dropped a whole foot, then he started going round in circles like a madman, saying, 'Tell her, tell her!'

"I agreed to spend a couple of nights with Jacqueline in Paris to tell her about Lorca and the Arab poets, but Fernando, the rogue, took me aside. 'Why should you commit yourself right now?' he asked. 'What looks so alluring on a ship in the middle of the sea may not appear equally so in a room in Montparnasse.'

"May God have mercy on your soul, Abeed; and Rakis, and Thuaylibat and Dhatu Firqayn, Montparnasse, Boulmiche, Boulevard Raspail... Some Arab soul may still be there..."

Luma, Luma, Luma! The whole ship talked about her, or so it seemed to me. In fact, she was not exactly a woman to fill the world with mirth and laughter. She was hardly the central figure in men's circles, hardly the one to tease and joke with the wolves. Not because her husband stayed so close to her all the time or because he was on guard and used his devotion to throw a magic circle around her which no man could break. It was rather because she herself chose to stand aside, to turn her face away from onlookers and stretch her beautiful long neck over their heads. She had a sort of aristocratic flair which I could not explain. Even in Baghdad I heard from those who knew her before her Oxford days that she was so proud that only those who knew her intimately dared to talk to her. At Oxford she was even more proud, but at the same time it was the kind of pride that might easily dissolve into shyness or disappear completely if her interest was aroused. She was like someone who would inveigle passers-by into stopping at her door, and then keep them waiting there without so much as a glass of water. And they wouldn't complain, either. Thirst! It's curious, but thirst always reminds me of Luma. Her very name stirs the depths of thirst in me. That's how our love was: thirsty. You could drink gallons of water and yet remain thirsty. It was a divine thirst that, despite your unworthiness, gained you an entrance into the company of mystics.

The whole ship talked about Luma because everybody was taken by her loveliness and because she never got close enough to anyone to dispel this interest in her. Everyone on the ship seemed to be asking me about her. Is she from Iraq? Baghdad? Baghdad is a magic word for Arabs and non-Arabs alike. Wadi Assaf, for one, sang the praises of Arab eyes, the wide eyes of gazelles that had maddened poets, paupers, and caliphs. He confessed to me openly that he looked for Luma every morning because he regarded black eyes and long, slender necks as good omens for the day. Emilia Farnesi inquired about her too, because Baghdad and Luma brought back to her mind the fantastic world of slave girls, of the harem, of the Sultan's daughter and Sindbad the Sailor. "Did Sindbad ever fall in love?" she asked me. Before I could answer, she gave her own response. "Impossible!" she said with conviction. "He never knew love because he was a sailor. Otherwise, how could he have left Luma and sailed the Seven Seas?"

Jacqueline asked about her too. "Does she love her husband that much?" she asked. "Beautiful women don't love anybody."

"How could you be so cruel?" I said.

"Monsieur Isam," she replied, "beautiful women are like the narcissus: they die of thirst because they cannot drink from the wells of their own beauty."

As for Fernando Gomez, the Spaniard who shared Wadi's cabin, he laughed loudly, his paunch moving up and down with his laugh. "The Arabs and the Spaniards," he told me, "have the same blood. They will kill men for the sake of a woman and kill women for the sake of love, jealousy, and honor. The Arabs and the Spaniards alone have mastered the worship of beauty. They alone can live and die for the sake of a beautiful woman and leave everything else to others. As for Señora Luma, her beauty will only end in tragedy."

No one knew about my relationship with Luma.

Every time we approached the sea coast, we heard the screams of gulls. A sharp scream would rend the air, catching us by surprise. The sky would break open, and flights of gulls would swoop down to the sea like arrows. Then they would soar upwards into the sky once again, scatter about, and circle around; their broad outstretched wings would allow them to glide effortlessly. Once again, without the slightest warning, they would swoop down, bridging the blueness of the sky and the greenness of the waters and filling the air with the noisy squawks of their freedom.

In Baghdad, in my younger days, I used to watch the gulls in the spring from the banks of the Tigris, as they swirled about above the waters and then charged down toward the muddy shores where I used to swim and play with my friends. At times, we would throw some bread crumbs in the water and watch the gulls flutter and compete with one another like birds of prey. Then they would fly away to other shores and other children. Emilia and I were leaning against the railing of the ship watching the flight pattern of the first few gulls that appeared. She was telling me about her life in Beirut, about her marriage that had not lasted long, and about her husband who had decided in a fit of madness to become a monk in one of the monasteries of Mount Lebanon.

How quickly people become friends on a ship! They imagine that the friendship will last a lifetime. They laugh easily, they love easily, confess to each other easily, then forget everything just as easily. What else could they possibly do, with the Greek Islands studding the sea like green gems? Fernando Gomez carried his paunch with all the agility of a dancer. Emilia strutted about, her breasts almost popping out of her blouse. Jacqueline Durand, her buttocks stuffed like fruit halves into tight yellow pants, strolled on deck with the dark, hairy, large-nosed Wadi Assaf, who would no doubt rape her some night on the ship's prow, under the big, bright stars.

The passengers began to emerge from the bowels of the boat. There were kids chattering in Greek, and Egyptian students telling jokes, playing cards, shouting, cursing and laughing endlessly. At times smoke emerged from the funnels like some enormous genie; it would roll away, swirling, and then disappear just like a genie. Now and then, the ship's fog horn sounded and was answered by another ship. The passengers took pictures of one another by the life-boats, on the stairs to the bridge, and alongside the swimming pool.

Emilia and I kept talking and smoking; we were becoming better acquainted. I must admit that I was using her, with not a little malice, to keep my mind off Luma. We started playing the games that lovers usually play on short, enjoyable cruises. If I touched her hand, she would turn her palm to feel mine; if I came close to her, she would lean back so I could smell her perfume. When I edged even closer, she clung to me and I buried my face in her long, scented hair. I took a deep breath and laughed.

"*Balenciaga?*" I asked.

"*Le Dix*," she answered.

I moved back a little.

"You're an adventurer, Isam," she continued.

"I wish I were."

"Beware of big trouble!" she admonished.

I squeezed her hand gently. "Thanks for the advice," I said. After dinner we used to watch a movie or dance while scores of people sat around satisfied just to watch the dancers on the floor. Shawkat Abu Samra, for example, never missed a dancing party, but he himself never danced. He would sit in a large chair near the dance floor and watch every step and movement. His head would fall on his chest in a doze. Laughing, I would lean over and startle him awake.

In Alexandria, Emilia and I visited the city. We hired a carriage with two vigorous horses driven by a garrulous driver who commented merrily on everything we saw. We drove along the Corniche, past sunny beaches that swarmed with bathers. On the other side of the road the sea wind gave some relief from the heat to the crowds of people who lounged lazily on chairs in the cool shade of the sidewalk cafés.

In Heraklion, on the island of Crete, we went to Knossos, accompanied by Falih, Luma, Wadi, and Jacqueline, and visited the Palace of Minos and the labyrinth of the Minotaur. What a magnificent sight! The stones of the palace erected by Daedalus, whose ruins had stood there for some four thousand years! There they stood, still catching the rays of the sun, preserving the secret of a terrifying sensual love, even though much of their mystery had recently been dispelled. We thought of Ariadne, who had betrayed her own father for the sake of her lover, Theseus, and then someone mentioned Icarus.

"But where is Icaria, the island where Icarus perished after he flew over its waters?" Wadi Assaf inquired. "Do we pass by it?"

"Icarus was another escapee," I said. "Unfortunately, his wings betrayed him."

"No," he said. "Icarus was a hero of my youth. It was the sun that really betrayed him, not his wings."

In Piraeus I was alone with Emilia. We traveled by train to Athens and climbed the hills of the Acropolis under the searing sun. I took pictures of Emilia posing by the ruins of the Acropolis, that miracle of marble that always got me talking about its architectural wonders. "And yet," I said, "the present ruined state of the architecture is part of its fascination."

"Maybe then we should thank the sailors of Genoa who bombarded the site," Emilia said.

"Or the Ottomans," I added, "who couldn't think of a better place to dump their bloody explosives."

Among the Ionian pillars, I spotted Luma and Falih. I made every effort to take pictures in which Luma appeared in the background, while she craned her tempting neck to look at the Caryatides supporting the lintel of a temple on their heads. Nothing could match the beauty of the pillars except Luma's perfect figure. She and I were playing cat and mouse, consciously or unconsciously. Emilia seemed irritated every time Luma and her husband moved closer to us, but I could only laugh at Emilia, who obviously wanted to monopolize me despite the fact that she barely knew me. At least this was how I interpreted her irritation. More than once she asked me about Luma and her husband. "Is he a successful doctor? Is he well-known in Baghdad? Is he rich? Well liked?" And so on and so on, the usual questions asked without much thought and answered casually and not always accurately.

"Aren't you getting tired of this woman clinging to you like a leech?" Luma asked me once when we were alone.

"She's interesting," I replied. "She's telling me about life in Beirut. I don't know much about it. She's pretty, don't you think?"

"You're a trickster and a liar," Luma said.

I was enjoying her jealousy. "No," I continued, "she really is pretty and intelligent. She knows a lot about Mediterranean civilization."

"You talk like Falih," Luma said. "I didn't know men were so fond of intelligent women."

"Falih? Why? Does he like her too?" I asked, feigning innocence.

"I'd wring his neck if he did," she answered quickly, and then with a laugh joined Wadi and the others.

I did not know how interested Wadi really was in Jacqueline. He talked so much one could not sort out truth from fantasy in what he said. I felt he wanted to unburden himself of his thoughts without ever getting to the end.

"What are you going to do with Jacqueline at the end of the voyage?" I asked him.

"I hope to be rid of her altogether," he said. "She demands a lot of attention, and that's something I can no longer give to anyone, man or woman."

"You're a narcissist!" I cried.

"Strange! That's how I described Jacqueline! 'You are narcissism personified,' I told her. 'You desire yourself, and I'm the mirror.'

" 'And what about you?' she asked.

"I said, 'I desire you narcissistically too, as a mirror for you. I mean, I take great pleasure in reflecting for you the desire that shimmers over your body.'

"And she said, 'The trouble with you, Wadi, is that for you the word is the body.'

"And what's wrong with that, Isam?" Wadi reflected. "Is there anything more beautiful than the body? Why should we blind our eyes by reading all our lives? Jacqueline herself agrees. She wants to learn the words for every part of the body, from the hair, to the breasts, to the buttocks, to the thighs, in all three languages— English, French, and Arabic. She pronounces every word as if she were singing, or eating apples, or drinking wine. I hear her crunch every letter, and I feel the hot flow around her tongue. I told her that. She said she'd never laughed in her whole life as much as she had laughed the last three days. She said I took pleasure in exposing the secrets of her sex life. What she held to be so solemn, so incommunicable, she said, I would play with as frivolously as with an innocent child. 'You turn love into a game,' she told me. 'You make fornication sound like eating apples.'

"Imagine, these were Jacqueline's words, even though she knew quite well that she would have to confess to her priest next Sunday. 'To whom did you say this?' the priest would ask. 'To an Arab I met on the ship,' she would tell him. 'You must say the Ave Maria and the Lord's Prayer one hundred times. And beware of Arabs from now on; none of them is ever satisfied with just one woman.' "

Most probably Yusuf Haddad and Mahmud Rashid boarded the ship in Beirut, but I only started noticing them after the ship had left Alexandria and the Greek Isles loomed into sight. The first time I met Yusuf Haddad he was complaining about the short time we were allowed in each port, despite the fact that the *Hercules* was actually more of a cruise ship that sailed slowly in order to afford its passengers the chance to relax, sleep, talk, and get involved, if they so wished, in all kinds of relationships. Yusuf and Mahmud: Don Quixote and Sancho Panza, or at least that is the way they looked to me when I first saw them together. They were inseparable. Yusuf was a poet, tall and gaunt, with a goatee. His eyes had that strange glint which suggested that they never quite believed what they saw. Mahmud was fat and short, wore

32

thick glasses, and had a guttural laugh which would every now and then wheeze its way over and above his friend's dreamy voice. He always gave the impression that he had to run to catch up with Yusuf. Mahmud was fond of quoting lines of poetry on every possible occasion, while his friend only recited his own poetry, and on rare occasions at that. Yusuf was Lebanese, but I could not be certain about Mahmud's nationality because he spoke a mixture of Egyptian and Syrian dialects. Wadi and I suspected he was from Damascus, but, when one of us (I forget who) asked him what country he was from, he replied inconsequentially that he was traveling on a *laissez-passer*. Later, I found out that he had a doctorate from the University of Geneva and that he had published in Beirut a book entitled, *The Legality of Government between Constitution and Revolution*. He gave me a copy of his book, but, needless to say, I had no time to read it at that point.

He, too, was fond of Luma. It was as though admiring Luma was the bond that brought us all together. However, I also got the impression that Dr. Falih and he were involved in an intermittent political discussion about the Arab countries. Nevertheless, Mahmud was certainly not unaware of a group of Greek and Egyptian girl students who had boarded the ship in Alexandria.

"My tragedy," Mahmud said, "is that I've never really hung on to a woman. I love them all—good looking, bad looking, blondes, brunettes, what have you, anything with a skirt on, as the British say. Now, my friend Yusuf is the maker of poetry: he can be as difficult as he likes about females. But I'm a consumer of poetry, and women in my creed simply are poems: metrical, free verse, unrhymed. Just as in poetry, everything about them is sheer magic, but I never really get deeply involved with any of them. I suppose I lack the resolve to carry on with an affair. In any case, since the world is exploding with women, it seems silly to hang on to one woman and exclude all the others, don't you agree? In politics, in philosophy, I espouse one line of thought, one ideology. In everything else, I prefer plurality. I wish I were a pluralist in politics too! Politics has given me hell. I feel like someone who is whipped by his wife every night and still becomes even more attached to her. As for women... do you know I haven't so much as written a letter to a woman for ages! Why? because I was afraid if I wrote a woman I might make love to her, or she might construe my words as love-making. I don't deny I've often been tempted to write, but somehow I've always managed to push my hand away from the paper in case my words betray more meaning than I intended. Anyhow, when I write, I prefer to beat about the bush in order to keep a lot unsaid. But let me confess... Recently my resistance has failed me, and more than once at that. When I've started writing, I've felt myself overcome by a sweetness, a refreshing warm sweetness. It appears in slow motion, like a waterfall, threatening (or better, promising) to engulf me from head to toe. I've tried to keep a safe distance from this waterfall with its playful water eager to caress the body so wickedly. To do that, I've clung fast to my reason and sense. But then I see myself telling the woman that I feared, 'Why shouldn't I invade the waterfall and bathe in its happy waters? The waterfall, my love, is you. I want to bathe in you, in your words, your arms, your lips. I want you to fall, cascade, all over me while I stand firm in your downpour,' etc., etc., etc."

I could not help laughing as I imagined Sancho Panza swimming in his poetic waterfalls. I could see him completely naked, with his flat, bald head moving to left and right and his belly shaking up and down as he splashed his dear waters over his spherical body. Yusuf laughed too, and kept encouraging him to tell us more. "You know, Yusuf," Mahmud continued, "Once, in Beirut, I was fond of a blonde woman who wrote poetry in both French and Arabic. She read me all her poems, but I didn't understand a single word.

" 'Your poems are beautiful,' I told her, 'but you're by far the most beautiful poem of all. I want you to read it to me with your whole body, from the top of your hair to the soles of your feet. I want your tongue to communicate your poem to my tongue, but then what would you say, I wonder? In what language would you say it?'

" 'Would it be necessary to say anything then?' she asked.

" 'Your arms would say it all with the greatest poetic originality,' I replied. 'My mouth would scan you, line by line, verse by verse. I would trap you the way heaven traps the earth on a dark night. Then I would search out all your secrets as I extract you like a large pearl from your clothes.' "

"This is too much, Mahmud," said Yusuf.

"The important thing is that I extracted the pearl from its shell," Mahmud continued.

"And the blonde lady gave up poetry altogether, didn't she?" I said.

"For that night, at least," Mahmud replied with his wheezing laugh. He looked around him, sampling the legs of the college girls who lay in the sun. "Dear God! Give me strength!" he exclaimed.

The whole atmosphere seemed to be contagious, for no sooner had Mahmud finished his story than Yusuf started reciting a poem. I had no doubt at all that it was Luma to whom he was alluding:

> *Her lips are lovely laughter*
> *That stirs delightful appetite:*
> *They tend a bed of pearls*
> *And promise a drunken kiss—*
> *And a barbaric, lustful bite.*

I noticed that Dr. Falih Haseeb hardly uttered a word in this coterie but preferred to be alone, even though that was well nigh impossible. He used to walk around carrying a book, either alone or with Luma. More than once I saw him sitting at a table with a drink, writing. People went past him, but he did not notice them. Meanwhile, Luma would talk to some of the passengers or lounge alone in a deck chair, wearing her dark sunglasses and reading. Sea gulls would swoop down out of the blue and devour anything they could get their beaks into. No matter how much Luma tried to be alone, she was the target of hungry beaks, too. I watched her from near and far. When she was not around, she lived in my imagination, like lust, hate, and bitterness. I was sure her husband saw everything while he wrote, drank, and made sarcastic remarks. What was he writing all that time, I wondered?

I did find out later, at the end, when I read some of the things he had written. But he was aware of the games the gulls were playing around the ship. "You should see them in the North Sea and in Scandanavian waters," he said to me. "They're cruel and horrible, like white crows. In Iraq, as you know, people call them 'water crows' because they caw like crows despite their magnificent whiteness, and because they flock around dirt and leftovers, just as crows flock over corpses. They are the crows of the sea. I hate them."

I was almost afraid to talk to Falih. I felt like a dreamy boy talking to a man who had grown weary of sinking his fingernails into reality, into the fibers of diseased flesh, a place where there was no room for dreams or emotional nonsense. It was that damnable emotional nonsense that Luma dragged me into again as she feigned complete ignorance, innocence, even.

"Emotions, Isam? Are you making fun of me?" Falih asked.

"You mean sex. Please, talk to me about sex and leave all talk of love and infatuation to little children. How is your sex life?"

"Terrible!" I said.

"Fine, now I understand. Luma, did you hear what Isam just said? His sex life is terrible!"

Blood rushed into Luma's face. "Haven't you heard of the problems of intellectuals in Baghdad?" she asked.

I could not help but ask slyly, "You mean the married ones or the unmarried?"

"The married and the unmarried," she responded quickly. "It's one and the same."

Falih broke into a fit of laughter, which was very unlike him. "The married ones more than the others, I bet," he said, trying to still his laughter. He finished the rest of his drink with one gulp.

"Your laughter's unnatural, Falih," I said to myself. "I wonder how *your* sex life is? How many times have you achieved that glorious madness with Luma that I did so many times?"

Wadi Assaf

"Abandon hope, all ye who enter here!"

According to Dante, that is what is written over the portals of Hell. People find it painful to abandon hope, but droves of them enter Hell weeping and moaning because they have done just that. Or perhaps it is hope that has abandoned them. As for me, I no longer care. I have been one of those "who enter here." I have experienced Hell from top to bottom and come out again. Hope? I know nothing about it any more. I do have two or three articles of faith which I cannot abandon, but the rest have assumed an altered significance or else have become like a closed book to me; it is as though they were being spoken in a language which I had forgotten. Despair? What does it mean? Hell? What if someone manages to get out of Hell? A man lives a perpetual nightmare. Then suddenly, God bestows His blessings on him and, like Dante, he gets a glimpse of Paradise and Beatrice brought to him by a hurricane, with the waves of the sea raging behind her. Then the nightmare vanishes and its terrors are all forgotten. Once or twice, during the course of a night or two, I have glimpsed Beatrice. The sight of her was an inner revolution more intense and violent than anything else I have experienced. Hope? Despair? No! There is some other region beyond all this where hope and nightmares come to naught. I entered Hell. When I emerged, I found myself in a world quite different from the one I had known before. Everything seemed more incandescent and of greater brilliance than before: strange cities gleaming like pearls, their blues and violets the color of the sky after rain, their mists as translucent as lace on the breasts of beautiful women, their commotion a blood-red color, roaring like fire, pierced by women's sibilant voices.

Sometimes I almost feel I am cheating mankind or God. I can travel from country to country, continent to continent, take active interest in what is going on around me and have a good, hearty laugh. All this as though I were still one of those millions of people who have never entered Hell and who would shake with fear if they ever saw what was written over the portals.

This is my third sea trip to Europe. It is my sixth or seventh trip, if you count air trips as well. But when I travel by air, it's more like a dream; and, like a dream, it's soon over—a quick nap between one period of being awake and another. So I will often say to myself, "Come on, Wadi, travel, see the world." Then I go by sea, not only because the sea is a whole world unto itself, but also because ships give you a bodily sense of gliding simultaneously through time and space. Airplanes almost eliminate time and thus destroy in you that human feeling of growth, of mellowing and of change. They emphasize the fact that you are traveling on a commercial, not a mental, enterprise. At any rate, I have had my fill of business.

I can almost say I am a businessman in spite of myself. I inherited the business from my father without any preparation. Even so, I have a good job, and my commercial office in Kuwait is doing very well. I feel almost jealous of myself; the tables have been turned on Fate! Since the mid-fifties my company has been more successful than I ever imagined possible, and I have an important branch in Beirut. So I lost my land in Jerusalem and gained an import office in Kuwait! Exiled from my roots, I was rewarded for my exile with a business in buying and selling! When Naima died during labor and my son was born dead, I never married again. Getting married a second time when you are over thirty-five is difficult enough, but especially when you are cut off from your roots and spend your time importing iron, cement, sugar, and rice into a country far away from your own birthplace, where the only women you see are married. After forty, marriage is even more difficult. And if you're obsessed by the dreams of your youth and the thought of the girls of Jerusalem whom you may only see two or three weeks a year, or every two years... I can see myself trying to justify the fact that I have not married again. Actually there are fifty reasons for it. All those years! Maha al-Hajj knows how many, my dear Maha, Doctor Maha—I don't even know whether she is in Beirut or Rome now. Every time I returned home to see my old mother in Shaykh Jarrah Quarter, she would return to the same old theme: "When are you going to get married again, Wadi? You loved Naima, we all understood that. But it's been a long time since she died—God have mercy on her!

Don't you want to make me happy by giving me your children to see? How many years does a husband have to stay in mourning?" Anyone would think the whole thing was just a question of mourning for a wife or a matter of time. She does not realize that I crave children even more than she does. So far I have refused to mention Maha al-Hajj to her in case she starts pestering or embarrassing us when neither would do any good. But of course I've talked to Maha about her. Maha is both sympathetic and cruel. She will weep when you tell her a story and then behave toward you as though her heart were made of plastic. She accepts the idea of marriage in principle, but keeps on stalling. She sends me impassioned letters in Kuwait, and then, when I come to Beirut, she excuses her own indecision by saying that she needs more time to think. A decision made one evening is rescinded the next morning. It's as though I wasn't forty-three years old at all and had another forty years of youth and vigor ahead of me, or as though the money which I have amassed was just not enough for what she has set her mind on. In fact, I only undertook this trip because I thought Maha would be coming with me, if not as my wife, then at least as my fiancée or girlfriend. She was the one who reserved a place on the ship for me and then left me to the sea by myself. When I came on board in Beirut, I was furious. I kept cursing all women and all men who crave a wife and children in this savage, oppressive world. Very well then! Let me roam and enjoy myself! Long live freedom in an era when it has disappeared. Maha can fly to Rome on her own, attend her international conference and talk about women's diseases. And I hope it makes her throat sore! There's one more chain I have severed from around my ankles.

The land which I have bought in the hills beyond the vineyards of Halhoul is better than a thousand women. I shall cultivate it with my own hands. I shall abandon the prostitution of commerce and cultivate vines, pine trees, tomatoes, and apples. I shall dig some artesian wells. The twenty thousand dinars I have amassed should be enough to allow me to strike a deep root in my land once again.

So I shall wander once more. It does not matter if I am to be away from the office for several months; there is someone who can be trusted to keep things running smoothly. In the first place, I have a Kuwaiti colleague, Khalid al-Fahd, whose monetary assistance was essential to the expansion of our business. Then there are Ibrahim Isa and Fakhri Safiya. Ibrahim in particular is an ambitious boy: he is intelligent and persevering, and knows the jargon of commerce inside out. He is hoping that I will make him a partner in the office management, and so I shall if he continues to be as reliable and productive as he is at the moment. He is a Palestinian too. He started out with a job in Baghdad first and then joined my office. His wife is a decent girl from Ramallah; she is called Maryam and she completed her studies at Bir Zayt College.

Ah! God bless freedom! Let me enjoy this illusion of mine. My philosophy on such matters is quite plain; there is no pretense: You can enjoy any illusion you like as long as you realize that it is an illusion. But as soon as you start thinking it is real, then you are in trouble.

My trip on this ship, thanks to my dear Maha, is one of my pleasant illusions. The sea always gives me a feeling of adventure, but I realize that adventures at sea in this age of ours have no connection with Sindbad (I don't think, for example, that the ship is going to sink and that I will be the only passenger to survive). The best thing about it is that you may get to know—or else never get to know at all—two or three people whom you would never otherwise have dreamed of meeting. You may enjoy their company for a while and even become friends. You may like one, while another may hate you. When you reach the port of your destination, you will have a fresh address in your notebook. Later on, you may even send them a postcard or, at the very most, a terse note saying that you're fine, and how are they, and what have they been doing, and various other polite phrases that commit you to nothing.

There are, of course, other reasons why I am especially fond of the Mediterranean Sea, and they are entirely emotional. I was telling a young Iraqi from Baghdad named Isam Salman about them today while we were en route to the ruins of King Minos's Palace. Among the scores of passengers on the ship, he attracted my attention because he looked like an English lord in Arab disguise or vice versa—the two are indistinguishable, and it hardly matters in any case. He took an immediate liking to me, and seemed to seek refuge in me, without realizing that it was a case of from bad to worse. I imagine he is about thirty. He asks lots of questions, but is a good listener too. He makes fun of himself, and, when he does, it is with a flair that must be the result of some intellectual training that rejects self-delusion just as much as delusion in others. I am almost certain he is getting away from

Baghdad for some political reason or... I don't know. All these people under thirty, they seem at a loss. They imagine that we have found our way and that our own confusion is at an end simply because we encountered it ten or fifteen years earlier. It was Emilia Farnesi who introduced me to him. She is a friend of Maha's in Beirut whom I met two or three times. According to her, she discovered him at the stern of the ship at night counting the stars and started counting stars with him! As soon as she saw me, she asked about Maha with a display of astonishment. She pretended not to be aware of the fact that Maha and I had had a bitter quarrel, and that only three days before we sailed, she had decided not to come with me. I told her that Doctor Maha would be flying to Rome in a few days to attend an international conference on gynecology. "Ah!" she exclaimed with a phoney laugh, "so you'll be meeting there." "Maybe," I replied. "But it's more likely that I'll go to Paris without her."

Paris. The idea had sprung to my lips all of a sudden without any volition on my part. At the time I had been talking to my cabin companion, Fernando Gomez. He had suggested that I should go to Madrid. However, I did not follow up on either my idea or his suggestion. If only I could be like Fernando, going back to a country that no witless sword had split in two! If only, like him, I could return to my home town after a trip abroad, with the proceeds of my travels in my pocket. I could put down my bags, pick up a violin just like him and then look for two or three friends to accompany me. We could make up a small orchestra. People would dance, and we would dance with our instruments while they danced with their women. Our roving eyes would flirt with the pretty ones among them... From a Beirut nightclub, across the crashing waves of an eastern summer, to a land full of grapes and apples, with presses for wine that men and women would drink together. This is Fernando Gomez, forty years old, with a fine paunch and a ready laugh. A devout Catholic who believes in God and the Virgin Mary, for him the Church can ward off the pains of sin.

But nothing wards off the pains of sin from me. I accept its consequences without regret or complaint. From the very first moment when I climbed the gangplank to the ship, I felt as though I were discarding Maha like an old overcoat. This trip was meant for her, but she refused it at the last moment. Maybe she thought that I too would decide to stay in Beirut courting her pleasure and taking her from one restaurant to another.

I bumped into Jacqueline face to face by the custom's officer, and we went aboard together. We exchanged a few words in a mixture of Arabic, English, and French. She is a tourist going home after visiting Jerusalem and Bethlehem; she wears a small cross round her neck. She spent some time in Lebanon and tried to learn Arabic or, rather, add some colloquialisms to her knowledge of the written language, which she had studied at a French university. She had the tanned features of one who loves long hikes regardless of the heat or cold. She hardly used any make-up at all except for a little eye-shadow. I used to like girls who wore full make-up and loved the kind of hair that a girl would think nothing of wearing in a new style every day, even to the extent of adding some false braids to it when the occasion demanded. Nevertheless, I have found in Jacqueline, with her short hair, tanned skin, and boyish beauty, a certain pleasure that makes me enjoy her conversation, her voice, and her wire-taut, athletic body. Her conversation, did I say? Perhaps I'm exaggerating. We talk in a mixture of three languages. I do not speak hers very well, nor does she mine. But we understand each other to a certain degree.

Or maybe we do not understand each other after all. Thus, our relationship remains both evasive and dynamic. If Maha knew about it, she would, of course, be angry. Who knows? Perhaps Emilia has already sent her a letter from Alexandria, saying that no sooner had Wadi turned his back on you than he had his arms round an adventuress from Montmartre! Whatever the case may be, mutual understanding is always difficult in the best of circumstances. There may be tolerance, indulgence, or even indifference, but genuine understanding is something rare. Perhaps I no longer care whether people understand me or not; then at least they will not expect me to understand them. Leave me on my island, please, in my own fortress, in my private desert. Call it what you will. It is exceedingly difficult to refuse to be deceived by anything. You can see them all standing like so many actors, gesturing and grimacing. Their laughter peals forth and their shouts burst your eardrums. You join in with them as though you were one of them, but you're well aware that behind it all are minds the size of the palm of your hand, or even smaller. Even the grief-stricken among them cannot convince you. Bereaved mothers and those who know what it is to have your roots torn up, they are the only ones who really know grief. For the most part, the rest swim in their own shallow water, surrendering to the "waves" of their imagination. And, if they were real waves, they would avoid them like a plague. After all, why get close to pain? Shun evil and sing to it; shun life and sing to it. Discretion, as they say, is the better part of valor. Thus, mutual understanding is not really important, since the exchange takes place between obscure, unknown quantities, causing neither benefit nor harm. However, I don't always succeed in putting a distance between evil and myself. If the real significance of evil is a surfeit of life, it sometimes attracts me like a magnet. Maybe it is because more than once I have hailed death from close range; it in turn has hailed me and then gone away. It is as though my fate is wary of me, just like the poet Al-Mutanabbi. Yet I recall that in the end he too was killed. Never mind! I am not yet fifty-one, the age at which Al-Mutanabbi was killed. Perhaps it is wary of me because up to now I have always looked it square in the face. Let me say something here quite frankly: I am an inveterate gambler; I am not easily bluffed, and I dislike losing. I have lost a great deal, but I do not accept the fact. I refuse to accept my expulsion from Jerusalem by bullets and dynamite; I refuse to accept the sight of my friend, Fayiz, soaked in his own blood right in front of me; I refuse to accept the sight of tents huddled together on the hillsides as a shelter over my family's heads; I refuse to accept the idea of going from town to town looking for some paltry morsel to eat or for a roof beneath which to house my mother and father; I refuse to accept that anyone should give me looks prompted by either pity or displeasure. Yes, many losses. I have gambled, and continue to do so in order to try to make up these losses. Then there are the small losses which I suffer every day. I cannot remain silent about them either. My speech may be silent, but my actions are not. I resist, in my own way, stubbornly and patiently. That is what Maha used to object to occasionally. She used to tell me how stubborn and headstrong I was because I would never give up for anybody's sake what was in my mind. I decided that, as soon as we were married, we would move to Jerusalem so that I could be near my new land and close to the real sphere of activity for which I am making preparations now. "And what am I supposed to do in Jerusalem?" she asked. "Practice medicine," I replied, "free, if necessary." "But what will we live on?" she asked. "We'll live the same way as everyone else!" She would push me away as though I were an imbecile. "I can't stay away from Beirut for a single day," she would say. How do you convince a woman that you have another love in your heart that in no way clashes with your love for her, especially when this other love inevitably will involve facing the enemy and even death?

This morning, Emilia seemed to be talking indirectly to her friend Isam (I wonder how much he really cares for her), when she told me that she had left her country because of Michel, but that things did not work out. If she fell in love with another man, she said, she would go into the middle of the desert to live with him if that was what he wanted.

"Even to Baghdad?" Isam asked with a laugh.

"Yes!" she responded avidly. "That's a city I dream about!"

An Iraqi doctor was sitting near us with his wife. She was brunette and had a marvelous figure, the creation of an Abbasid poet's fantasy. The doctor listened to what Emilia had to say. "Your dream will only cost you the price of an air ticket," he said.

"The price of the ticket's easy, Doctor," Emilia replied. "But there are other problems that are much more costly and difficult to solve."

"Go! You could stay in my house," Isam butted in quickly. "I won't be back for a long while."

Emilia did not laugh. Her look seemed almost pained. "I'll remind you of this invitation of yours at the end of the trip," she said.

When I mentioned to her later that Maha was attached to Beirut as if by an umbilical cord that refused to be severed, she chose to defend her friend. "How could you possibly leave her?" she asked. "You really came on your own. How could you let yourself do it?"

"We had an argument."

"What a joke. To think she was the one who reserved a berth on the ship for you!"

"You know that?"

"Of course! Don't you remember how the reservations were made? When I learned that she intended to go on a sea trip, I told her I was going on the *Hercules* and so why didn't we all travel together? When she agreed, we both went to the travel agent on Wigan Street and booked a cabin for her and me and another one for you. Maha said at the time, 'When Wadi comes from Kuwait, I'll have saved him this trouble if nothing else!' And now, after all that, you've come on your own and deprived me of my cabin companion!"

What should I say to her? Should I tell her about my stubbornness?

"Did you meet Jacqueline one day in Beirut?" I asked petulantly.

"Who? That French girl?" she asked, raising her hand somewhat angrily. "You men! I'll never understand you! Where on earth can we run to escape the horror you cause?"

"And what about you women? I'll never understand you either! Where can we run to escape the horror you cause?"

The narrow door. When you have managed to get through it after much hardship, you feel a sense of release into a vast expanse like that of the firmament itself, where sounds and fantasies revolve like stars in eternal, unknown worlds. That was what our passage through the Corinth Canal was like, that rocky straight which divides the Peloponnesus from the rest of Greece; it seemed like a sword's edge over which anyone who wanted to be saved had to walk.

The passageway for ships was so narrow that, when ours pushed its bow into the canal, you expected it to get stuck at the midships or else crash into the rocks that jutted out on either side. However, it had been through the canal several times before and was quite used to taking its travelers through this ordeal, each one to his own particular expanse beyond. As it proceeded cautiously through the canal, the passengers crowded by the railings and waved to the people standing on a bridge high above them. They in turn were waving back and shouting out their gratuitous greetings, almost as though their only purpose in being there was to perform this function for everyone traveling by ship. Hello! Hello to all you tourists! Meanwhile, the boat was gliding between the jaws of the canal, and loudspeakers were sounding a concerto for flute and oboe by Bach; the whole atmosphere was permeated with one of Bach's divine ecstasies.

We thus made our way toward the setting sun, gliding into the open sea where we plowed through the mingling reds and yellows of sea and sky. The ship headed toward the pale darkness of an evening where the remnants of daylight gave their last flicker and faded away, while the music sighed like the spirit in living things.

Is this what the entry into Heaven is like? Moisture, darkness, the ancient, lofty roofs, Byzantine chants sung by choirs whose voices sound like trumpets on the Day of Resurrection? The expanse, the height, the void, the darkness, the trembling flames through which the incense twists its way upward. Mingled with the pleasant odor is the fragrance of candle smoke, hundreds of candles. There are monks with square beards and long hair falling down over their shoulders draped in gold and silver copes, and words which can hardly be made out in the midst of the resounding Greek melodies and the hundreds of people praying. It is one of the processions during the Easter season. These resounding voices, these odors charged with time and ages long past, with human torments kindled like candles that two thousand years have not been able to extinguish. From the Church of the Resurrection to the Cave of the Nativity to the gloom of subterranean rocks that curve over like the womb over an embryo, topped by high, polished pillars. Generation after generation of worshippers has made the pillars shine as each sought a blessing by touching them with their hands.

Christmas night. It is intensely cold. Snowflakes fall intermittently. In the flames of small stoves, hot chestnuts pop and burst. Voices are singing and bells peel cheerfully. One of the bells has a special angel who comes down from heaven to ring it. At the low, narrow entry, men and women bow down low in order to pass through the stone wall into the spacious darkness among the pillars. Thousands of people in the flickering light of lanterns and tiny candles beneath a huge cross very high up, watching the new birth. Fayiz and I are crammed in the middle of the crowd because rebirth, like resurrection after death, has particular meanings that bind us to this cold, rainy night, to these ancient choral songs, to this ground in whose stone were hewn caves, cells, and mosques to announce the eternity of the city throughout the ages. Could it be that there is within the rock a fire which refuses to be put out? Such is the case with some of us. There is a fire which may descend on each of us from an early age. It leaves no traces like Christ's wounds on hands and feet, but settles in the heart to remain there forever restless, just as it does inside the rock itself. Sometimes it even makes the body melt away, and then only the defiant rod remains, with the strength and flexibility of steel. And the question remains: Where does this fire come from, and who can receive it?

Near the Sultan's pool, the Friday market used to be held, where cattle and riding animals were for sale. On one of my visits to the market, I noticed a young boy sitting in the sun on a rock against a wall and drawing with a pencil. He was wearing a shirt and short trousers. He had put the drawing book on his knees and was focusing his attention on something in front of him. His hands moved with short, deft strokes. I went over and looked at what he

46

was drawing. It was a mule that had stopped quite by chance in front of him.

When he noticed me standing over him, he laughed. "It's neither a donkey nor a horse," he said. "I have to draw in the details carefully so that it doesn't end up looking like either of them!"

"Why are you drawing it?" I asked rather stupidly.

"Why? I don't know. Maybe because he's another of God's creatures."

"'But, if you'll excuse me," I said, looking closely at the picture, "it looks exactly like a mule!"

He looked up at me and smiled. It was as though the likeness he had drawn was a foregone conclusion. "Do you draw?" he asked.

"Occasionally," I replied. "In school, to please the teacher. An eggplant, a pitcher, a football. You know."

"That's what we do in school too," he said. "But I like things that move, people, girls, animals, vendors, peasant women...."

He had a thin face, so thin that it made his eyes seem very large. There was a sparkle and a warmth to them, a look that suggested enthusiasm, a love, something akin to longing that would never cease flowing.

He went back to his drawing, shading in the mule's head with his pencil and accentuating its jaws and the curvature of its reins. I felt envious of him, the kind of envy which made me love him. Even so, I left him without saying a thing and wandered around the market listening to the arguments of people as they bargained. But his eyes were still gleaming in mine, and almost involuntarily I found myself going back to him.

"Didn't you find anything to buy?" he asked.

"Why should I buy anything?"

"Why don't you sit here on this stone beside me," he asked, "till I've finished the picture?"

I sat on the stone and stared at his face while he was busy drawing. He had an elongated face, and his nose seemed big, maybe because his cheeks were so hollow.

"Do you live near here?" I asked.

"Yes," he replied, "in Jurat al-Annab. What about you?"

"I live in Shammaa," I replied, "up there."

"God! Way up there?"

"Sort of. Do you come here often?"

"Occasionally. I like the pool; it reminds me of the sea."

"Have you ever seen the sea?"

"Once at Jaffa. Have you?"

"No."

"It's incredibly blue. Many years ago when I was a child, one of the monks took a group of us on a trip to Jaffa. In the port we went on board one of the ships they were loading with oranges. One of the boxes fell off the crane and crashed against the edge of a boat. Oranges were scattered all over the blue surface of the sea. I've never forgotten that sight. The porters were cursing and swearing, but I just stood there enjoying the sight of the oranges going backward and forward, bobbing up and down to the rhythm of the waves."

The colors started bobbing and dancing in my imagination too. "I must go to Jaffa to see it too," I said. "My father works in the import-export business. He has an agent there. I'll fix things with him. When I go, will you come with me?"

"I'd love to, but...."

"But what?"

"It'll be difficult for me to find the taxi fare."

"Simple. That can be arranged. Where's your mule?"

"It bucked and wandered off. What do you think of it?"

He showed me the picture with a good deal of pride. With a certain amount of envy, I had to admit it was an excellent mule! "I can't even draw a donkey!" I told him. "I tried once too, but failed miserably."

We both stood up and walked together. We went up to the road. After a few minutes, we were at the threshold of an old building with dilapidated walls. Village women had come back from the market at Jaffa Gate, where they had sold their fruit and vegetables, and we were sitting in the shade with their circular baskets.

"This is where we live."

"In the whole building?"

"No, just one room. In the basement on the other side. That's the window of our room."

On a level with our feet there was a square opening in the wall no higher than fifty centimeters. "If I want to see you again," I said, "will you let me come here?"

"All you have to do," he replied, "is to bend down and call me through this window. My name is Fayiz Atallah."

When the breeze blew across the shady part of the building, it was pleasantly cool and reached from the doorway to a short stone passage at the end of which was a stairway going down to the lower courtyard. We sat on the threshold by the doorway. A pretzel seller came by, and each of us bought a piece for half a piaster. As we started eating it with some thyme, Fayiz leafed through his note pad which was full of drawings. He stopped at one of them and held it up for me to look at. "Look!" he said, "isn't it like him?" It was a picture of the pretzel seller.

"Exactly," I replied. "Have you drawn everyone in the quarter?"

"Even the old women!" he nodded with a laugh.

A few days later, I went to see my new friend and did just as he said. I bent down to the low window and shouted: Fayiz! Fayiz! A few moments later, he came up to see me and we spent the whole day talking about a lot of things.

"Do you know the picture of Saint John the Baptist by Botticelli?" he asked.

"Who?"

"Botticelli, an Italian Renaissance painter."

"No!"

"I saw the picture in a magazine and cut it out. I'll show it to you."

"What's that to you? Do you go to church a lot?"

"That's not the point. John, as you know, used to live in the desert by the Dead Sea, surviving on locusts and honey. He was almost entirely naked, his face was so hollow that his bones stuck out, and his eyes were as wide as the desert. He used to see visions and talk in riddles, about baptism by water, baptism by the Holy Spirit, baptism by fire. The ribs of his chest jutted out from his body and looked like arches of steel."

"You seem to admire him?"

"Admire? Sometimes I think I'm like him. I see myself as John the Baptist, with his body melting in the heat of the fire which burns inside his heart."

"The voice of him that crieth in the wilderness?"

"Exactly! Don't you think that's the quintessence of poetry— the voice of one crying in the wilderness and, eventually, a voice which all humanity listens to?"

He was like the portrait of John the Baptist that he had painted verbally. Later on, whenever I saw the picture he had mentioned, I could only think of him in the image of Botticelli's Baptist. I began to compare other pictures like it to his own thin, boyish face and his fiery eyes, that would stare at you with a profound blend of yearning and delight.

49

Like me, he was fourteen years old at the time. However, he had an appetite for visions, an obsession for a saintliness far removed from the world, despite his real love for all the people around him. Unlike him I was ignorant of all this at that age. Such saintliness, I used to say, will one day lead to having his head cut off in front of a debauched beauty at the order of an obese, depraved ruler....

We used to meet after returning home from school in the afternoon. We only lived a few minutes' walk apart. Whenever he came up to my house, we went into a neighboring field that overlooked the Montefiore Quarter behind the King David Hotel. We sat on the rocks under the olive trees and talked till the sun set.

I had read Anatole France's book *Thais* and given it to him to read. When he gave it back, we had a long argument about good and evil: Is it in fact true that good exists only through the existence of its opposite, evil? That is what the Alexandrian philosophers in the book try to prove through brilliant sophistry. They said that the crucifixion of Christ was necessary to redeem mankind, but that it would never have happened had it not been for Judas Iscariot. Thus, mankind's redemption was achieved only through a kiss of betrayal! A most disturbing logic, and part of France's sense of irony!

Both of us liked the ascetic Paphnos and regretted his piteous behavior at the end, when Thais has repented and he starts lusting after her. How was this fall possible? We could perhaps comprehend the repentance of the aristocratic courtesan, but we were unable to understand how a man could fall into the devil's clutches when his whole life had been spent in a victorious struggle against him. That is what cities did! What would John the Baptist have to say about Paphnos? Ah, we were not all made of the same stuff as prophets. Our bodies were consumed by the fires that surrounded us, not the extinguished fires within us. Woman was a temptress, deceitful: She brought us down and then saved her own skin, and so on and so on....

We were deep in such a discussion in the doorway of the building, when Fayiz's father came home with a heavy sack on his back. We helped him take it off and then carried it—Fayiz and I— into the passageway and down the stairs into the lower courtyard. This large courtyard was surrounded by four or five rooms in each of which there lived a family; the members of each one—men, women and children of all ages—sat by the door. When we opened the sack, we found it was full of things which looked like lead cartridges. "They're battery cells," Fayiz told me. "My father collects old batteries, wherever they may be, breaks them up, and takes out the lead cells."

"What does he do with them?"

"He melts them down here."

In one corner of the courtyard was the door to the room where Fayiz and his family lived, close by a filthy lavatory. Nearby were some tripods which were still full of ashes. This was where Fayiz's father melted the lead. There could hardly have been a more primitive way of doing it; just a fire was lighted around the lead cells, causing them to melt. The metal would then flow in between the burning wood, and when the fire died down, the lead would be left solidified into lumps of various shapes and sizes, some of which looked like statues. His father then sold the lead for a few piasters to people who ran small foundries. This helped his family stay alive.

Meanwhile, a boy two or three years older than my friend came out. "That's my brother, Ibrahim," Fayiz said. Ibrahim joined us as we resumed our conversation about Thais and Paphnos.

"Have you read the book, Ibrahim?" I asked.

"Of course," he replied with a laugh. "When Fayiz does his homework in the evening, I take the books he has brought home and read them. It doesn't matter whether they're school books or not."

It was then I learned that he was a carpenter who had been forced to give up going to school many years ago. One by one, I met their neighbors. There was a stonemason whom Fayiz had taught to read but who had given it up when his eyesight became too weak after he got a stone chip in his eye. A shoe shiner who coughed a lot and was about fifty years old; he had a daughter who stood by the door staring at us in her school uniform, her eyes as wide as the world itself. A house painter had at least six children, as far as I could tell, who would fill the courtyard with yells and screams. In the far corner was another man, young and strong looking, who was telling his wife a story about one of the customers in the forge where he worked. He kept yelling as though he were still amid all the din and hammering of his shop, and complaining about how stingy people were. His wife's laughing was just as loud.

This scene has remained imprinted in my mind ever since, with that slender boy occupying the center of the stage, drawing, reading, melting lead with his father, and spending the evenings working in the glow of an oil lamp. Waves of yelling, laughing, and weeping tossed him up and down, and all the while his eyes gleamed with visions. He seemed just like his favorite saint, as he tried to grasp the meaning of baptism by water and by fire and looked to a Messiah who would come and bow down to receive the water he would pour over His head; all this after He had been weighed down by the sufferings of mankind.

Ah, the sufferings of mankind! The self-same burning phrases poured forth in a melody of anguish and love, rejecting bitterness and hate. Life was bitter in those days, and conditions in Palestine were in a permanent state of turmoil and rebellion. But the cool breeze wafted its way across the shady area and the pretzel seller came by with his sesame-filled circles impregnated with thyme. My friend talked about the beauty of people's voices, faces, and hands and the eternal endurance of mankind. Then we would discuss *The Sorrows of Werther, Faust,* and *Julius Caesar.* I admired Antony's shrewdness, whereas Fayiz liked the idealism of Brutus.

One evening, as we were returning from the olive grove to Shammaa, we were carrying on our conversation. Fayiz and I went down a dusty slope in the direction of his house in al-Jura. To our surprise, we found the slope sprouting, not with crops, but with men! I could not believe that this was happening a mere five minutes from our home without my having any idea about it. Every man had dug for himself a shallow pit big enough to throw himself in as protection against the cold wind after midnight. Wrapped up in their torn *abayas* they would sleep in the pits till dawn. But who had brought them there, and where had they come from? In the morning, they would all disperse to earn a living that would barely keep them alive. Then they would return once again to their pits and spend the night in them, telling each other stories, returning the greetings of passers-by, waiting for the next day and the time to return once again to the same pits. At least, that pinpointed for them a place in the land to which they could return. "Is there no end to misery, Wadi?" Fayiz asked me.

"Have you sketched these people too?" I asked.

"Yes," he replied, "from memory. They have huge hands, as if they were hewn from rock. And they're as steadfast as rocks too...."

Like rocks. We turned the idea of "rocks" into a secret code between the two of us. We told ourselves that they symbolized Jerusalem, which was itself shaped like rocks. Its contours were those of rocks, and rocks were to be found on the edge of every road in the city. Wherever we went, we saw people breaking up rocks to pave roads or to build houses. Rock quarries were all round the city. Palestine was a rock on which civilizations had been built because it was so solid and had such deep roots connected to the center of the earth. The people, who were as solid as rock, were the ones to build Jerusalem and all of Palestine. And whom did Christ choose as his successor? Simon Peter, "The Rock." What did the Arabs build so that it would be one of the most beautiful buildings made by man? The Dome of the Rock. And what about those people dotted around on the slope? On moonlit nights you could see their heads and shoulders showing about the pits. They were of rock too! And the Sultan's Pool, what was it we like about it? The rocks, which were surrounded by water every time there was any. So let us now praise the virtues of rock!

One spring day when the rocks were exploding with flowers, the students from all schools congregated in the courtyard of the Dome of the Rock. The intention was to set out from there in another demonstration to protest the British Government's allowing Jewish immigration to continue. I ran into Fayiz there among the hundreds of students just as they were all adopting their protest resolutions. When we moved out into the narrow streets of the city and surged forward in bands, Fayiz and I were together. The close-packed roofs echoed our slogans and people closed their stores and joined in the procession with us. At Jaffa Gate, we found British soldiers and police standing ready to break up the demonstration, but the human flood of shouting youth went on without letup. Then the soldiers fired at us and charged. Stones, sticks, and even shoes were hurled from every direction. There was a slogan on everyone's lips. One of our colleagues fell to the ground, wounded in the leg. Blood was streaming down his leg into his shoe and painting weird red butterflies on the asphalt. We carried him on our shoulders, still shouting, "Rocks!" The whole country was on strike for six months afterwards, and the rock of Palestine burst forth everywhere with revolutionaries.

During that long summer, Fayiz and I spent many days wandering among the rocks and olives. For a while, we loved the village of Ain Karim because it had rocks, trees, and water and also, perhaps, because it was the birthplace of John the Baptist. But then we have lots of verdant, rocky villages in Palestine. One hot day around noon, we reached the village of Salwan, feeling very tired and thirsty. We headed for the spring. There were only two or three women around it since the rest had already finished filling their jars and cans in the morning. The spring had a big cave with slippery steps to it, but at that hour there was no one in it. It felt cool and refreshing, and that made it very inviting to the weary on a hot day.

"Can there be a cave anywhere else in the world with such life-giving water?" we asked. "Can any cave be older than this cave of ours?" It was just as though we had discovered a new continent. From that very spring, in the very same cave the builders of Jerusalem had drunk at the dawn of history. They had provided life to the city, established it on its rocks and raised it up like a stone ladder to the top of the hill which became a heart of Jerusalem. We descended the slippery steps to the floor of the cave. Water was pouring down the sides through a large opening that broadened at the base and narrowed at the top to a point where it was slightly above our heads. The rocks in the cave were a smooth, rosy yellow, as soft to the touch as the skin of the women who came there every morning and evening. Feeling hot and sticky, we flung ourselves face down in the cold water and gulped the pure, gleaming flow. In no time we had taken off our shoes and shirts, and sat on the ground. With our feet dangling in the water, we proceeded to splash each other. We kept licking it into our mouths in succulent drops as it poured over our lips. "Do you think anyone will come here now?" Fayiz asked suddenly. Before I could answer, I saw him take off the rest of his clothes and jump naked into the opening of the spring, yelling, "Hey, hey, hey!" like a lunatic. I sat there, laughing at his antics. His body now seemed to have the same color as the rocks whose domain he was now invading. I can still visualize his gleaming shoulders and back and the ripple of his buttocks, which looked like two pieces of rose-colored rock. He kept wading through the water, following the bends in the deep fissure. Light flickered around him reflected by the water as it flowed down the cave. "Hey, hey!" a moist echo, pulsating and alive.

The only thing I could do was to take off my clothes too. I leapt into the bubbling fissure. The water came up to our knees, and the bottom felt smooth and responsive to the feet. Fayiz penetrated still further round the bend, that began to get narrower and darker. "So here is the root of it all!" Fayiz yelled when the roof finally became too low for him, "this is the very womb!" He was bending over as far as he could to touch the secret of the city's birth with his own two hands. "Water and rock!" The sound of our laughter reverberated around this dark tunnel while the water rippled fresh and inviting around our thighs. We sat down in the cold water till our mouths and eyes were completely immersed. Then we started singing and thrashing the water like idiots. From our wading spot we made our way back to the cave before a group of women could arrive and surprise us. They would probably think that the spring had produced from its fissure a couple of young, naked genies immersed in the baptism of water and rock.

All this time we did a lot of drawing too. We drew whatever we saw. I found myself venturing into lines and colors. Where had this talent been hiding that now came raining down on me so suddenly with just a gesture from Fayiz's hand? (He had beautiful hands. No one who saw them could possibly believe that he used to carry heavy loads of lead, blocks of wood, and cans full of water from the public tap in the middle of the quarter.) I took to drawing now as I had done to studying before. I drew hills, olive trees, the Fortress of the Prophet David, village women selling the grapes, radishes, and tomatoes they grew among the rocks of the land. The rocks... a gorgeous woman, stunning, moving up and down like breasts, bellies, and thighs.

Some time later, when my father bought a piece of land in Upper Baqaa, I used to flirt with the rocks—as I always did when Fayiz and I were together. We built a house on one part of the property while I flirted with the rocks. I ran after beautiful girls because they seemed like rocks, like the earth from whose firm surface we extracted our gorgeous vegetables and sweet-smelling fruit.

I went to the American University in Beirut. Fayiz stayed in Jerusalem as a civil servant in a government department. He did not have enough money to support him through university. However, when I came home during the summer months, we would have long discussions about the books we had read. No! He had no need of teachers. The fire inside him was always burning, and he tested every idea in its flames. His will was like rock itself.

I used to see myself carrying him wounded, sometimes in my arms and other times on my back. The wound was in his chest. I felt that my knees were about to collapse under the weight of his body and the impact of the tragedy. I knew, as a dreamer would, that he was not just wounded but was dying in my arms. And there I was, carrying him, not knowing where I was going. Sometimes I would see myself taking him up a rocky hill with the stones and scree spilling under my feet. I could only go up a little at a time. With every step I took, the top seemed to retreat further away and I would push on upwards. Sometimes I would be taking him down through narrow passageways, leaping over the walls of vegetable gardens with him on my back and running among the olive groves, but the branches would hang down low and impede my running. Other times, I'd put him down on the ground and then, suddenly, he was someone I didn't know or else my father. I would try to recall how he was wounded, but all I could remember was a vague fear. A bomb, a bullet, or a mine which exploded under his feet. And then I'd see us being chased and have no idea who was chasing us. But we were always alone, the dead man and I. I'd yell and yell, but no one would answer. Then I'd wake up from my dream to the sound of my own yelling, with something like a sobbing sensation in my throat.

At the beginning of May 1948, modern Jerusalem was a battleground between Arabs and Jews. Actually, the British army had not departed yet, but it had left things to the Arabs and the Jews, thereby feigning "complete" neutrality. The Arab freedom fighters had secured control of the Old City and were now concentrating on certain quarters in the modern city, especially the section between Talibiyya and Upper Baqaa where our house was. Nearby was a large piece of land filled with pine trees, which we did not have sufficient money to build on. Close to where we lived was a large British army camp, one of the largest in Palestine. It was understood the army would be withdrawing on the fifteenth of May and that the camp and everything in it would be handed over to the Arab freedom fighters. Upper Baqaa was on the road to the south, the one leading to Bethlehem and Hebron where groups of freedom fighters had control of the region. Since we knew all that and were expecting the Egyptian army to move in our direction as soon as the Arab armies entered the country, Fayiz and I decided to stay on in our house like many young people of the quarter. We bought a Sten gun, some hand grenades, and a quantity of ammunition. We fired some of it from the Sten gun, by way of practice.

My father, mother, and sister went to my uncle's house in the Old City. Fayiz rented a room there for his mother and brothers (his father had died two years earlier). It never occurred to Fayiz and me that we would encounter the slightest difficulty in getting in touch with our families again. It would all last a few days at most.

The freedom fighters and defenders were all furiously busy. There were battles going on in the western part of Jerusalem, and we kept hearing conflicting reports about them. However, we were all waiting for the fifteenth of May, the day when the British army would finally withdraw and the Arab armies would enter from the south, east, and north. We would then clear Jerusalem and the rest of Palestine in two or three weeks.

The appointed day approached. Our morale was high and communications with other parts of the Arab world were still good. However, early on the morning of the fourteenth of May, we were surprised to see the British army moving its vehicles and equipment and withdrawing a day earlier than agreed. We suspected something terrible was happening: The army was withdrawing and actually handing over the modern city to the Jews, step by step, under its protection. We suddenly became aware of the Jewish advance from every direction, filling the void which the British were leaving behind them.

Fayiz and I went out in our car and toured round the streets of Baqaa with some of the young men from the neighborhood. We had a Sten gun and some hand grenades in the car. A group of freedom fighters came past us in a truck, rushing in the direction of the British camp from Talibiyya. The streets were deserted, and the noise of shells and gunfire could be heard from every direction. We did not know exactly what was going on around us. The district of Taury (just outside the city) was in Arab hands and faced the Jewish district of Montefiore. On the opposite side of the valley where the road leading into the city clung to a ridge, there arose the walls of the Old City of Jerusalem and the Fortress of the Prophet David from which the fighters were firing shells on the Montefiore district. The city's tragedy, indeed the country's tragedy as a whole, was that the Jews had laid out their kibbutzim with military precision in between the different Arab districts. Over the years, they had set up command posts in them which were fully equipped for warfare. The local people had been totally unaware of this fact. That is how the Jews were able to cut Arab communications whenever necessary. Even the British camp, which was behind us and which we confidently had expected to take over from them, was attacked from a Jewish quarter to the east of it. We now came to realize that Baqaa, in the space of a few hours, had been totally cut off, a disorganized pocket, completely encircled, around which the enemy would be tightening its stranglehold before nightfall.

Then we heard some news which caused us considerable alarm: The Arab fighting forces had decided to withdraw to the south toward the Monastery of St. Elias and to the northeast to Taury. The purpose was to consolidate at strategic points, allowing the Arabs to regain some control over the situation that had developed so unexpectedly that day.

It was three or four o'clock in the afternoon, as I recall. Fayiz and I decided to leave the house in order to see what our position was like. We headed in the car toward Bethlehem. Some distance away we saw Jewish armored cars on the highway, but they paid no attention to us. They were starting to occupy the modern city. Maybe every time they saw a civilian car, they felt sure it would surrender to them sooner or later anyway.

"What now?" Fayiz asked, with the Sten gun under his feet in the car.

"We're not giving up that easily!" I exclaimed.

"Let's go to Taury!"

I reversed the car, and we headed toward Taury by way of secondary roads. We passed through al-Baqaa and the German colony, where we saw some foreigners looking out windows, anxious and uncertain. By the time we approached the district of the Government Press close to Taury, we thought we were safe because there were some detachments of armed Arabs there. However, the shelling was more intense than anywhere else. What scared us was that we had no idea where it was coming from; actually we got the impression it was whizzing over our heads. We soon discovered that the battle was going on about half a kilometer from where we were, across the valley which led to the Old City between Taury and Montefiore.

When we reached the nearest road to the right that went through the district of Taury, we took it. But a gray armored car was coming round the bend, heading straight toward us. When we spotted it, it could not have been more than three hundred yards away. We knew at once that it was certain death for us to stay in the car on a road where all the houses were locked up, apparently deserted, and a Jewish armored car was chasing us. At the point where the secondary road turned off the main road, it ran parallel to the valley ridge, which sloped away to the east and continued its downward incline in the direction of the Arab area, joining up eventually near Salwan. Without a moment's thought, I stopped the car. "Hit the valley, Fayiz!" I yelled at my friend as I opened the door. We bolted from the car. Fayiz was carrying the Sten while in my jacket pockets I had two heavy hand grenades. We leaped from the road on to some rocks at the top of the incline, which was very steep at that point and ended, way down, with three or four old stone-built houses scattered about at random.

Just then, a hail of bullets hit the stones, raising up dust all around us and whistling over our heads. The armored car had stopped near our car and was shooting aimlessly in our direction. However, the sharp angle of the incline and the ancient stone walls did not allow the man at the machine gun perch to get a fix on us. The bullets kept splaying off where he did not intend them to go. We stayed where we were, shielded by the wall, and did not move an inch. We were hoping that some of our people in the houses higher up, overlooking the road—if, indeed, there was anyone in them—would spot the armored car. But it stayed where it was without opening fire again, apparently waiting for us to come out into the open again. Nearby, the rattling of bullets and the sound of shell explosions went on all the time, something we could not understand.

"Where the hell are they, where the hell are they?" We could only speak with difficulty.

"So this is it at last," Fayiz said.

"What do you mean?" I asked.

"Face to face with death," he replied.

We lay low where we were; every second seemed like an age. As the tense silence continued, we started assessing our options one by one. My mind began to function with a weird clarity: Can we face an armored car with a Sten gun when we are on lower ground? Impossible. Can I hit it with a hand grenade? Can I possibly hit the target that high up? Also impossible. If we crawl upward on our stomachs between the rocks, there is a big rock up there full of cavities. Maybe we could get to it and strike from there. Maybe the best thing to do would be to stay where we are till the enemy gives up and goes away. Time must be valuable to him as well as us.... I clutched a hand grenade in my shaking hand, and my friend Fayiz had his hand on the Sten, ready for any surprise move.

Then we heard the armored car roar, apparently moving in reverse because it could not turn around where it was. Immediately afterward, we heard a prolonged burst of fire; they were shooting at our car to put it out of commission. We ran toward the rock at the higher level. Then suddenly we saw the armored car just above us. What happened? Till today, I still do not know exactly what happened. All I do know is that Fayiz opened fire on the armored car and emptied a Sten magazine in a single, brutal burst of fire. At the same time, I took the safety pin out of the grenade I was holding and threw it with all the nervous energy I could muster. We heard it fall under the armored car, and then it exploded with a terrifying bang. "Scram, Wadi!" Fayiz yelled, "Run and don't look back!" We started running, leaping from one rock to another without looking behind us. "You only die once," I told myself, "if it comes... and it won't come, we've hit them! We'll soon be in Salwan."

Not long afterward, it struck me, to my horror, that Fayiz was lagging behind and groaning. When I looked back, I saw him lying on his face among the stones and thorns. Blood was flowing all over the ground, and his gun lay beside him.

"Fayiz, Fayiz!" I yelled.

I went back to him and turned him over on to his back. "No, no!" I found myself shouting out, "For God's sake, no, it's impossible."

He raised his head, all in a sweat, and looked at me. "What happened?" he asked.

I opened his shirt to have a look. My hand was immediately covered in gushing blood. There was a gaping wound under his left shoulder, and the flesh was exposed as though it had been lacerated and become viscous. The blood was drenching his shirt and flowing slowly now. "It's above the heart," I said. "No, it's not a serious wound, it's above the heart." Forgetting entirely where we were, I tried to stop the bleeding. I took off my coat and used parts of it to staunch the crimson flow. Fayiz was having trouble breathing; perhaps the bullet had punctured his lung. What was I to do? I took the second hand grenade out of my coat pocket and rolled my coat up like a pillow. Then I put it on a rock and leaned Fayiz's head against it. I tried to remember what I had learned about first aid when I was a boy scout, but I could not remember a thing. Fayiz kept looking at me pleadingly, as if to say, "Can't you do something?" All I could do was to look back at him helplessly like an imbecile.

What was I to do, for God's sake?

The afternoon sun was still infernally hot. I looked around me and noticed that we had come a long way from the ridge of the valley. Even so, there was still a considerable distance to cover before we reached the floor below, green with olive trees. Once again, I became aware of the sound of gunfire going on in crazy repetition all over this rocky, deserted landscape and around the Old City some distance away from us. I had to get my friend to the city before sunset. The wound was not in his heart. I would carry him in my arms. I was slightly taller than he was. When I was young, I had been a soccer player and used to swim a great deal in Beirut. I had once carried a girl in my arms for a long distance into the sea to prove how strong my muscles were. Yes, I would carry him.

I lifted Fayiz. He groaned, but said nothing. I picked him up with some difficulty and started walking. As I walked, he kept moaning quietly. I was sweating profusely, and the drops of sweat fell on to his bloody chest. The blood had stopped flowing by now. He felt heavy, but my knees did not give way under the weight; they managed to carry both of us. The ground sloped downward—thank God for that! We had to reach Salwan before darkness. Then we could go to the spring and descend to the cool cave which we had not seen for many years.

But I could not keep walking for long. I tripped and could not move another step. I put Fayiz down on the ground so that we could both have a rest. His face had turned a dreadful yellow color. "Wadi," he mumbled, "I'm thirsty... thirsty." I burst into tears as I looked at his tormented, pale face, the lean, beautiful face of Fayiz. I wished that I could give him my tears, my blood even, to drink. "Fine, Fayiz," I said, "I'll go and look for some water."

But there was no need to look. He started shaking uncontrollably; I could not stop him. His mouth kept opening and closing in jerks in a desperate quest for air or water or both. I kept shouting, "Fayiz, Fayiz...." Then a thin trickle of blood flowed out of the corner of his mouth, and his eyes remained fixed on the walls of Jerusalem like two glittering stones.

My friend had been killed, and I had stood there by him as helpless as a child. The sun set, indifferent to the wounded city. I remained beside him, brushing off the flies. This vast earth—how

61

tight it really is! The sounds of death fill the air, and there is not one person to help me move my friend, even a few inches.

I stood up and carried him on my chest, just as one carries a baby. I took him toward the olive trees. I could not see where I was walking, but I kept moving. There he was, the lover of rocks, heavy as a stone on my chest. I put him down again to take a short rest and then carried him some more. We fell down together once again. All I wanted was to die.

I put Fayiz on his back and threw myself face down on the ground beside him, inhaling the smell of the earth and the stones. I was panting hard, and could not slow my breathing down, however much I tried. I was unable to think about anything any longer. Let them come, I thought, let them come and bury us together! Let them come? Who? Who on earth would come to this valley abandoned by God and man? Where was the Sten gun? Where was it?

Just then, I remembered that the gun had been left on the ground where Fayiz had fallen for the first time. My coat was still there too and so was the only hand grenade I had left.

I got up at once, unbuckled the cartridge belt Fayiz had around his waist, and put it on. I leaned over to talk to him. In the gray darkness of that moment, he was just sleeping; he would wake up again when I got back, no doubt about it. "I'm just going for a short walk," I said, "then I'll be back, I promise." I retraced my steps up the loose earth of the hill, looking for the weapons we had left behind.

The coat was still there, rolled up and stained like a tramp's. Close to it shone the steel gun stained with Fayiz's blood. I picked it up, wiped off the blood with the coat, and then threw the coat away. Not too far away, I found the grenade, that death pomegranate. I picked it up and hung it on my cartridge belt. When a man is resolved to die, everything seems simple and possible. I filled the magazine with the bullets I had and went up the hill, toward the same rock as before. I crept forward in the dark, feeling that the noise my feet were making in the earth must be echoing throughout the entire valley, however soft it really was. No matter! It might attract some of Fayiz's killers. But they should not see me, at least not until I had finished the task I had set myself.

The road above was illuminated, but seemed empty. The battle had to be going on somewhere else, since I could still hear the sound of firing. I reached the rock a little bit beneath the road and waited. Then I crawled up toward the edge of the road. There was the armored car. But, now that I had put it out of action, it lay there silent and deserted, like an ugly giant cockroach, dead. Close by it was my car, which looked like a murdered child. I walked over to it and looked it over. The glass was shattered, and the metal was perforated like a sieve. I walked round it and gave it a pat as if to encourage it to carry on. If anyone had seen me at that moment, with the gun in my hand, he would have assumed I was guarding it. But nobody came. I started walking backward and forward, listening carefully. All I could hear was the exchange of fire between the Fortress of the Prophet David and Montefiore.

Suddenly I heard a loud noise, the sound of an armored car or truck approaching. With a single leap I was behind my rock again beneath the edge of the road. The sound got louder and louder. I tightened my grip on the weapon and waited. A large truck appeared. Terrific! Fantastic! It came up and stopped by the disabled armored car. Some men got out of the truck, talking to each other in Hebrew. What were they going to do on this deserted road? Maybe they would just take a look at the armored car and then leave. I had no time to lose.

I was crouching in the dark, while they—three or four young men wearing khaki clothing—were on the lighted street. I could see them as clearly as if they were acting on a stage. They took out a thick, metal cable, and the driver moved the car so that the back of it was opposite the front of the armored car. They had come to take the junk away! I took the grenade from my belt and crawled upward to a point just below the edge of the road. I took out the safety pin with my teeth and yelled: "Take that, you bastards!" I threw it right in the middle of them. When it exploded, I felt my own head had exploded with it; my teeth chattered at the power of the explosion. I climbed up on to the road at once, stood up over the smoke-filled scene and unleashed a single burst from the Sten, screaming, "That's for you, Fayiz!"

Slowly I turned toward the incline. I stepped slowly at first and then started leaping among the rocks and thorns. I was going back to my friend to tell him what I had done. I looked for him in the dark and for a moment thought I had lost him, but then I found him and knelt down beside him. "I've killed the people who killed you!" I said. It seemed to me that he heard what I said and even moved a little. My head fell on his head and my face touched his face. It was cold, cold as stone.

I could not move. I dug my nails into the earth, and waited in case there should be any sign of life from Fayiz's body as he lay there on his back with his arms spreadeagled. He was smeared all over with the blood that I knew must be on my face, hands, and shirt. Rocks. Terror. I felt my soul splitting in two parts, one of which I gave over to the earth and thorns. The noise of gunfire filled my ears. I had to take him somewhere, to the nearest place in Salwan.

Eventually I got up. The slopes were all dark, and I could not make out any path to follow. From time to time, the darkness would be shattered by a sudden explosion that would then be followed by the clatter and rumble of gunfire throughout the valley. I was not going to leave Fayiz on his own even if it meant my falling into enemy hands. I sat him down on a rock with his legs apart and then squatted down if front of him so that he fell on to my back with his arms dangling over my chest. I grabbed hold of one of them and, using all the energy I had left, stood up. My other hand lifted up one of his thighs around my waist so that his body collapsed on to my back like a big child. Had the fire in his heart really been extinguished, so that all I had to do now was to carry his molten body and let his head rest on my neck? I walked through the olive trees, over thorns and among the rocks, with the Sten gun hanging over my shoulder and under the dangling arm of Fayiz. I fell over, but gathered my breath and picked him up again. I heard my own voice talking; it seemed to be coming from some deep cave. I talked to him in staccato breath. Our families. Salwan. Jerusalem. Two crazy people in a desert of death. When I took him off my back to take a rest, I swore that I would come back, somehow, as an invader, as a thief, as a killer; I would come back, even as a casualty. That I swore on a rock.

It was a long, foul night.

At dawn a group of our fighters came by. We handed over the martyr to his own folk along with the afternoon's other martyrs. Amid the weeping and sobbing, I stifled my own grief with an oath that I still remember every day and have remembered for over fifteen years. Can you understand that, Maha?

The Corinth Canal is behind us now. The Greek Sea now envelops us in its moonlight, a night full of tales of love and murder. The smell of the earth attracts Ulysses as he roams amid the perils of the sea. There has to be a return.

There was a dance. Jacqueline danced in my arms as lightly as the breeze even though the hall was crowded. When the music became more insistent and wild, she threw herself on to my chest

64

as if she wanted to squeeze herself between my bones. I remembered Fayiz. I remembered the rocks. I remembered death and birth. All this while my mouth was caressing Jacqueline's short hair and feeling her tiny ear. Then she withdrew her ear from my lips. "Oh!" she whispered with a laugh, "you excite me. Are you really thinking of me?"

Isam Salman

It was almost midnight when Wadi Assaf took me to his cabin. I did not realize that he wanted to reveal a secret to me. We had spent most of that evening dancing. In the cabin Fernando Gomez lay on his narrow bed reading. We apologized for the intrusion, but with typical Spanish hospitality, he expressed his pleasure at seeing us.

Wadi produced a big portfolio. For a moment I thought he wanted to show me some maps or architectural drawings that might interest me, since he knew I was an architect. But when he opened it, it was full of paintings. He took a few out and laid them flat on his bed. As I looked at the first picture he took out, I stood transfixed for a few moments, not knowing how to react.

I sat on his bed. "Who painted that?" I asked.

"I did," he replied.

"You? Is this what you do when you are not importing and exporting?"

"Yes."

Yet before I had a chance to comment on the painting, he took another one out and laid it flat on top of the first one. Then another, and another, spreading them out right and left. They were horrifying; I cannot really claim that I understood them. They were full of faces—half faces, sleeping faces, dead faces, green, red, and yellow faces, surrounded by suns and moons, dry twisted branches, and large hands with horrible fingers.

"I usually paint on paper," he said, "because paper is easy to carry when I travel."

"But they're horrifying," I said. "Anyone who has the slightest acquaintance with your good humor would never be able to understand how your mind can depict such dreadful thoughts."

"Nightmares, rather," he said, to correct me. He seemed to be poking fun at Fernando and me or else at himself. "That's pre-

67

cisely why it's difficult for anyone to live with such paintings," he continued.

"Yet, you carry them with you wherever you go?" I asked.

"Yes, the same way a man carries his cross with him, wherever he goes."

Fernando was silent all this time while he examined the paintings carefully. "Is it possible?" he asked suddenly. "You're an Arab Goya! These are the *Horrors of War* all over again. If you don't mind my saying so, there's a touch of madness in them. Not so?"

Wadi laughed. "A lot of madness," he replied. "But then even people who paint rivers, mountains, and wheat fields have a touch of madness in them too. In fact, even those who paint pretty faces, large, naked women, and beautiful thighs and breasts may have a touch of madness in them. No?"

"This calls for some whiskey," Fernando said. He took a new bottle out of the little cupboard and poured the whiskey into plastic cups. "I only drink it straight," he said.

As I enjoyed the marvelous kick of the whiskey, Wadi continued. "There is a touch of madness in each one of us, more in some than in others. We escape from this ugly reality of ours into a world that is hidden inside and filled with all that we desire, and, at times, all that we dread. Just like lunatics."

"It's a defense mechanism," I said. "We need it in order to keep our wits about us when we leave the world of lunatics, even for a few brief moments."

"In my opinion," said Fernando, "the world we escape into is probably more truthful than the real world. This morning I was sitting in the parlor leafing through *Vogue* magazine. There it was, a "hidden" world filled with all that we could possibly desire: soft, silky women, with wide eyes and big mouths. You know, I work in a nightclub in Beirut, so I'm no stranger to the world of women. But the women there, off-stage, are as hard as nails and as sharp, too. Everything about them is false—it's all dyes, make-up, wigs, and they would do anything for a good Lebanese pound. The world of *Vogue* is different. It's a world of... er... affluent lust, where sex is more refined than prostitution, or so it seems. The most beautiful of God's creatures in the most beautiful postures, on velvet carpets, with flowers, among ruins in Lebanon, Italy, Greece, under evergreen trees in England, fully dressed or half-naked, it doesn't matter. They all seem oblivious of the fact that their seductiveness stirs in us sex, lust. They devour men, these tender houris, without betraying a single emotion. They are our shortcuts to stupor, to fantasy, to withdrawal from the jaws of vicious reality. Give me *Vogue*'s illusory women, and you can keep all the reality of this world! Is that madness?"

"Perhaps, to a certain extent," Wadi said, "or at least, an illusion forced upon us by nature itself. Look, what is sleep? It's a kind of withdrawal into the inner depths, into the sweet recesses of darkness. Illusion is the twin of forgetfulness, and forgetfulness is the best balm for wounds, as the saying has it, till nightmares come to shock us. And that's the crux of the whole matter. A large part of civilization is devoted to the organization of illusion, the enjoyment of illusion. Yet the nightmares remain, and they are, in the final analysis, the really creative forces: women, as hard and sharp as nails, multiplied by a hundred million, raised to the nth degree."

"You mean your paintings, your life, and mine," I said. "But, the real question is: Do we escape from or into this civilization of illusion?"

"It seems to me," Wadi replied, "that we've been wronged by nature. It has left us relatively little illusion. Can't you see how I pour out all my nightmares into these paintings like a cloud unloading its rain?"

"But why do you force your nightmares on other people?" I inquired. "That's what people usually ask. Everyone seeks a little forgetfulness, a little self-deception."

"If art has no connection with the hell that is in the soul," Wadi said, "it can have no connection with the heaven either. Artists who always respond to what people want are mere dabblers, dyers, whores, call them what you will. They know nothing about the concentration of black clouds, the thunder and lightening, or the rain and fertility that follow. A painting which cannot produce fertility in the soul of the beholder is nothing but a big joke. Our tragedy is that we try to renounce our civilization because it is based on illusion, while we, despite ourselves, are part of the civilization of fantasy—until the nightmare suddenly returns. The enemy we elude in order to forget him or make him forget us materializes in front of us. And so we fall back into our vicious circle and resort to some sort of illusion."

"Perhaps to some sort of truth?" I asked. "I am a rejectionist: I escape in order to seek a reality that suits me."

"Are you prepared to kill?" Wadi asked.

"Kill? I don't see how the question is relevant to the subject."

"So you too prefer to escape just for the sake of escape."
This persistence annoyed me. I knew too well that I was an escapist and that I did not want to kill. I remembered then what I had always dreaded remembering: What my father had done when I was a little child. Killing? Perhaps Wadi was thinking of Palestine, of killing the enemy there. Yet, when he mentioned killing, he opened inside me a wound of another kind. Why did my father kill Jawad Hamadi and inflict a curse on me for the rest of my life? He rebelled, he killed, and then he lived in exile far away from us. Everybody said he had done well by killing Jawad Hamadi. Everybody said he had done us proud by doing so. Fine, but the gods hankered for vengeance in a shameful manner. The gods forced him to live away from us and turned him into a mere legend. They were not above making me lose the one woman I loved and keeping me pining for her.

"I prefer to escape in a positive way," I said. "Is that possible? Perhaps it's like the army commander who retreats in order to regroup his men and prepare for a fresh assault. I really don't know. I'm confused. Have you ever really killed?"

Wadi raised his eyebrows in his usual fashion and gave me a strange, penetrating look. He did not answer my question. Instead, he said, "Alright, we're agreed, then. You're confused, I'm confused, and so is everybody on this ship. Let's go back to the question of madness."

Since some of our conversation was in Arabic, Fernando busied himself with a thorough examination of the paintings. He picked them up one by one and shook his head, sometimes to express contentment, and at other times the opposite. Then he clapped his hands.

"When I don't understand a painting," he said in English, "I enjoy it. Take this one, for example. I don't understand it, but I feel that it penetrates me. It hurts me, but I enjoy it. Masochistic? Why not, as long as I enjoy it?"

"My own sense of enjoyment is purely intellectual," I said, studying the painting carefully. "I love to observe relations, proportions, contrasts between lines and masses. It's the kind of thrill one experiences after solving a difficult mathematical problem."

"But," Wadi said, "there are no solutions in art. The problem is what counts. The solution is always in the next issue that you never buy. I enjoy anything that tears me apart within, that makes me feel I'm walking to left and right at the same time. You know, most of us are like a man in love with two women at once, a

70

brunette and a blonde."

Fernando burst into a guffaw. "It's a good arrangement," he said, "if you can take care of both women at the same time!"

Wadi took another gulp of whiskey. "This kind of man," he continued, "regards each of them as a paragon of beauty, and in his solitude he sees in each one all that he can possibly want in a woman. He sees himself moving back and forth between them, kissing one while the taste of the other woman's kiss is still fresh on his lips. He thinks they know nothing about each other, that his game is one of his own closely guarded secrets. But, in a devilish moment of fantasy, he sees them both making love strangely to each other. The idea strikes him as ludicrous. It upsets him, and he dismisses it from his thoughts. One day he discovers that they are indeed in love with each other, that they are lesbians, torturing him for their own sport, and finding true pleasure only in each other. He becomes aware that he is jealous of each of them, jealous of a woman whom he loves and whom he thought he was able to deceive and use in order to deceive his other woman. This is how we constantly tear ourselves apart between the things we love (or imagine we love) while these things actually love themselves and hold fast to their own logic and eccentricities much more than they care for us or our desires. Our way of life in society is one example of this. Power and its contradictions, money, possessions, marriage, children—they're all constantly tearing us apart. In the end, what a pleasure it is to seek refuge in the world of *Vogue* where there's no pain, no tearing apart, just a dream that lasts for an hour or even less!"

"I should grow a beard then," I said.

"I should become a monk," Fernando said.

"Become a monk, grow a beard," Wadi continued, "that's alright. A little madness is better than total insanity, which is the end result for many people. They are born crying, as a poet once said, and they die in a tempest of horrors—some hidden, others visible, some psychological, others physical, with intermittent spells of clarity, rather like the brightness you get at noontime in the desert—a never-ending sky over a never-ending earth—and silence fraught with the dreams of mystics, until the tempest strikes again. Today the tempest swept me away. The nightmares that I fear and pour out onto my paintings whenever I can, have begun to haunt me once again. People say that, for a man, the nightmare is an incubus, a lustful woman who attacks him at night, sucks his life out of him for her pleasure, and makes him see whatever she wants him to see. But my nightmares are different. All I see are human massacres. I fight my way through them, but only manage to escape to places that are full of ruins and garbage. What is the meaning of escape anyway? Where are we escaping to? I may escape into these paintings, which I only show to a very few people, or I may withdraw into silence that lasts for many days, flirting with my own thoughts. These thoughts usually revolve around my homeland, and my silence—a kind of internal silence, like a cosmic night whose spaces cannot be spanned.... Many years ago, I wrote something about the bells of memory ringing in subterranean caves, silent like the endless time that enfolds the history of man, the clamorous, raging history of man. It is the kind of silence that is filled with memories and visions, with forty years of turmoil, forty thousand years of tumult, love, and anger. And visions are very important, no matter how obscure they may be. How many people throughout the centuries have held fast to their visions or even become martyrs because of them? This evening as the sun was about to set, I experienced a vision that is almost impossible to express. It cannot be described: layers of clouds, blazing hot with the colors of twilight, like rampant flames and molten gold, like the sky in the paintings of Tiepolo, surging with drama for no apparent reason. But what exactly did I remember? What did I see? Cascades of pleasure? Oceans of yearning and of conflict? Maybe. Or was it, perhaps, a haze, a luminous dust, flashes of light, and volcanoes? It was a dizzying silence, the silence of intense joys and agonies that came to an end and yet were about to start anew, just when they had reached a conclusion. The devil inside me exploded. Neither he nor God could be exorcised by prayers or poems. Forty long years of my life flared up, raged, and collapsed at their hands, while the clouds were being torn asunder by split gold and blazing fire.

"Music was blaring on the ship. People came and went, watching the sunset, sighing, laughing, flirting. I stood there like an idiot, completely absorbed by the scene. Perhaps I was suffering from an illusion, debating both God and the devil at the same time. You would probably say, along with Freud, that the whole thing was sexual. Sexually deprived people often imagine they're either the world's giants or its vermin. But the issue is not that simple. For me, it's a question of life, the very matter of survival. What I mean is that, however pretentious a man may be, illusion is still something that he cannot avoid. It is as though he would say, 'Take away illusion, and darkness will prevail.' So let man sing as

72

long as he wants. Singing is all illusion. Illusion is all the sweet things in life. Remove it, and the final pleasure reverts to nought. Only salt will be left. Illusion possesses me, and I become filled with the desire to say things in endless words, even though the words are mute. But illusion is soon dissipated. Words falter in my throat, then cease. What is it that afflicts me? What is this fascinating, evil phantom? Does it have a pulse, teeth, a nose, arms, legs? Does it crunch like an almond or a peanut? Does it echo with sound like bells? Does it soar to great heights and then plunge to the ground? Does it fill people's hands with peaches and grapes? It is probably just another lie that comes to me like a fruit from far-off lands; I put it in a basket full of other fruits of all kinds and colors. The palace of silence is stocked with such baskets. The harvest is better than I thought!

"All the time I see myself running over the hills, walking among the mountain crags or even on the waters of Lake Tiberias. Christ keeps me company. I see His large, bare feet, His long, slender fingers flowing with miracles, while He himself hardly utters a word. Then the hours of serenity brighten my vision. People and things slowly take shape. Everything becomes sharp, clear, hard until it almost hurts. Where are we? What fools' paradise is this? At this very moment, we who are burdened by philosophies and illusions are about to leave this cabin for the open sea again. Meanwhile, someone else, an English or French explorer perhaps, is crossing the Empty Quarter, risking his life in the trackless sands, trying to master a language that eludes both his tongue and throat, and finding a singular pleasure in drinking camel's milk from a container washed with camel's urine. What do we know about our own deserts, those wide expanses that are open to all kinds of adventures but closed to us? What do we know about our own Bedouins, for example, who mark their way with a heap of stones here and there in an ocean of sand, like someone charting the course of this ship by a floating cork? And those foreign adventurers, what are they looking for? Oil? Minerals? Perhaps they're serving their governments' secret designs. Maybe. But what matters is that they venture into the unknown in order to return with something knowable, communicable. In the meantime, they will have defied the scorching sun, lived with the stars, overcome thirst, subsisted on a handful of dates, and worn out their buttocks on camel saddles that are not made for them. No doubt some of them are also running away from something or other. Certainly they are escaping from societies where they don't feel at home, or women whom they are afraid to marry, or some kind of comfort that has bored its way into their hearts like woodworms in a piece of wood. But this kind of escape is toward something yet harder, something more intractable—and more worthwhile. One explorer will spend five years among Bedouins learning a dialect of a language that he will never read or write. He then returns to London or Paris, like a victorious general from distant battlefields, in order to describe a black goat-hair tent at early dawn and the way in which pebbles glow like jewels in the first rays of the sun, casting behind them long, blue shadows. In the desert he discovers man in his very essence, satisfied with the very least. One beautiful word can please him, while one scorching word sets him aflame. He discovers that in such surroundings chivalry manifests itself every day, that life is synonymous with courage in a constant state of rejuvenation, and that the only fate of the coward is his own ever-recurring death. In the end, the explorer writes his book and publishes it. We read it in his foreign language to learn something new about ourselves, to learn where some of us are."

Fernando reached for the bottle and poured us some more whiskey. Wadi was lying on his bed as he spoke. I sat facing him on Fernando's bed, with the paintings scattered at our feet. Gradually I began to follow this Palestinian's train of thought. At first, I felt he was contradicting himself, but then I realized he was being consistent with his own kind of opaque logic.

"In spite of everything," I said, "these adventurers of yours remain runaways, or as you said, escapists. They're in search of something more difficult, intractable, worthwhile; fair enough. But they're "escaping" nevertheless. They're strangers in their own countries and in other countries as well. They discover the unknown in distant places in order to forget their own alienation, to put an end to it, and to return victorious to a world that they dearly wish would embrace and accept them. Like all adventurers, however, like every Sindbad, they can never remain among people for long. This feeling of alienation and this lust for escape soon takes hold of them again."

"But don't you see?" Wadi interjected, "they have a place to go back to and be measured by. Henry Layard goes back to the British Museum with winged bulls, and Sindbad returns to Baghdad laden with jewels. Real alienation is alienation from a place, from roots. This is the crux. Land, land, that's everything. We return to it bringing our discoveries, but as long as we hang on to the racing clouds, we remain in this fools' paradise. We are continually escaping, but now we must go back to the land, even if we are forced later to start off again. We must have *terra firma* under our feet, a land that we love and quarrel with, a land that we leave because of the intensity of our love and our quarrel—and return to once more."

"Land?" I asked, interrupting him and moving involuntarily in his direction. "My father was a farmer in southern Iraq. He went to Baghdad and killed an "important" man. He stabbed him to death because of the land."

"I know that," he said.

I was surprised. "How do you know?"

"Dr. Falih Haseeb told me. That was more than a quarter of a century ago, wasn't it?"

"It's all over now."

"The important thing," Wadi continued, "is that the land remained yours."

"A little part of it," I replied.

"And yet, you're...."

I interrupted him before he could finish his sentence. "Yes," I said, "I'm running away from it. I reject it. I reject the destructive, useless struggle for it."

"It's strange, Isam," Wadi reflected. "No matter where I go, no matter what fancies possess me, I'm forever running toward my land, which has been separated from me by a thousand kilometers of barbed wire. I run toward it carrying a hand grenade. Yet you reject your land?"

"I was delighted to sell most of it," I said. "I had no regrets."

Wadi drew close and stared at me with his deep-set eyes. "What exactly are you running away from?" he asked.

"From Luma," I answered without reflection.

He was silent. He inhaled deeply from his cigarette and then pursed his lecherous lips as he puffed out the smoke. "From Luma!" he exclaimed.

He got off the bed, stooped down, and started picking up the paintings scattered all over the floor one by one without uttering a word. I watched him, hoping that now that I had divulged my secret to him in a couple of words, his silence indicated he was thinking of what was bothering me. But no sooner had he put the paintings in his portfolio than he looked at me.

"No problem!" he said.

"What do you mean?"

"I mean, forget it!"

Fernando did not understand the last bit of our conversation, but his eyes moved from Wadi to me as though he understood everything.

"Luma?" he asked in English. "Does she interest you? Too bad. Too bad!"

Wadi would not relent. "Land, land, that's the secret in your life, with or without Luma. The land will drag you back to it no matter how much you resist, no matter how far you go. Luma is the soil, the trees, the water. She is the land, no matter how much you imagine otherwise, no matter how you fail to hold her in your arms, and despite all her philosophizing."

I do not know why I laughed just then. I laughed happily. It was as though Luma had suddenly appeared in the cabin and sat in my lap as she used to do in London.

"Land interests you," I said, "because you were forced to leave it. Don't you see, Wadi, your deprivation has nothing to do with sex; it's a question of land. People who are deprived of women think about women all the time. You, on the other hand, are deprived of your land."

Wadi laughed. He grabbed my arm and led me out of the cabin as we said goodbye to Fernando.

"But I've spent all these years wanting to marry her—the land, I mean," he said as soon as we left the cabin. "I collect one penny after another for the sake of her beautiful eyes. My exile has almost come to an end. I have transferred my money to Jerusalem and bought a large piece of land in a village near Hebron. I shall buy another piece in Bayt Hanina, build a big stone house, and plant tomatoes and apples. I'm not a farmer, but I shall use the latest farming techniques. I shall dash the rocks to pieces and cover them with our red, fertile soil. I shall force plants out of the rocks, I swear! I shall dig an artesian well. I shall collect every drop of rain. As soon as I return home I shall get married— to bring woman and land together. There is still time enough in my life. I want to have children before I am sixty. I shall look for a woman who is well-known for her fecundity, a widow perhaps. I shall plant anything, even radishes, and I shall paint, paint a lot. I shall paint our rocks, our olive trees, the walls of our vegetable patches, our village women in their blue and orange dresses and their white flowing headdresses. Come and visit me there! Make sure you bring your hiking boots because we shall walk through rocks and mud. Of course, I shall buy a thousand records and listen to Vivaldi, Bach, Telemann, Josquin des Près, Brahms, Sibelius, Stravinsky, and modern electronic music. Music is my hashish; I'm addicted to it. But I shall live with the land, with the soil and the rocks. You'll visit me there two years from now, eh? I'll write you long letters. Let other people enjoy traveling by sea and air. I'll only travel in my own country. Every time humanity goes mad, I'll plant a hundred more trees. I know I won't be able to stay away from the world, but I'm going to do my best to stay close to it. There will be strife all around me, I know. I'll hide a couple of guns and a grenade in my house, but I'll plant trees, paint, and breed a dozen children who will contribute to the beauty of life—although they may add to its tragedies too. From there, I shall work to bring the decisive moment closer.

"By God, I shall be able to stand on the top of one of our hills, among the ancient pine trees, high above the terraces of grapevines, fig and azarole trees. I'll raise my hands to the heavens like a madman and cry out at the top of my voice, "Hosanna in Excelsis! Glory to You, my God, for this bounty, for this marvelous outpouring from Your cup of bounty on to the earth, for these hills and valleys that You grace with Your blessings and fill with oceans of love, radiance, and enchantment! But I know I'll be surrounded by lamentations caused by hunger, woe, ruin and tyranny—lamentations that will confound every word I utter like vicious atmospherics that spoil the reception of a program on the radio. So I shall raise my voice even louder. I'll even split my throat open with my screams so that God may hear me and listen to my gratitude—and my protest.

"And now, Isam, this beautiful woman from Iraq, what exactly is your story with her?"

Wadi Assaf

Faith needs no justification. There are not many things that I believe in, but I don't feel that I have to put myself out in order to provide convincing proof.

A group of us—Doctor Falih Haseeb, his wife Luma, and I, along with three or four others, including Yusuf Haddad and Mahmud Rashid—were talking. When the sea was not too rough, we used to go to the bow of the ship before dinner; sometimes, Isam and Jacqueline would be with us. We would lean against the railing right by the bow and look down at the deep, blue sea. The ship would be ploughing its way through the waves which would then recede along the sides of the ship and come together again at the stern. They looked like some living thing that refused to relinquish its life and so was constantly renewing itself in a white marble wake of foam stretching away into the distance. In the clear water below us, we often saw large fish intently swimming away from the pointed prow as though to escape a savage beast trying to devour them. Groups of them proceeded on their way with superb abandon, but in the end even they became exhausted, each moving aside and disappearing. Other fish too were being chased by the ship as we watched. It all seemed like an endless game.

"Poor fish!" Luma commented, "fugitives of the unknown."

"They know how to dodge," her husband replied, "or do you think they learn it at the last moment?"

"Don't they die when they bump against the side or bottom of the ship?"

"Of course not! Just look down there!"

Dolphins were playfully leaping out of the water on both sides of the ship. Their heads kept popping out of the water like so many balls in the hands of a juggler. Up and down they went, appearing and disappearing in a never-ending game.

79

Suddenly Luma looked at me with those eyes of hers; eyes that spoke of inaudible things, incomprehensible things. Nevertheless, they stirred something in the depths of one's soul; at least, that is what they did to me, even though it obviously made Jacqueline feel very jealous.

"What do you think, Wadi?" she asked, looking at me. "Do fish believe in anything?"

"Of course they do!" I replied.

"Their beliefs are just like Wadi's," Yusuf Haddad commented, "purely poetic!"

"All belief is poetic," I said.

Luma turned her back on the sea. She was wearing a sleeveless orange summer dress with a plunging neckline. When her hands came together, her long, brown arms and her chest made a luscious naked circle that enclosed her magnificent protruding breasts.

"This poetic belief the fishes have," she asked, "is there no speculation or logic to justify it?"

I had no idea whether she was being serious or joking. "Faith needs no justification," I replied. "There aren't many things I believe in, but I don't feel I have to put myself out in order to provide convincing proof."

The languid, reckless expression on her face changed. She looked animated and radiant, reflecting the radiance of the water all around us. "But Wadi," she said, "haven't you read your St. Thomas Aquinas, or what is it they call him in Arabic, Tuma al-Aqwini?" As she spoke, I felt that her white, pearly teeth would grind the very logic out of me.

Her question staggered me. I might have expected her to ask a thousand different questions, but not that one. Tuma al-Aqwini? "Luma," I replied, "you've stunned me, destroyed me! Can you remember what Thomas Aquinas has to say about faith? Good heavens! It's been ages since I read him. Do you realize what I studied at the American University in Beirut a long time ago?"

"What?"

"Don't laugh, please. Philosophy. Even though my father wanted me to study medicine. Thomas Aquinas and his colleagues were more fascinating to me than the anatomy of corpses. But what does Aquinas have to say about faith? I don't suppose he insists on backing up his arguments with proofs and evidence, does he?"

Amid that collection of men, Luma held forth on Thomas

Aquinas. The way she kept gesticulating with her hands was a constant confirmation of the liveliness in her eyes, her face, and her thoughts.

"Maybe you can remember his method of logical argument. He begins with what he calls objections and then proceeds to answer them one by one. 'Faith without proof is a virtue—that is the way his first objection begins. Exactly the same as you said. He finishes the objection and then comments that, for this very reason, if faith comes as a result of some proof, then it loses its virtue."

I began to remember the method, and recalled a number of other things along with it. I remembered my whole career as a student in Beirut and the trips between Jerusalem and Beirut, traveling south by car along the coast from Beirut to Ras al-Naqura, then to Haifa and then to Jerusalem. God have mercy on you, Thomas Aquinas! Every time I came back in the spring, the road smelled of orange blossom the entire way. "Doubtless he responds to that," I said, "by suggesting that proof amplifies faith and thereby its virtue."

Luma laughed. "Exactly, but do you remember his logical method for establishing that?"

Doctor Falih who had been watching the dolphins bobbing up and down in the sea below intruded at this point. "No," he said, "which logical approach?"

"The approach of Thomas Aquinas."

"The dark ages! It's all rubbish! If only you'd studied medicine, Wadi. Faith isn't a necessity; nor is it a virtue. There is scientific conviction or non-scientific. Only the former deserves further investigation."

"But... Falih," Luma began, then fell silent.

"I'm sorry, Doctor," I said, "but I have no scientific convictions whatsoever. Just faith, and in a very few things at that."

"It's a poet's faith," Yusuf Haddad said, "not a philosopher's."

"Funny!" said Luma. "I always thought the two faiths were very similar. It depends, of course, on your definition of philosophy. For example, Bergson places poetic insight on a higher level than intellectual proof."

Yusuf Haddad raised his hands in the air. "Why could I never find that out for myself?" he said. "Now I can carry on writing poetry without feeling any sense of shame!"

"You'd all better watch out, folks!" said Mahmud Rashid. "Whenever Yusuf says that, it means he's about to put his hand in his pocket and bring out his latest poem...."

Yusuf was about thirty-five. His "Lebaneseness" was very obvious—in a certain way. He had a beautiful goatee with white flecks in it, that gave his appearance all the respectability of a monk. However, his eyes were forever flashing. No, there was nothing of the monk in him. He told a lot of jokes and for most of them had to wait until the women had left our group.

"Your writing poetry," Doctor Falih suggested, "can be described in a completely scientific fashion. You could say, for example, that you were 'secreting' poetry...."

"Good grief, no!" Yusuf said indignantly. "Secreting something is... ugly, like secreting...."

"Like silkworms secreting strands of silk, sir...."

"Terrific!" Mahmud shouted with a laugh, "terrific!"

At that moment there was a sudden shout a short distance away from us in a language I did not understand. Then there were other shouts. People started running to the right hand side of the ship, that made a loud, mechanical noise as if it had struck a rock. It almost turned completely around before coming to a stop in the middle of the waves. We all moved quite spontaneously toward the stern where everyone else had run. Unexpectedly large numbers of sailors appeared, yelling in Greek and other languages.

Out there among the cavorting dolphins you could see two hands bobbing up and down, human hands. The head was barely visible. He had thrown himself in. We had seen him leap from the side of the ship. We threw him a life-jacket and then another and another. He is Polish—no, Czech—no, he is Hungarian, or....

There was continual whistling. After a while, the chaos turned into more orderly movement. A sailor jumped into the sea in the direction of the man. A lifeboat was lowered incredibly quickly with two or three sailors in it. Suddenly, a doleful, anxious silence came over everyone. The repetitious beating of the waves assumed a cruel, hostile sound as the boat struggled with the waves to reach the man who had tried to commit suicide.

As I turned around in the middle of the crowd, I found Luma right beside me. Isam was on her other side; I had not seen him all morning. They were whispering to each other, and Luma looked alarmed and distressed. "Wadi," she asked all of a sudden, "don't you think this man has demonstrated his faith?"

"You mean his despair?" I replied. "What does Saint Thomas have to say about that?"

"I'll tell you what I think. That man did the right thing. He's got courage."

"He's a runaway, no doubt," Isam said. His expression was full of hate, and his lips were almost quivering.

"We're all runaways," I answered. "Eh, Luma?"

"What can you tell me about running away?"

"A great deal. Even though I've constantly tried to reject it. Ask Isam, Luma."

"Isam? I hardly even know him."

"You don't know him?"

"Where does a man run away to?"

"To the waves of the sea," I replied. "However, the eyes of the curious are ever alert. They'll pick him up, empty the water from his stomach and restore him to good health, and all that just to punish him."

Isam turned toward me. "Do you hear?" he said in a loud voice. "Punishment is like whipping a dead horse. Our friend in the water there will certainly die."

But he did not die. The lifeboat came back toward the ship while some of the sailors gave the man first aid. It never even occurred to anyone that he might live. Even from that distance, his face had a glazed look, something like blue wax. They brought him up to the deck and took him to the infirmary. As people split up, everyone wanted to know what would happen to him. The question on everyone's lips was, How do they get rid of a dead man on board ship? Will they keep the body till the ship reaches the next port, or will they wrap it in a shroud and throw it into the water where its final resting place will be the rocks and the insides of fish?

The ship started moving again, and the passengers proceeded to the bar to grab a drink. No one knew for sure the identity of the man who had tried to commit suicide. People said he never mingled with anyone and spoke very little. Maybe he was a diplomat from one of the Eastern Block countries. Fernando, on the other hand, insisted that he was from one of the Northern countries, Germany or Scandinavia. "Every time a man gets near the Mediterranean, his attachment to life increases; every time he moves away from it, death becomes less of a problem. Have you ever heard of a Spaniard, an Italian or an Arab committing suicide? They might be killed in a duel or something. But commit suicide? Impossible!" I reminded him that rumor had it he was Polish or Hungarian or Czech. He laughed, something he always did when he wanted to scoff at someone else's ideas. "For sure!" he replied. "That's a rumor put about by enemies of Communism."

It emerged later that the poor man was Dutch and that he had survived.

The good news was broadcast over the ship's loudspeakers in a number of languages and with some pride. The man who had attempted suicide had been saved, they said. The announcement came just before dinner. When dinner time came, everyone felt happy that the unknown man had been restored to his unknown existence and his unknown problem. The only exception was probably the unknown Dutchman himself.

That evening, we all gathered again at the bow of the ship. The ship's movement is always at its strongest at the bow and stern; they keep going up and down however calm the sea may be. Most passengers usually avoid them for fear of getting sick. However, our group was no longer afraid of getting seasick; in fact, the sea treated us very kindly on those clear June days. When we met again that night, the sea was so calm, it was almost frightening, unbelievable. It looked just like one big pool of oil. Little phosphorescent waves shone like droplets of silver. The moon rose late, and its greeny-silver glow was enough to drive the mind to a frenzy. What did this sea want from us, with such stunning magnificence, such mysterious, tyrannical beauty? The frenzy inspired by the moon brought with it a certain amount of melancholy, anxiety, fright even, and also an obscure feeling of love shared among us.

There had been no advance planning, and yet we all felt attracted to our remote corner. I arrived with Isam. We were talking about the Greek Islands, about card games—something my friend could not stand—and about the suicide attempt, which Isam had not stopped talking about since midday. Then along came that Italian woman who kept hovering around him, running toward us from the distance. She was wearing slacks and had a large part of her bosom exposed. Then the Doctor and his wife came, walking slowly. Luma was wearing a tight-fitting black dress that came to above her knees. They were followed by Fernando and Jacqueline. Fernando had in his hand the one thing I detested about him: a transistor radio that never left him, as though it were a part of his arm. After a while, the circle widened as more passengers came and joined us; some of them we knew, others we did not.

We sat down on chairs; some sat on the deck. I offered Luma a chair, but she refused and sat down cross-legged on the deck beside her husband and opposite Isam. Everyone looked happy. Most of them had been drinking Greek ouzo in quantity before and after dinner. In fact, Doctor Falih took a plastic half-pint of whiskey out of his pocket and had a swig; throughout out the conversation, he kept drinking. Fernando was turning the dial on the radio from station to station. Every time he found an Arabic station, they were playing Umm Kulthum. When it's midnight in the Arabic world, the voice of Umm Kulthum fills the air everywhere, even in Greek waters. Even though Fernando was looking for some other kind of music, we kept insisting that he leave the radio tuned in on Umm Kulthum. All of a sudden, Emilia got up and started doing a belly dance in her own style to the music. Fernando got up and joined her, doing a caricature of the dance, shaking his stomach to left and right. The sound of clapping began to rise and people started getting boisterous. Just then, Luma—Luma of all people—rose and began singing along with Umm Kulthum. Could this be the same Luma who that very morning had been talking about Thomas Aquinas, Ibn al-Arabi, and Eliot, and who had held forth in an ironic tone on the frenzied, blinding, hellish world of Dostoevsky's characters as they experience the misery a man feels when he finds himself incapable of love?

Fernando withdrew to watch. He gave me a wink and moved his lips in a manner that seemed to be saying, What a beauty! Pretending that she felt tired, Emilia moved away too and sat down in Luma's place. Luma was laughing, laughing, laughing all the time, and did a belly dance just like a professional. My tongue stuck in my mouth. Everyone was watching that sensational body bursting out of the tight-fitting dress, twisting, undulating, and wriggling. Without the slightest sense of shame, Luma danced on—her breasts quivering, her waist swaying, and her buttocks flexing above those long, slender thighs, that kept bending and straightening in time to the music. It was difficult to decide which part of her body to concentrate on. She kept raising her hands to tease her hair with the same alluring movement that belly dancers use. The difference was that she was doing it for fun, and that made it ten times more seductive than when performed by professional dancers. The doctor followed her girations with a mixture of pride and embarrassment. I noticed Isam riveted to the spot, not clapping or making a sound. His eyes were clouded by a dense blackness, but I could also see a burning fire that seemed to spring from deep inside his head. His mouth was open; his expression showed awe, alarm, and lust. Meanwhile, other people had joined us and gathered round. The clapping increased, and Fernando raised the volume to its highest level. Luma kept performing her vibrant, sexy dance without any sign of fatigue, and through it all she kept laughing and joking. I was rather worried that her dress might be ripped off her pulsating limbs.

The circumstances which surround whatever a man sees may give him exaggerated feelings: nighttime, the sea, the moon, whiskey, self-abandon on a ship, such things may affect his judgment. But all those details surrounding Luma faded away. She was something impossible, a goddess tottering between dream and reality, or a demoniac body that the waves had thrown up from an old gumgum.* Her eyes were made up with mascara, which extended in a line from her eyelids in the direction of her temples. They seemed very wide, as though they embodied the delectable fantasies of poets and painters: the devious beauty, the prey of passion who devoured her lovers; Circe, who turned her lovers into swine. But she was as delicate as moonlight. As she kept bending and twisting, and exposing the hidden and the luscious, her body seemed for a moment to dissolve in the breeze, to become diaphanous and vanish. What would Saint Thomas Aquinas do with those glowing lips and intoxicating breasts? What happens to those philosophical ideas while she stiffens herself from the waist down and shakes her shoulders so as to focus her attention on her bobbing breasts, and then stiffens her torso to concentrate on her buttocks?

The doctor began to fidget and in a barely audible voice said, "That's enough, Luma!" His expression was now a mixture of distress and anger. "Luma," he said again, "that's enough!" But Luma did not hear him (or else she pretended not to), and kept undulating to the sound of Umm Kulthum. The song, in a reckless grip of passion, was getting wilder and wilder. Suddenly Falih leapt to his feet. Kicking away the transistor radio like someone demented, he grabbed Luma by the wrist and dragged her away through the crowd of clapping spectators. The radio went on with its song even though it had landed among people's feet. At once everyone stopped clapping and in the silence that ensued, the

* An allusion to a story in the Arabian Nights in which a fisherman hauls up in his net a *gumgum*, a large copper pot, from which a great genie comes out and terrifies him.

voice of Umm Kulthum seemed to fill up the entire sea. It was accompanied by the sound of retreating footsteps as Falih dragged Luma away as fast as he could.

Isam took my arm, and we headed for the center of the ship to get away from Jacqueline, Emilia, and the others. "What's the point of all this persecution?" he asked, quivering with rage. "What's it for?"

It was not hard to sense the tension between Isam and Luma, but I responded as though I was not aware of it. "A husband exerting his rights," I answered.

"Fine. Let him do what he likes to her, or vice versa. It's none of my business. But why is she persecuting me?"

"That should make you happy."

"Happy? Why?"

"Love is the greatest persecution of all. If she really is persecuting you, then it's obvious she loves you."

"My friend, I don't want her love if it means living through this persecution. Every movement she makes is a dagger thrust in my flesh. I can't take much more of it."

"I don't think her husband can either."

"What do you mean? Do you think he... knows?"

"Falih? I don't think so. Falih, in my view, is the type who remains blandly indifferent up to a point. If things go too far, he'll be unable to control his jealousy. He'll become jealous of you, me, and every sailor on board this ship—you just watch. But he must be used to his wife's whims by now. Perhaps he's used to her beauty as well. How long have they been married?"

"Three or four years."

"Listen, Isam, I don't want to meddle in your affairs, but I'm going to ask you a question. You don't have to answer it if you don't want to. Did the two of you arrange to meet on this ship?"

"Certainly not. It was quite by chance, an inconceivable chance. It never occurred to me that she would travel by any other means than by plane."

"Strange, very strange!" I paused for a moment and then changed the subject. "We'll soon be at the Straits of Messina. It's a beautiful spectacle by sea at night."

I changed the subject for two reasons: first, I did not believe what he had said, and second, I did not care to talk much about Luma and Falih. However, I found myself asking him, "Why were you so distressed this morning when the Dutchman tried to commit suicide? Luma too looked rather alarmed."

"Really?"

"Forgive me. I'm probably meddling."

"Not at all. If two lovers are prevented from marrying, is it surprising if they talk about suicide?"

"Oh, then it's an old story."

"Very. And I hope it's all over. But—did you believe me?"

"Why not?"

"Actually, Luma was telling me that her husband had threatened to commit suicide more than once recently. Every time he hears of a suicide, he goes back to...."

I did not press Isam any further. I figured that things were more complicated than they seemed on the surface. I had no wish to get embroiled in a question for which there was probably no simple answer.

Fernando was sitting in his pyjamas on the bed when I returned to the cabin. He was holding a large glass of whiskey, and the radio had been put away. He said nothing at first, but from the moment I entered the cabin, I could see anger written all over his face. Then he addressed the cause of his anger head on. "The doctor never even apologized to me, do you know that?" he exclaimed. "I thought he was a gentleman. I'll tell you, after that display of temper with his wife, I felt like running after him and giving him a punch in the nose."

"Why didn't you?" I asked with a laugh as I took out my own pyjamas from beneath the pillow.

"Because I'm a gentleman." ·

"He'll apologize to you tomorrow. I'm sure of it."

Gradually, his anger subsided. "It seems that things between the two of them are in a bad way, doesn't it?"

"Right."

"Poor devil! He should keep drinking. It's the best cure there is. What do you think he'll do with her till tomorrow morning?"

"I really have no idea how married couples solve problems of this sort."

"If he doesn't sleep with her...."

"You'll know tomorrow. If you see him drinking first thing in the morning."

"What else can he do? And while we're about it, why did you leave Jacqueline and come away? I think she was delighted by what she saw...."

"I'm sure everyone was. If they had seen the poor woman struggle free of her husband and throw herself into the waves, they would've been even more delighted."

"Actually that's just what they were saying, that she would do what the Dutchman did. But what they don't know is that Arabs don't commit suicide. Right?"

"Just like the Spaniards," I said as I threw myself on to my bed.

Isam Salman

If Wadi had asked me to jump into the sea, I would have done so. This is the feeling I had every time he and I talked. I almost hated him for controlling me so; it felt as though he had hypnotized me and paralyzed my will. He was around forty, with a face difficult to define, as if it were hewn from a piece of rock. His hazel eyes glittered like precious stones, like the eyes of a cat mesmerized by the headlights of a car at night. Suddenly his face would crack and crumble, and the hero would collapse into a victim. No, it was not possible to define his identity. Those gushing words, wherever did they all come from? I often felt that he made fun of me, that he had tricked me into believing his imaginary stories the way he had tricked his two village friends with the story of the veiled woman he imagined meeting at the cemetery. In just a few days, he had managed to create a net; every time I saw him, he cast it over me, and I enjoyed being caught in its mesh. Every time I remember this, I feel both amazed and furious. Perhaps my relationship with Luma had drained me of my willpower, and so he was able, demoniacally, to take advantage of my weakness and submission. If he had asked me to jump into the sea, I would have done so, because I would have saved myself a great deal of agony. But I was also (and how could I possibly deny it?) in an ecstatic trance of the dangerous type—a trance that made one accept anything, even degradation, to avoid its being dispelled. I saw him as a giant, a very important person, indispensable to life. Why? How? I don't know. A man like him could not possibly be a runaway. He attacked, never retreated. I envisaged him striding toward the barrels of rifles, and none of them would be able to hit him. I was not surprised that Jacqueline attached herself to him like a dog to its owner. Even Emilia fluttered around him like a bird that enjoyed being trapped. Nor were Yusuf Haddad, Mahmud Rashid, Fernando, or any of the stewards and crew on the ship safe from his imposing personality.

Despite his secretiveness, I got the impression that he was involved in a special mission to enlist a select group of commandoes who would be trained to infiltrate enemy lines and strike at the Zionists inside the occupied territory. The way he talked incessantly about land could not simply be some sort of mystical obsession. It was clear that he wanted the Arabs to return to the land, to stick fast, organically, to the soil. It is easy for anyone who had spent his younger days in Jerusalem to identify God with the land or, as Wadi would say, "To unite Christ with the rocks." But Wadi united himself also with Christ and the rocks, and he saw the need to preserve this trinity as one whenever it seemed to fall apart. Wadi Assaf would only be himself, he said, when he returned to God and the land. So when the Jews had conquered Palestine, they had also conquered him and his God. He was, therefore, like Jerusalem, torn apart, and he had to reintegrate the self; to reclaim the whole trinity—with blood. Hence the need for action, for martyrdom.

With this kind of logic he tried to convince me of his point of view, although he knew quite well that I had little use for his mystical idiom and that I preferred what I imagined was scientific objectivity. But I no longer needed to be convinced. If he had said to me, "Pick up your gun and follow me," I would have done so without much reflection. I was sure that the sea played a supportive role in such matters, just as it did in our relationships with women. The scenes are always the same except when we reach port. Eyes get used to the various decks on the ship and the blue of the waves and the sky; ears become attuned to the roar of the breakers and the monotonous throbbing of the ship's engines. With everyone's heart bent on exploring all that is new and exciting, feeling intensifies for all those things that are variable: people's shapes, their figures, faces and voices, what they say and how they say it. Hearing sharpens and words become unusually clear and powerful. One hears everything that is said, and reaction, whether of pleasure or otherwise, is immediate. Even the least bit of anger or any other emotion seems too important to dismiss lightly. And so when arguments are presented loaded with all the warmth, the voice, and the confidence of Wadi, they take hold of the mind and strike root there.

Yet, what could I do to please him? He ignored the seriousness of my problem. After long years of reflection, I had discovered that I would only solve my problem by leaving it where it was and seeking a future where it would not figure at all, no matter what it had put me through.

One man alone, Dr. Falih Haseeb, rejected Wadi and found him irksome. It was impossible for Falih to be on Wadi's side, because he knew, no doubt, that Wadi was the secret power lurking in the enemy. If he joined him, he would lose Luma; not to Wadi, but to me, since Wadi had not cast his net in her direction. Falih was well aware that Wadi provided me with some support; he also knew that Luma was rapidly falling apart. This was why he started drinking so heavily after we left Heraklion. He drank continuously and swore at everything and everybody. This went on all the time, so much so that I got the impression he loved no one, including his wife. At times he would pretend that his nerves were made of steel. He would play cards with anyone who wanted to play (including Wadi Assaf) without betraying a semblance of hatred and annoyance. Perhaps he put up with his ordeal because he believed it would last four or five days at the most. Once it was all over, he would give vent to his anger and collapse any way he wished, away from those "friends" on the ship.

Falih was only two or three years older than I. He belonged to an old rich Basra family, most of whom had moved to Baghdad. We had known each other since school days. Both of us graduated from the same secondary school in Karkh, but he graduated three years earlier than I. Our relationship had since remained that of an older student to a younger one, which made him assume he could always treat me as his junior. I heard he had an excellent reputation in the College of Medicine, both as a student and as a society man: he was a star at college parties and debates, wrote for the University magazines, and stood out in that he seemed to have read dozens of books, the titles of which his colleagues did not even dream of knowing. He and Luma were related through his mother, a fact that placed the young, promising doctor very high in the estimation of Luma's parents. After he graduated from medical school, he spent one or two years of internship in Edinburgh, and then returned as a surgeon well-suited to the new social position that he felt he had earned, not inherited. When he married Luma, I wanted to disappear and never set eyes on him again, except by chance. I never knew whether Luma ever told him about us. It was unlikely, but then rumor-mongers were capable of anything.

He knew, of course, that Luma and I had been in England at the same time and that we were friends. But on this trip, the serenity of the Mediterranean and the raucous gaiety of the ship made him sense what any husband would dread contemplating. An overwhelming sense of suspicion got hold of him and seemed to alienate him from all the other passengers.

In fact, I had expected matters to take this turn the very moment I met Falih and Luma on the ship. I tried hard not to display any emotions toward Luma which might give rise to suspicion. Even Wadi failed to notice anything, although it was difficult to keep a secret from him. How, when, and why did the doctor start regarding me as an enemy? I don't know. But one morning he took me aside. His face was pallid and his lips were pale as wax; he admitted that he had not slept all night and had not shaved that morning. "How on earth can you put up with that idiot, Wadi Assaf?" he asked. Whereupon I realized that he was expressing his position loudly and clearly.

I, too, had been unable to sleep that night. Luma had danced like a whore and had set every vein in my body on fire.

"Wadi?" I replied after a moment of silence. "It's been some time since I met such a great man."

"He's conceited," Falih said. "Maybe he's made a lot of money in Kuwait, and so he regards the whole world as a pawn in his hand."

"It's strange," I said, "but I don't think he's conceited at all. Maybe he loves life more than you or I?"

"No, Isam," Falih insisted. "He's like most Palestinians, obsessed with himself."

"Obsessed with his past, definitely," I said. "Most Palestinians are obsessed with the innocence they've lost and want to regain."

"In a couple of days you'll be making a hero out of him," Falih scoffed. "Listen, Isam!" He hesitated, and his eyes wandered over my shoulders toward the azure of the waking sea as it reflected the first rays of the sun. "What brings you here at this early hour?" He did not look at me.

"No matter how little I sleep," I said with a laugh, "I always get up with the dawn. It's a habit I've never been able to shake. What about you? What brings you up so early?"

"I wanted to watch the seamen clean the deck," he said. "I didn't sleep. But, tell me, Isam...."

I could see he wanted to ask me about Luma. In his mind, all our names must have become connected with Luma. When he had dragged her away the night before, I thought he was going to accuse her of having slept with all of us and then kill her. But he did not quite ask me about her.

"How many years did you spend in England?" he asked instead.

"Altogether? Seven years. Luma was in Oxford then. She was very lucky. I was in London, as you know."

"Yes," he said, "Luma told me about that. Was Luma popular among the students? The Iraqis, I mean."

"Hardly," I answered quickly. "I think she studied philosophy. It was a difficult subject and took up a lot of time. I don't think she mixed much."

(I was lying through my teeth, but why should I inflict another wound on an already wounded man?)

All of a sudden Falih's face changed. The pale, hard features gave way to a terrible expression of humiliation. I felt his lips were about to stretch sideways to let out a cry of pain. Instead, he pursed his lips with determined spite. "When will this cruise be over?" he asked.

"You want the truth?" I asked. "I don't want it to end at all."

"I can't stand the sea for so long."

"Do you get sea-sick?" I asked with malice.

"Sea-sick? Never! I'm claustrophobic. I can't stand being trapped on a ship or anything else."

"Yet the whole sea is around you!" I said.

"And all of you, too," he said, but then apologized quickly. "I'm sorry, I'm sorry, Isam. My nerves are on edge. Every time I realize that in the morning I'm going to sea...."

He did not finish the sentence. I said nothing and was about to leave him, when he took a pack of cigarettes from his pocket.

"Forgive me," he said. "When we reach Naples, Luma and I will catch a plane to London. What do you think?"

"Why not?" I replied.

He offered me a cigarette, and I took one. He lit mine first, then his.

"It seems you don't like us," I said.

"No, I am sorry," he was quick to say. "But what's the use? If I don't drink, I die. At any rate, it's stupid of me to interrupt the trip now. Have you noticed the Frenchman who sits with Luma and me at the dinner table?"

His disjointed thoughts surprised me. "What Frenchman?" I asked.

"The man who's been sharing our dinner table since Piraeus."

"What about him?"

"Do you know he insisted that his wife accompany him on her last trip?" he asked.

"Last trip?"

Falih smiled. "His wife died in Athens," he said. "He insisted on bringing her body along with him to Marseille and then to Paris. Now she's in an iron box in his cabin."

"Horrible!" I exclaimed.

"I asked him why he didn't send her by plane," Falih continued. "He said he was afraid to travel by air, and that for emotional reasons—whatever he meant by that—he felt she should accompany him on the ship, exactly as she had always done when she was alive. Imagine! He told me all about it at the dinner table, and hasn't uttered a word ever since."

"It must be love!"

"Love?" he said as he threw his cigarette butt in the sea. "Horrible!" He walked away dragging his feet and repeating, "Horrible, horrible!"

Around midday we met at the bar. Falih had not stopped drinking since the night before, but now he was freshly shaven and smartly dressed, while the rest of us were dressed rather casually. I suspected he was observing us all with a great deal of boredom or maybe spite; I wasn't sure which. Mahmud Rashid was trying to convince him that politics was like medicine: it too resorted to drugs at times, to suggestion at others, and sometimes to radical surgery.

The first thing I noticed about Mahmud was how short he was. But in spite of that, he was a man who could hardly be ignored. He had a large head, and his short hair was like an old flattened toothbrush with uneven bristles, worn out in places. His eyes were also large, or so they seemed when they twinkled behind his thick eyeglasses. He spoke with a monotonous squeak that made you nervous until you got used to it. Then you started paying attention to him and soon forgot the sound of his voice. You felt yourself faced with a challenge and forced to weigh your words carefully, or else he would make you sound like a fool.

Mahmud and Yusuf seemed to be traveling together. They occupied the same cabin, kept together, and leaned on each other. It was as though Mother Nature had arranged it all by making them very different people. Yusuf was tall, well-dressed, had a beard, talked gently and quietly, and drank very little. He spoke only when the conversation revolved around music or women. He was not interested in forcing you to listen to what he said, unlike Mahmud, who constantly gave the impression that he was afraid you did not quite hear or understand him, and so repeated every single word he had said, just to be sure. We were all listening to Mahmud. All of a sudden his eyes twinkled behind his lenses and he addressed himself to Dr. Falih. "Do you know what is the most important thing in life?" he asked. He looked round at each of us.

"Dear God, protect us!" someone murmured.

"The most important thing in life," Mahmud continued, "is to be able to endure pain without uttering a sound. In politics, it means that people should not tell on one another, no matter what happens."

"You mean man should learn to swallow the knife and not utter a word?" Falih asked.

"More, more than that," Mahmud explained. It's a strictly ethical question. Any policy which does not have an ethical foundation is bound to fail."

I was certain that Mahmud had been involved in a great deal of political activity; most likely, of the clandestine kind—the kind that had a lot to do with the upheavals that had swept us all in the last few years of fickle uncontrollable passion—we the innocent ones. Given the chance, Mahmud could talk to us all day about the subject. Instead, however, he singled out Luma.

"I think," he said looking at her, "that Madame Luma agrees with me."

"Your basic premises already scare me," Luma said with a laugh. "Are you trying to lead me to an unexpected conclusion?"

"Doctor, please rescue me!" he said raising his glass, begging for Falih's support.

Wadi looked over his gin glass and his cigarette, which was giving off strands of smoke around his face. He laughed.

"Rescue yourself," Falih said, "You're in a fix."

"Do you know what Ahmad Shawqi* said in his eulogy of Ali Pasha Ibrahim, the famous surgeon living in Cairo during the twenties and thirties?" Mahmud asked, then recited:

"Ali, you have been called healer of wounds.

How apt the name! Your hands are cure for misery:

One hand cures pain, the other poverty;

*A famous Egyptian poet who was later in his life called the Prince of Arab Poets. He died in 1932.

As though you were the death of death—
She sees your face and runs away."

"Excellent!" said Luma. "I hope you mean Falih by these lines. You're all safe from death now. Isn't that so, Falih?"

"Mahmud," Falih said, "you've a confession to make, don't you? The symptoms are obvious. Speak, and we will try to ward off the angel of death. Have you had to 'swallow the knife'?"

"Many knives, Doctor," Mahmud replied. "It's strange, though. All I can remember now is what another person suffered for my sake, not what I have suffered for the sake of others. I was a little boy in fourth grade when it all happened. I shared the desk with a classmate. One day, during the last class period, we were tired of schoolwork and of squirming about on our hard wooden seats. The teacher asked us to keep quiet because the new principal was going to visit our class and give us some words of advice before we went home. We sat quietly for a few seconds, then started squirming again. Soon we were talking, pinching, poking, teasing one another. Some laughed, others complained. "Silence! Silence!" the teacher shouted. The noise stopped miraculously— for a few seconds more.

"The principal is late," the boy who shared my desk whispered to me. "Have you seen him?" he asked, trying to smother a smile. "He has grown a nose the size of a camel's!" I pressed my lips together hard and held my nose with one hand in an attempt to suppress a laugh that almost broke loose. At that point the principal entered the classroom. The teacher sprang to his feet and ordered us to stand up and then to sit down. I stood up and sat down with the others, carefully studying our new principal's face and his gigantic nose. In spite of myself, the imprisoned laugh burst out of my lips amidst the deep silence, like a scandalous explosion. The principal looked in our direction—my friend's and mine.

"Who laughed?" he cried out.

My friend and I looked at each other feigning ignorance.

"Who laughed?" he asked again, as he walked slowly toward us. "The laugh came from here," he said. "Isn't that so, boy?" he asked, pointing an accusing finger at the boy sitting right in front of my friend.

"Yes sir, from behind me," the boy said trying to vindicate himself.

"You are the one who laughed," said the big-nosed man to my friend,

98

"No sir," my friend responded quickly.

"Who else, then?" growled the principal. "You're the one who laughed, you dog!" The principal moved forward and gave him such a slap that the walls echoed with the sound. My friend knew very well that I was the culprit, but he did not say so.

"No sir, no sir," he kept repeating as the principal slapped him again and again, shouting, "Confess! Confess!"

My friend's face was red all over. I was scared to death. I could have owned up and saved him, but I was sure he was going to tell the principal himself and that my turn would come anyway. Yet he told him nothing.

"Who laughed then, you dog?" the principal asked as he pressed furiously for an answer. He refused to let the matter go and slapped him for the fifth or sixth time. We were often beaten harshly in those days. "Stand up!" he barked. "I'll make an example of you for the others. Come along to my office. I'll teach you a lesson with the cane."

The principal had no time for the class. We were dismissed, but my friend walked out in front of him, like a lamb before a butcher. As for me, I barely knew how to get out of the classroom. Somehow I pushed my feet forward, leaning against the walls of the hallway. "He's going to get it for sure," my classmates said. I edged closer to the principal's office, but stopped short. "What a coward I am," I thought to myself. I heard the principal shouting, "Confess! Put your hand out! There, one, two, three. Confess! Four, five. Confess!" I could hear the cane ripping into my friend's palm. He was crying out in pain.

"Yes, yes, sir, I was the one who laughed. I did it, I did it," my friend pleaded.

"I swear, if you ever laugh in class again, I shall expel you from school," the principal shouted. "Here's your punishment: I want you to write on a sheet of paper, neatly and clearly, 'Laughing in the presence of the principal is a crime.' A thousand times, do you hear? What's your name?"

Before my friend left the office, I ran through the hallway into the open court, and out through the main gate. I waited for him. He came out a few moments later, his cheeks blue and his eyes bloodshot from the tears that he tried to hide. I ran to him and tried to embrace him, but he pushed me away. "Are you happy?" he asked. "Satisfied?" I simply did not know how to apologize. "I hope you'll do the same thing for me some day," he said.

Mahmud removed his glasses and revealed his bulging eyes.

He looked exhausted. He took a handkerchief from his pocket and proceeded to clean the lenses. Wadi looked at Luma and smiled. "Should we believe him?" he asked her.

"Why not?" she replied.

"Mahmud," Wadi said, "are you sure you were not the one who suffered the punishment and swallowed the knife? It was your friend who remained silent, wasn't it?"

"No, I swear," Mahmud said.

"God knows how many knives you've swallowed since that day," continued Wadi.

Mahmud put his glasses back on and filled his glass again. "Ever since that day," he said, "I've had to expiate my sin toward my friend. And I've done so several times, not simply by suffering a few slaps on the face or writing some silly sentence a thousand times. It has not even been for the sake of the same friend, who has since left for Argentina, but for others. I've had to."

"What?" Luma asked, "You've had to suffer for others and confess to crimes that you have not committed?"

"Yes," said Mahmud, "under torture, Madame. But I never implicated anybody. That's what counts."

"But how many people can withstand torture?" Luma asked. "God, if I were to get beaten up, I'd confess to every imaginary crime in the book. Under torture! Can you think of any period in history when people experienced more pain and horror than we do these days? This is the age of informers, accusers, defamers. Phew! Let's talk about something else."

"This is the age of worms!" Falih said, as he took a sip from his glass and then set it down with a trembling hand. "I curse this age. In this atmosphere filled with the recorded sound and sexual groans of the Beatles and their like, every man, everyone of us is Christ and Judas at the same time. Everyone of us is betrayed, crucified, and given gall to drink, and he does the same to everyone else. I no longer care about who tells on whom. One worm devours another. We are in the kingdom of worms."

"Since we're in the kingdom of worms," Wadi said (and for a moment I thought he wanted to defuse the situation), "we're in the best of times, when frontside is backside. O happy days of somersaults, and spiderwalks.... May God have mercy on your soul, Awad Shnuda, great master of the Kingdom of Worms."

I thought the doctor gave Wadi a nasty look. He must have felt that Wadi was poking fun at him.

"Awad Shnuda, my dear doctor, was a Bedouin from the

Taamar tribe. Whenever he came to our quarter, the women and children would say, 'Here comes Awad; here comes the poet.' We would all go, sit around him on some doorstep and listen to his poetry, or rather, his rhymed prose. We would each give him a crust of bread, a bunch of grapes, or a tomato, and he would pay us back with words. He knew the stories of the legendary Zir and Abu Zayd al-Hilali word for word, and he would recite them to us in rhymed prose. He had huge black eyes and a thick white moustache which he kept twisting up and down like an Ottoman army officer. His long flowing hair showed beneath his headdress and covered his forehead. 'This is the age of spidering,' he would say to us. And when I asked once what 'spidering' meant, he answered me in rhymed prose: 'How come, my learned son, you've never heard of spidering and somersaulting, of scorpioning and grasshoppering? These are the qualities of our times, our crazy times, when frontside is backside....' It's only now, after thirty, forty years of working hard and living with people of all kinds, that I've come to understand what Awad was talking about, and to remember him again with affection. As you said, Mahmud, if politics or any kind of work has no moral foundation, it is, in the final analysis, nothing but spidering and somersaulting, of—"

"Since we're talking about spidering," interrupted Mahmud while turning to Yusuf, "where is that spidery poem of yours which you read to me this morning?"

"Forget it," Yusuf said. "Let's talk about Awad Shnuda instead."

Mahmud was drunk by then. "Give it to me," he insisted, "and I shall read it for you. It's in your pocket, isn't it? Your pockets are always bulging with papers. Don't be shy, man; we're all brothers on this ship, whether we're sober or drunk."

Yusuf took a stack of well-folded papers out of his pocket and searched for the poem. When he found it, he threw it at Mahmud. "There," he said. "You read it!"

"The problem is that it's written in free verse. May God have mercy on your soul, Ahmad Shawqi! Please read it for us, Yusuf."

Yusuf gave in reluctantly and started to read slowly, monotonously at first, then with gradual variation, bringing out the expressive power of his words:

Which one of us is the sun, which one the moon?
Which the spider and which the fly?
You be the spider and I the fly,
Or you be the fly and I the spider;

I devour you and you me
As do the rocks and the sea.
I'll be the rocks, you be the sea—
Or I am the sea
Roaring wildly around you everyday
While you give and withhold,
Contain the waves and set them free.
And if I am the rocks,
I'll softly embrace your violence
As it charges and retreats.
Is it a battle of love or hate?
He who knows the difference, let him say!
Let him describe the mutual devouring of spider and fly,
Of rock and sea, out of love and out of hate,
Ever-renewed, like night and day:
Which one of us is the sun, which one the moon?
Which the spider and which the fly?

Out of the blue, the doctor gave a muffled, malevolent laugh. "Spider and fly!" he said. "A worm devouring a worm! I curse this age of worms!"

He banged his glass down on the table and walked out of the bar alone, leaving Luma behind.

At that moment I mumbled something that I soon regretted, because the others heard it clearly. "Luma," I said, "who is the spider? Who is the fly?"

Fortunately, Luma was not angry. "What does Thomas Aquinas have to say about Satan and the temptation of Christ?" she asked Wadi, evading my question.

"Ask Isam," Wadi replied.

"Aquinas says there is no virtue without temptation," I responded, glad to change the subject.

"O happy days of spidering!" Luma said laughing and shaking her lovely head.

We all left the bar together and climbed up the narrow stair-case to the deck. The sun was bright, warm, and pleasant. A few steps ahead, I spotted Emilia talking to the doctor. He did not wait long. Luma caught up with him, took him by surprise, and put her arm around his waist. A sailor passed by striking his gong. It was lunch time. Emilia and I walked toward the dining room.

"The sun is gorgeous," she said, "the sea is gorgeous, and gorgeous Emilia is simply famished."

102

Wadi Assaf

The doctor does not get along with me; that much is obvious. Or maybe I do not get along with him. It is also clear that he is resentful of life itself. He has his own particular reasons, but his resentment is projected on to all of us, even on this tiny ship.

His tremendous intelligence clearly gives this resentment a number of dimensions and meanings, even though, as far as I am concerned, his wife is the principal cause. Falih is a Puritan, prim and proper, scared of pleasure. And yet, he has insisted on marrying a woman who positively exudes notions of freedom, pleasure, and lack of restraint. Her intelligence gives her beauty, too, a thousand dimensions and meanings, all this in the face of his resentment of life.

Even if I had a choice, I could only take her side; that was obvious too. But I was a stranger to their world, and so were they to mine. So why was there this tension which had no need of any of us? It would be just a few days, and then everything between us would be over.

But then, opposites attract despite themselves. Falih would meet me and pat me on the shoulder, and I would do the same to him. We'd differ, we'd argue with each other. If I had been living in Baghdad, the antagonism between us might have ended up with some kind of mutual understanding which I could not envision. The appetites for life and death might then unite through some extraordinary coincidence without either of them becoming any weaker.

"We're in pretty bad shape," he would say.

"It's up to us to change it," I would reply.

"How can you be an optimist," he would ask, "when we're on our way to the guillotine?"

"I'm an optimist because we have a mammoth task in front of us that has to be completed."

"And what about the guillotine?"

"We'll destroy it."

"Because the mammoth task is waiting for us?"

"Like a harbor, with us hurrying toward it."

"Keep dreaming!"

"There's no harm in that, but the whole thing's a purely arithmetical problem."

"Is that the way you do your commercial calculations?"

"And I make a profit too!"

"Then I'm afraid you cheat."

"There's no need to cheat anyone. The thing I find useful is a little bit of philosophy."

"Cheating has any number of names."

"So philosophy is one of them?"

"I'm sorry! I didn't mean to imply that you do it consciously. One's entire mental being keeps adjusting itself in order to double-cross reality. That's what I meant to say. That process of double-crossing has any number of names."

"But making a profit is a process that involves facing reality."

"Exploiting reality, you mean."

"Submitting to reality. That brings us back to that guillotine of yours. We'll overpower it, destroy it and then complete our task."

"What task is that?"

"The task? It's everything. Palestine. The future. Freedom."

"Can you see some connection between these things?"

"That's what I see. I see nothing else."

"What about the guillotine?"

"As I understand it, the guillotine is the enemy."

"So we agree then!"

"Do we really, Doctor?"

"What will you drink?"

"Whiskey."

When the whiskey came, we'd start another dialogue.

"One night," the Doctor told me, "I was called to the telephone at about midnight. There was a very urgent case. In the usual way, the sick person's family explained to me how to get to their house; you know: in such and such district, two streets on the right after the illuminated mosque; in the middle of the street you'll find a large vacant lot, take the road to the left, and so on. Baghdad is a city that is continually expanding; its empty spaces can still be numerous even in the built-up sections. I told my wife I would be no more than an hour, and drove off in the car following the directions. As ill luck would have it, I took a road with a number of vacant lots along it. I soon decided it wasn't the road I wanted.

"Just then, I got a flat tire! The wheel of the car started clattering, so I stopped. I got out to look at the useless tire. The road was totally deserted. All the houses were far away. Never mind, I told myself, I can change the tire in a few minutes. I then discovered that the jack was not in the trunk. It had been stolen! I started swearing, and waited for awhile in case a car came by. But no car appeared, so I locked my own car and headed toward the main road—I'd be more likely to find a taxi there. I had barely walked more than twenty meters from my car when a dog came rushing toward me, barking. Behind it came another, then a third and a fourth. They were all stray dogs living in these empty spaces that were sometimes occupied by mud huts and hovels. Just imagine, six or seven huge, black dogs. I could see their teeth gleaming even in the dark as they made ready to tear into my flesh. They formed a hideous circle around me, and their howling alone was more than enough to scare a complete tribe. I have never been as scared as I was at that moment. My whole body was shaking. I screamed like a madman and thrashed the air with my empty hand. I could not even find a stone in reach to throw at them and maybe scare them off. Hopeless. One of the dogs came dangerously close to me, and my screams began to tear my gullet apart. My throat and tongue had both gone dry. I whipped off my coat and started thrashing it around, spinning around rapidly on my heels in the direction of the car. As I turned round and round, I kept brandishing the coat around me as though it were a piece of armor. Well may you laugh, Wadi; later on I was able to laugh too. But, when I got to the car after all that sheer torture, I found it was locked. The key was in one of the pockets of the coat I had been using to keep those vicious teeth at bay. When I thought that the key might have fallen out of the pocket while I was brandishing the coat in front of me, I panicked. As I was looking for it and at the same time kicking out at the dogs, one of them bit me in the calf of my leg. When I used my utmost strength to get it off me, it ran away taking with it a piece of my trousers and a bit of my skin too. However, I had found the key and was able to open the door. Panting, I threw myself inside and locked the door...."

"What a piece of luck!" I said.

"Ha!" Falih exclaimed, "the adventures of a doctor! You see what I mean by the guillotine?"

"The enemy?"

"You're thinking of the outside, and I'm thinking of the inside. We find it difficult to understand one another. We have to be prepared to face the enemy outside; fine, we agree on that. But what about the enemy inside, the solid teeth that stick into your flesh as you're on your way to save people closer to death?"

"What happened to the sick man you were on your way to see?"

"I have no idea. I spent the next two weeks in the hospital. But don't change the subject. You understand what I mean, but you're changing the subject."

"You know, Doctor, I was chased by dogs too. They attacked me and chewed my flesh. One afternoon, some dogs killed someone who was dearer to me than my own brother, and they almost killed me too."

"Are you being serious?"

"Yes, but don't ask me how. I was able to kill some of them, but I'm not going to tell you the story; it's too long."

He gave me a quizzical look and then smiled.

"Another drink?" I asked.

The morning's activities were in full swing. The ship's passengers were all moving about as though the warm sun had released their pent-up energies. They were running, laughing, shouting, playing table tennis, and lying on their fronts and backs in every direction. Transistor radios in every hand blared out all kinds of music—each one a tiny world of its own, establishing its individuality and its incompatibility with everything else.

Mahmud Rashid joined us. Soon afterward, Luma came up with a big book.

"This is the novel," she said to Mahmud, referring apparently to some previous conversation they had had. "I haven't finished it yet, but I've underlined the passages I mentioned to you. Bye-bye!"

And with that, she left.

"It's *The Devils* by Dostoevsky," said Mahmud. "I haven't read it yet." He thumbed through the pages, looking for the specific passages. "I want to see what is arousing Madame Luma's interest so much."

"Let me tell you," Falih said. "It's the views of Shigalov. These days, Luma keeps repeating his phrase, 'I begin with limitless freedom, and I end up with limitless despotism.' Then she starts arguing with me and everyone else about the idea. It worries her."

Mahmud found a page full of underlining. He asked us to listen and then read out the following passage in English: " 'As a solution to the problem, he's proposing to divide mankind into two unequal parts. One tenth would be granted absolute freedom and unrestricted power over the remaining nine tenths. The others would have to be deprived of all individuality and become something like a herd of sheep. Since their subjection would also be limitless, they would be regenerated time after time till they achieved a state of primeval innocence, as though they were in some new Garden of Eden....' Woe to you, Rousseau! Here's something else: 'He's suggesting a system for spying. Every member of society will spy on the other members; it will be his duty to inform on them and denounce them. In that way, everyone belongs to all and all belong to everyone....' and so on. Further on, he says, 'Despotism is the only thing of which great minds are capable; they have always done more harm than good. So they will either be eradicated or executed. Cicero will have his tongue cut out, Copernicus will have his eyes gouged, and Shakespeare will be stoned to death....' Listen, there's more yet...."

We tried to stop him from reading any more, but he went on a few more sentences: 'So down with education! Enough of science! We have materials enough without science to last us for a thousand years. But man has to learn some discipline. The only thing the world lacks is order. The desire for education is aristocratic. As soon as you set up family ties or fall in love with someone, the desire for private property begins to show through. We will destroy that desire. We'll use drunkenness, slander, and spying; inconceivable corruption, we'll use it all. We'll throttle every genius in the cradle. We'll reduce everyone to the lowest common denominator! Total, undiluted equality!'

"The guillotine!" Falih commented with a laugh.

Mahmud continued to peruse the book and then shook his head. "If Dostoevsky gets annoyed about something," he said, "he talks with the fire of prophets."

"What you've just read is not the fire of prophets," Falih said. "It's a vision of the terror which is certain to come."

"The whole book," I said, "is a view of the nihilism which Dostoevsky feared would sweep through not just Russia but the entire world if it was deprived of the teaching of the Russian Orthodox Church."

"The book has the most horrible suicide in it that I've ever read in a novel," said Falih, "a studied death. The suicide prepares for it just like someone going on a journey or concluding a commercial deal. He's quite sure he'll reap the profits, political or human, I don't know which. Most people who commit suicide do it without being able even to determine the causes. Mahmud, have you ever contemplated suicide?"

"Never!"

"What about you, Wadi?"

"Sometimes," I replied, "as a philosophical question. Which is better: Sisyphus pushing his rock up the hill every day to no effect, or suicide? Of course, Albert Camus surpasses all of us in his investigation of the whole question."

"I've read his book *The Myth of Sisyphus* and wasn't convinced. Suicide, as far as I'm concerned, is still the major challenge."

Mahmud shut the book and put it in his lap. "I haven't had enough time to consider the question of suicide," he said, his thick fingers strumming on the illustrated cover of the book. "As far as I'm concerned, the major challenge is authority, authority as a principle agreed on by mankind since the times of the Sumerians and the Pharoahs. What's the dividing line between authority as protection, and authority as exploitation, authority as the execution of the will of the people, and authority as the execution of the will of one tenth of them, as our author here says, over the rights of the other nine tenths?"

The Doctor stared at Mahmud's lips like someone whose heart strings had found some sympathetic reverberations. "Do you mean," he asked, "authority as the opening up of a blocked road, and authority as guillotine?"

"I'm aware of what you're after, Doctor. Our modern history is complicated and involved."

"Not at all!" Falih interrupted. "It's as clear as the hand in front of your own face. But too bad for you if you even try to define its identity!"

Mahmud kept calm and continued his contemplations as though he were eager to carry on his train of thought in spite of the digressions. "History has always been like that," he continued. "According to some people, it's the story of the struggle between freedom and tyranny, a battle between spirit and matter. But in my view, the amount of tyranny in any one period of history will be the same as in any other, and the same probably applies to freedom as well."

"You mean, the two amounts remain the same then," I asked,

"even though tyranny and freedom are in conflict?"

"One country may have more freedom, another more tyranny; one group will be set free, another locked up, and so on."

"It's true, of course, that there's often confusion in terminology. Tyranny will be called freedom. Isn't that so?"

"Certainly. There are very few tyrants who are prepared to admit that they are tyrants."

"Only the crazy geniuses, Caligula, Nero, and Al-Hajjaj. If what is called freedom is, more often than not, tyranny, don't you agree with me that the two entities, as I said, are not equal?"

"It's the desire and the struggle for freedom that are really important."

"And what about us?" the Doctor asked nervously. "Where do we fit into all this?"

"We move from one to the other, sometimes here, sometimes there. Actually, we—I don't mean just us but mankind as a whole—we're moving around in vicious circles. Humanity dreams of absolute equality and launches revolutions in every generation. But, in spite of them all, equality remains a dream. History meanwhile carries on, a struggle between tyranny and freedom, and we have to keep up with it. Struggle cannot be avoided. It's proof of the fact that the people are alive. Whenever the people become ossified and the struggle loses its vigor, then all that remains is the individual will. And when individuals emerge who are prepared to carry on the struggle with what they say, with what they do..."

"Defying the guillotine..." interrupted Falih.

"Then the people have to start thinking about moving towards the future once again. In our lives, individuals are still the ones involved in the struggle."

"And what a struggle! In a world full of evil. They say that, if good is not faced by the challenge of evil, there's no civilization. Fine! But, if evil keeps a stranglehold on good, what kind of civilization is possible? It's Shigalov's world, a world full of spying, slander and abuse, a world of slaves."

The Doctor clasped his whiskey glass in his hand, and I noticed it tremble as he spoke. He was talking like someone who had just managed to get his head out of a snake-filled ditch; he was trying to clamber out but without success.

"I reject a world," he said, "which does not permit me to raise my voice in protest, which does not allow me to petition or insist on my human rights without bashing me on the head."

Mahmud looked a little distressed. "Needless to say," he commented, "Wadi and I both reject it too."

"No, Mahmud," the Doctor said, "you don't understand me. I feel as though I'm living in a world in which I'm supposed to choose between silence or the guillotine. Why am I forced to repeat exactly the same things as the people in the dark ages: 'If speech is silver, then silence is gold?'"

"But there are many speakers, Doctor."

"Of course there are! When speech is unadulterated hypocrisy or pure lies, there will be lots of speakers. What's the harm?"

Mahmud gave a subdued, coarse laugh; it was almost as though he were unwilling to give vent to all the sarcasm pent up inside him. He kept strumming on the cover of *The Devils*, trying not to arouse Falih any more than he had already. "Maybe that's all part of the struggle?" he said.

But the Doctor had now reached a point of no return. "The struggle?" he said. "Lies can only be lies. They can't stand the noisy sound of defiance, of pride. And those who really make life what it is are the defiant ones, the people with pride. Ugh! Those liars! Journalists lie, politicians lie, professors lie—endless hypocrisy, all of it! They talk about opportunism! Give me what I want and take all the talk, abuse, and praise you want. You only have to lie two or three times in order to savor the taste of it. If you are good at lying, people are afraid of you. Lying leads to more lying, up, down and in every direction. Soon life as a whole is molded on pretense, false claims and swindles; the tongue becomes mightier than the sword. How can I possibly read a newspaper in such circumstances? How can I listen to a patriotic, political or social speech? Words mean their opposite, and the opposite doesn't mean anything. Everyone knows he's lying. I lie to you, you lie to me. The clever person is the one who makes his lies better, more terrible, more lethal, or more trivial, as dictated by circumstances—and he can provide fifty different types of lying. One person will say he believes in freedom. He's lying; he's getting a prison cell ready for you. Another will say he believes in the people; he's lying too—just take a look at his bank account after a while, look at the house he's had built, at the bottles of perfume stacked up on the dressing table of his wife or mistress. Every time circumstances change, a new group of liars appears. Only one person in a thousand tells the truth, and he remains naive, lost, despised and baffled. He cannot understand why he makes no progress in his life. Wave after wave of liars keeps crashing against both him and other waves, and all the while he's completely unaware. At times, he does not know what to believe. Eventually he closes his ears to the hubbub. He closes his mouth and would dearly love to close his eyes too, except that he has a native desire to see through his eyes rather than his ears, and let happen what may. No! I'm fed up, disgusted, nauseated. I have no desire to read a newspaper, hear a radio broadcast, or go to a public gathering. Let the liars marry and bury each other to their hearts content."

"So what's left for us?" I interrupted.

"Great books, they're the only things that don't lie. The body, it doesn't lie either, nor does the scalpel. To be sure, the scalpel may make mistakes, but they are honorable ones because it doesn't lie. You know, Wadi, sometime when you're feeling really happy, you the great optimist, you may say that I, the Doctor, keep on talking like a naive adolescent who's just seen his mother's backside for the first time. No matter. Like a naive adolescent I want to tear the trappings of delusion off me, but every time I see the truth or what seems to me to be the truth, I get horrified and angry. So now, I actually have no idea which cancer is crawling around this body, truth or falsehood."

"We're in a real quandary, Doctor. If truth can be a cancer too, even potentially, then what can we do about it except face it with your scalpel?"

"Exactly, exactly!"

"What if the operation's a failure?"

"The tragedy will have fulfilled itself. And, however heart-broken people may feel, tragedy is always noble."

"To a certain extent, I agree with you," said Mahmud.

"To a certain extent?"

"Yes. I can detect the smell of suicide in what you're saying."

"And why not?"

"Because I totally reject suicide. Sometimes, certain classes get the idea that everything in the world is threatening them, particularly when they sense that their own interests are in trouble. So they go to all kinds of extremes, even suicide."

"Mahmud, that's an old tune I've heard many times before. It's all part of the process of intimidation aimed at anyone who says, 'I've tested your data and found them false.' That's when they tell him that his class is threatened with extinction. Shit! I may well commit suicide, but I won't be doing it to protect 'certain classes' as you put it. It'll be because I am Falih, son of Shaykh Abdul

Wahid Haseeb, who has looked at the world and found it to be a ball full of poisonous, foul-smelling gas deflating slowly under his nose. So he has kicked it away from him to perdition, thereby confirming that he rejects it of his own free will...Another whiskey?"

Meanwhile, I had noticed Emilia walking past us more than once. I felt that she wanted to sit with us, but was discouraged from doing so by the intensity of our conversation. In fact, no sooner had I gestured to her than she came over, her rosy cheeks aglow and her blue eyes flashing. We all three stood up, but she did not sit down.

"Excuse me for interrupting," she said.

"On the contrary, we're grateful to you," said Falih, managing to conceal his fully aroused emotions. "Please join us."

"Actually, Doctor," she said, "I would like a word with you in private."

"Are you going to deprive yourself of the pleasure of the company of Mahmud and Wadi?"

"No," said Mahmud, "we are the ones who are denied the pleasure of her company."

She blushed once again (I had not expected her to be so bashful). "I've a request to make," she said, "which no one should ask a doctor on his vacation: a medical consultation."

Falih did not reply. He ordered another drink for us and then asked our permission to leave. "I'll be back in a while," he said, and then left with Emilia.

"Doctors have all the luck!" Mahmud commented slyly. "There he is going to her room now, and yet what can we say except that he's doing it as a service for tortured humanity?"

"But when he has a wife like Luma, do you think he would..."

"Man is evil by nature, Wadi, but I was only joking in any case. As far as I can see, Doctor Falih is the very last person to behave flippantly with women. He's too busy being angry."

"These types who are so busy being angry can have a terrifying emotional capacity. They're consumed by fire inside and out, and in a variety of ways. Towards women, too."

When the waiter had refilled our glasses, Mahmud pulled his chair towards me and put his large head so close to mine that his thick spectacles were almost touching my face. "I'm worried," he whispered, as though it were a prelude to something he was hesitant to divulge.

"About him?"

112

"Yes. A man of his candor, sensitivity, and intelligence can have an enormous influence on the direction of his country, if only he will participate in organized political activity. But he is independent, very independent. Nothing satisfies him. I've seen people like him all over the place, drinking themselves to death because they reject everything. Their own internal severity makes it impossible for them to approve of anything in life. The little that I've seen of him these last three or four days has convinced me—I hope you'll forgive me for being so frank—that he doesn't really love his wife, whom you all keep rhapsodizing about."

"I don't think he likes us so much either."

"I don't know. Every time I talk to him, I find him so intense, but in a way I cannot define exactly. As I said a while ago, he reminds me of the aristocratic group who sense intellectually that they are doomed and try to charge at death before it gets them. If he wanted, he could be a great revolutionary."

Mahmud was trying to imply, consciously or otherwise, that he himself belonged to a revolutionary group; more like an intellectual feeding his views into a secret movement that had not yet made its aims public. I would have liked to learn more about him, but every time our conversation came near the brink of a true confession, he managed to wriggle out of it like quicksilver.

"But he *is* a revolutionary in his own way," I replied. "Don't you think so?"

He shook his head sorrowfully and pursed his thick lower lip in an odd way. "His kind of revolution is like the steam that bursts out of a locomotive's boiler," he said. "It all comes to nothing, and the locomotive stays where it is. Energy has to be organized, Wadi."

"Just as Shigalov says?"

"As anyone who really wants to bring about change in society would say. There are evil forces in man as well as good. How can we rescue the one from the other?"

"By revolt, just as Falih is doing. Do you know, Mahmud, he claims he doesn't agree with my views. In fact, on more than one occasion, he's shown a distinct aversion towards me. I've no idea how either of us has managed to overcome it. But now I've started to see his point of view more clearly. I don't think he'll *ever* see mine. But then, that's not important since I've started to like him, or at least, to sympathize with him."

"This voyage is very short unfortunately. Soon we'll all go our own different ways and all these feelings will be dissipated as

113

though they had never happened."

"Really, you think so? As far as I'm concerned, every experience leaves its mark on me. Now tell me frankly, are you running away?"

"Running away?" As he said these words, Mahmud stiffened his back and moved away from me, just as though I had slapped him on the face.

"Are you running away?" I asked again.

Mahmud pushed the novel away from him on the table, lifted his glass quickly to his lips and downed the contents in one gulp.

"Running away? Certainly not. Everyone has his own personal tragedy in life. Mine is that I don't run away. Why do you ask?"

"I've begun to see that running away can take an infinite number of forms. Our real tragedy is that intellectually we are escapists. We're all poets, even though we don't recite any poetry. Delusions work their allure on us, so we tag along behind them wherever they lead us. The effective realities are left behind us."

He looked somewhat relieved and happy at my response. The way in which I had generalized my comments made it possible for him to put a distance between himself and my probing questions.

"Do you think that I too am one of those poets who don't recite any poetry? No, Wadi! I may be fond of poetry, but I've a head on my shoulders which only deals with facts in a scientific way. That's the way I look at our friend, Doctor Falih, at you, and anyone else I meet. I believe that society must be changed. How and in which direction? These are details which I am also studying. What's revolution? Rebellion? Struggle? Power? The individual? As far as I'm concerned, these are all priorities that I'm trying to define clearly."

"Even so, you claim that in spite of man's continuing struggle, the quantities of tyranny and freedom don't change a great deal! How so?"

"That's from a purely historical standpoint. It's my realistic understanding of history."

"What about faith?"

"Faith in what? Faith's of no concern to me."

"You'd side with the tyrants then!"

"The ideology which I adhere to has no need of invisible factors. Mathematics, that's the way I look at it. The important thing to do is to define the quantities of what is known and unknown. Then you can work out the correct equation."

At this point, he stared out at the sea. His back sagged until it was bent over.

"When I was fifteen," he continued in a subdued voice, "I composed a poem. I can only remember two lines of it. I imagined myself in a small boat that I was steering through a stormy sea. The sea here is wonderful; just look at it! Its waves keep stroking the side of the ship like a woman caressing a lover asleep in her arms. But the sea I imagined myself rowing through was savage and wild; the waves played a vicious game with my little boat:

> To the left it was pushed,
> To the right pulled back again.
> And my heart so trembled
> Torn out by despair.

That's all I can remember: the storm, the trembling, the despair. I was still a young boy then; all I knew about life was what I had read in books. Ever since, I've been trying to save my little boat and put an end to the storm, the trembling, and the despair. After all that, can you still ask me if I'm running away?"

His gruff voice had become softer, and he sounded distressed. I sensed that he was shaking and that his glasses were probably hiding a few tears. He was wounded and was trying to disguise the fact. How is it that I find myself today squeezing the very deepest secrets out of these people? Or could it be that they have been waiting for the first opportunity anyone offered to pour their overflowing anxieties into his ears?

I will not claim, however, that I was able to squeeze a great deal out of Mahmud's heart. Doctor Falih did not come back soon, as he had promised. Mahmud and I talked for a long time. Two things had been on Mahmud's mind since I had become aware that he was on board the ship: politics and women. His approach to each was marked by considerable caution. It was as though deep down inside him there was a latent fear that determined how far he could safely stray in what he said. It was not difficult to deduce that both caused him pain, in spite of the head on his shoulders which took a strictly scientific approach to facts. Perhaps his real trouble was in that huge head of his. It was the head of a thinker—there could be no doubt about that—a head made of coarse metal, with an unpolished surface. It might well harbor some marvellous ideas, but it would never be able to turn the heads of any women as he dearly wished. His ideas seemed to be concentrated on the creation of a political system that would bring together a large number of Arab intellectuals who might be scattered not just across the Arab countries from the Atlantic Ocean to the Gulf but throughout the capitals of Europe and America too. Mahmud claimed that revolutionary intellectuals generally crystallized their leftist ideas in capitalist cities in the West. Basically, they could live only in a liberal atmosphere which afforded them opportunities to read books, study, and organize freely and without hindrance. The reason was, according to him, that those cities allowed a good deal of give and take in intellectual matters and had legal guarantees. He believed that revolutionaries were liberals deep down but were forced to abandon the liberal position under the constraints of imperialism, which they could understand better than anyone else because they had studied in the West. So they abandoned liberalism for some temporary political purpose, hoping as they did so that they would be able to return to the democratic principles they had abandoned as soon as things were going well again. But then they discovered that the way back was blocked—that, according to Mahmud, was part of the nature of things. The forces they unleashed could only be controlled by resorting to the very limits of the means which they employed: thus, violence became an unavoidable evil to them before the earth began to sway beneath their feet. But what actually happened was that later on the forces they unleashed would never yield, even to their own extreme methods. Their revolution rolled over on top of them. They were isolated and soon lumped together with the bourgeoisie, the idealists, and the reactionaries. Eventually they end up running away.... That was the problem that Mahmud, as a responsible intellectual, wanted to take account of. That's the question. He was going to spend two or three years at Lille University in order to have some time to himself to think and clarify this dialectical process.

I had taken this new friend of mine exactly as I found him. "Action, action," I said. "Confrontation, self-sacrifice, death, those are the only things I can offer as an answer to your analysis and explanation. But I'll take you just as you are."

He did not like that comment; it was as though I had scoffed at his endeavors from on high. But he gave his usual rough, sarcastic laugh. At that moment, Doctor Falih came back alone.

"Have you left any discussion for me?" he asked.

I ordered a glass of whiskey for him.

"How did you find Madame Emilia?" Mahmud asked him.

"Mahmud, please, if you don't mind!" the Doctor replied with a frown.

"Forgive me," Mahmud said. "I wasn't talking of her as a patient, but as a splendid woman I know."

"You know her?" Falih and I both exclaimed at the same time. "Where from?"

"Why the surprise, folks?" he replied. "I know her from Beirut. I used to know her husband, Michel Asad, before he married her, years ago. Then he had an attack of...I don't know what it was. In any case, it's not important. He left her."

I had no idea why this peice of news made me feel so happy at that moment. Maybe it was because his acquaintance with Emilia established some sort of connection between the two of us.

"We're old friends then, Mahmud," I exclaimed.

"Do you know her too, then?"

"For more than a year. I don't know her very well, but I've met her several times. She's the friend of another woman I've known for a while."

"And who might that be?"

"Do you want me to reveal all my secrets?" I asked with a laugh.

Mahmud did not pursue the matter, and Falih remained silent.

"If you twist my arm a little," Mahmud said, "I'll tell you all mine!"

"Important ones?" Falih inquired.

"Important to me. At least, they were. It all came to an end many months ago."

"You didn't betray your friend, I trust," I joked.

"I don't know, for heaven's sake. I was fond of her when they were married. I met her on one of my visits to Beirut, after her separation from her husband. I got the feeling I was falling into... Listen. If it weren't for all this whiskey inside me, I wouldn't be saying all this. In any case, I should be fair. This gorgeous Italian female did not respond to me at all. I spent two or three sleepless nights over it, but then I told myself that that was quite enough adolescent behavior and the whole thing came to an end."

"So you treated facts in a scientific way, I see!"

"How I wish! Love is the one and only thing which transcends science and politics. To be brief..."

To be brief, I was unable to find out any more about Mahmud's life. In fact, he succeeded in confusing the issue even more by adding, "I get similar attacks from time to time."

117

"You make it sound like attacks of epilepsy," I said.

"There's not much difference between the two. What do you say, Doctor?"

"Absolutely, absolutely," Falih replied, grave-faced.

"Then they disappear as though nothing had ever happened."

"What about now?" I asked.

"You don't mingle much with the young people who are traveling deck class, fourth class. They're the most enjoyable people on the entire ship. There's a girl among them, an Egyptian student, whom you really should take a look at, Wadi."

We continued our conversation. The Doctor did not say much. Thereafter, all I learned was that the Egyptian girl Mahmud liked so much was in her twenties or even younger and was studying drama. We took him to task for that.

"Every time I get a year older," he said, "I fall in love with younger women. Pretty soon, I won't even bother about any girl over seventeen. Seventeen, just think of it! The beginning of spring, the very first buds, nature's virgin gift, an act of mercy towards men whom the years are dragging ever faster towards their fifties..."

I woke up late and could feel that the sea was rough, unlike what it had been since the voyage started. Looking out of the porthole, I could see that the waves were higher and rougher than they had been the previous night. I had only just finished shaving when there was a knock on the cabin door. It was Jacqueline. Her face looked pale and her lips were blue.

"Didn't you hear the noise?" she asked. "Are you still in bed?"

I put on my clothes just as I found them and then followed her quickly up to the deck. We went into the middle lounge. A large number of people were gathered around a man who was still shouting and screaming angrily. It was Mahmud Rashid without his glasses, surrounded by a group of sailors and stewards from the ship. I was certain that he had gone mad: His eyes were bulging in a terrifying fashion, his black lips were swollen, and there was a glistening white foam at the sides of his mouth. He kept jumping up and shouting in his coarse voice in Arabic, "It's him, I tell you; it's him, people, him in person, the son of a bitch, Nimr al-Ajami! By God, it's him, look...look, here, this long scar on my chest, this long line across my stomach."

He had no coat on and had torn his shirt off. He was showing all the onlookers his body, which was covered with scars. They

118

meanwhile kept trying to calm him down. "Those black lines on my back," he yelled, "just look at them, people!"

Yusuf Haddad kept trying to calm him down, but it was useless. People's reactions ranged from revulsion to malicious glee. I rushed over to him. He started clinging to me and begging me. "Grab him, I beg you!" he kept saying. "Where's the bastard gone? Nimr al-Ajami. Where's he gone, Wadi? Two whole months, sixty days, that's how long he tortured me. With a whip. He hung me to the fan, he locked me up in the lavatory, he made me drink my own urine. Did you see him? He was wearing a Greek sailor's uniform, the bastard! He's even come here to spy on me. Grab him. I'll kill him, so help me, I'll kill him!"

Our Arab friends joined us, and we all tried to calm him down by talking gently to him. But he would not listen. In fact, he was roaring like a wounded bull. He kept addressing one person and then entreating another, but adamantly refused to accept anyone's pleas that he should calm down. Every time we tried to get him out of the lounge, he pushed us away with unusual strength.

Eventually we had to use force. With the help of some of the sailors, one person grabbed each arm. We then carried him forcibly to a small cabin that had only the usual porthole and an iron bed in it. The ship's doctor then appeared carrying a syringe and small tube. He filled the syringe. Meanwhile, we were holding on to Mahmud for all we were worth. We laid him down on the bed, and four men helped to keep him flat on his back just as he was. He kept pushing and writhing around; his yells had by now changed to a hoarse babbling. We tore the sleeve off his shirt, and the doctor showed tremendous dexterity in giving him the injection. Mahmud kept on shouting, cursing and babbling furiously, but before long he began to calm down. When at long last we were able to release our hold on him, he did not resist but simply stayed where he was, spreadeagled on the bed. Finally, he lost consciousness. The doctor recommended that we leave him alone, so we all left the cabin and he locked the door after us.

"What on earth happened, Yusuf?" we all asked. "Did your friend have an attack of epilepsy, or what?"

"No, it wasn't epilepsy," replied Yusuf, his voice still wavering. In fact, his entire body was trembling quite uncontrollably. "It wasn't epilepsy; it was anger, a hideous anger. After breakfast, we were together. He was reciting Shawqi's poetry, as usual..."

"What?!"

"That's right! Ahmad Shawqi's poetry. He knew his entire corpus by heart. He's been thrusting it at me for days. In fact, he's actually made me feel sorry that I neglected his poetry in the past. Then all of a sudden, he started yelling. One of the sailors had come up—I think he's a waiter in the salon where we had been sitting. Mahmud just took one look at him and started yelling. I didn't understand what he was saying at first. Then he grabbed the sailor by the collar. 'Even here, Nimr, you pimp,' Mahmud yelled. 'I'll kill you, by God, I'll kill you.' That's the way it was—no advance warning, nothing. Mahmud grabbed him by the neck. The sailor started yelling. He struggled with Mahmud and said some words in Greek and then a few others in Arabic. Passengers immediately gathered around us. All I could gather from his babbling was that Nimr al-Ajami had tortured him in some prison or other and that this sailor was Nimr al-Ajami."

Isam, the others, and I all came to the conclusion that he was probably imagining things. However, if he really had been imprisoned and tortured, then his experiences were, no doubt, horrifying. He was living a nightmare, a nightmare that suddenly catapulted him into a situation where insanity was a real possibility.

"Who is Mahmud Rashid?" I asked Yusuf.

"I've no idea," he replied.

Everyone was flabbergasted.

"But you're always together."

"I got to know him on board. When my companion got off the ship at Piraeus and he discovered that I was alone in the cabin, he asked if he could join me before someone elso was assigned to it. But I don't know anything about him. He hasn't told me what he does for a living. He seems to be well-off. Maybe he's a politician."

"What party?" Isam asked.

"I've no idea."

"Why couldn't the sailor whom Mahmud wanted to kill be Nimr al-Ajami?" I asked. "There are lots of things in life more peculiar than that. Maybe Mahmud wasn't imagining things. Or maybe the sailor really does look like this Nimr al-Ajami, so Mahmud thought his terror had become a reality."

When we went looking for the waiter, we were told he was suffering from shock and had been ordered to bed by the ship's captain. We went up to talk to the captain and asked to see the sailor. The captain merely laughed.

"What's the point?" he asked. "Is one of the young men I have on board supposed to be an agent in disguise from your country, or what? Our friend, Mr. Rashid, seems to be ill. We're quite used to things like this, you know. Please rest assured that we'll take good care of him. We like you, and you like us."

So saying, he gave a puff of pipe smoke out of one corner of his mouth while the pipe itself was fixed in the other. He made light of the whole episode, as though nothing had happened at all. He promised that, as soon as the sailor recovered, he would send him to see us with a glass of whiskey for each one of us.

"What precisely are you going to do with Mr. Rashid?" I asked.

"I'm hoping he'll be over his crisis before we reach Naples," the captain replied, "thanks to our excellent doctor. As you can see, the sea's rough today. The weather forecast says it's going to get worse. One of those rare storms that can blow up sometimes during the summer. I bet you that as soon as the sea calms down again, you'll find that the patient has recovered."

The sea did indeed get rougher and rougher. A warm wind began to blow, although you could hardly hear it at first. Then it began to intensify in both frequency and force. The wind started to howl, and the sound blended with the clashing of the waves as they surged against the ship, white and angry. The ship itself swayed from side to side, heavy and reluctant.

We found Emilia all by herself. She was leaning on the rail as the ship swayed this way and that. Her mind was far away, and her eyes stared out towards the distant horizon—in fact, she may have been staring at a yet more distant horizon than that of the sea and sky, which we were all looking at with a degree of alarm. When she turned towards us, her eyes looked the same color as the blue of the storm-tossed sea.

"Emilia," I said, "Mahmud claimed yesterday that he knows you and Michel. Is that true?"

She replied in the affirmative by muttering something and nodding her head.

"What do you know about him?"

"No more than you and Isam know. He was one of Michel's acquaintances during student days. He came to visit us from Damascus once or twice."

"Is that all there is to it?"

I remembered what Mahmud had told us about the two or three sleepless nights he had had because of this "gorgeous Italian female," but Emilia was not any help to us in finding out more details.

"I saw him once or twice after I left Michel."

"Ah!" exclaimed Isam, "now the facts are coming to light!"

"What facts?"

"Come now, Isam! What do you take me for? With all due respect to him, I never..."

The only way she could find to express her feelings about Mahmud was to purse her lips and flair her nostrils. "I don't know," she continued, "what brought him on board this ship."

"Love maybe?" suggested Isam.

"Isam!" she shouted, anger flashing in her eyes. "I'll never speak to you again if you make such an insinuation once more!"

"The truth is," I said, "that he's traveling to France to work as a professor at Lille University. So don't do him a disservice."

"I wish him well!" Emilia said, and then looked about her. "Funny!" she continued, "I've seen all the passengers today except your two friends."

"You mean the doctor and his wife?" I asked.

"Yes. Maybe the doctor is involved in treating Mahmud."

"I don't think he'd be at all reluctant to help if he were consulted."

"Of course not. His hands are like a magician's."

"How do you know?" Isam asked jokingly.

"He examined me yesterday. By the way, Wadi, do you think I was wrong to take him away from you yesterday?"

"Certainly not!" I replied. "Actually, you came at the crucial point in the discussion, but you managed to put an end to one of his rages. If he'd seen what happened this morning, he would not have been the slightest bit astonished. It all fits in with his cosmic disgust."

"Emilia," Isam asked, putting his hand on her arm with obvious tenderness, "do you admire the doctor?"

"As much as you all admire Luma. Right?"

"Touché!!" said Isam.

A sailor came up to us at that moment with an envelope in his hand. "Mr. Assaf?" he asked. When I said yes, he handed me the envelope. My heart sank at the sudden surprise, as though I'd been given a warning of something dreadful. I had forgotten that passengers on ships were not out of reach of telegrams, especially if the telegrams come from Beirut. I opened the envelope and read the following English words, which were stuck onto the sheet of paper:

Changed my mind. Traveling to Rome by plane. Will come to Naples Friday morning. Wait for me there please. If you wish I'll finish the journey with you by sea. I've forgotten everything that has happened. You must do same. Another start. Don't wire. Enjoy yourself. Dying to see you. Maha.

"Good news, I hope?" Isam asked.

"Good news," I replied as I put the telegram in my pocket. I turned towards Emilia. "Maha's coming to Naples," I said.

Her features burst into a sudden smile, and her eyes sparkled. "Maha's coming to Naples! That's terrific news! How marvelous!"

"Yes," I replied.

"What do you mean, yes?" she asked. "Aren't you happy she's coming?"

"Of course I'm happy she's coming," I replied coldly.

"Wadi!" she said, "Don't make things difficult for her. She's a wonderful girl. You know that better than anyone!"

I did not respond to her comment.

"So we're going to see Maha at long last," said Isam to break the silence.

I did not know how to take the sudden news. I felt as though a sharp sword had been brought down on a recalcitrant knot inside me and had severed it at one blow. Even though the storm was getting worse by the minute, I should have been leaping for sheer joy and announcing the glad news over the ship's loudspeaker system. But I found I had been more affected than I realized by what had happened to Mahmud. I could not forget that he had been tortured and that he was still in the throes of his agony. What law on earth allowed us to inflict such agony on other people? I've always had deep inside me an idealistic "weakness" that I cannot control in spite of all the organized and individual brutality I have encountered or witnessed: No man has the right to torture anyone else, whatever the motivating circumstances may be. I have been unable to comprehend some of the types of political struggle. Political, did I say? No! I have rejected the designation. Every time the struggle assumes a form that conflicts with man's basic right to be a human being whose dignity must remain untouched, the struggle ceases to be a political one. It's something else. The political designation is a shameful cover-up which can only lead to yet more agony and a more shameful cover-up.

But what did Mahmud have to do with Maha? That was what I could not understand. Maybe I was feeling tortured too and saw my own self in Mahmud. But I was a free man, free, free! I could travel where I liked. When I had a disagreement with Maha, my own will exerted itself like a giant, as it always did whenever I disagreed with anyone. But the agony of torture? How could that creep into the inner recesses of the mind and insinuate itself into your very blood? Maha? She really was a wonderful girl. She seemed as gentle as the breeze, but in fact she was harder than stone itself. So, in just a few nights (and I hope she did not sleep a wink) she had decided she had made a mistake and had given way. Even though she had sent such a specific and clear telegram, I was not sure she would really come to Naples by next Thursday evening when we arrived—she must have found that out from the travel agency in Beirut. The ship would be staying in port on Thursday and Friday and then resuming its voyage on Saturday morning. Maybe she would spend some more sleepless nights and change her mind once again. I could receive another telegram in Naples explaining it all to me. I had once written her a letter just like that as a comment on a letter which she had sent me. 'Wait for me sometimes,' it had said, 'and spend the night sleepless! That's exactly what I want! I want you to stay awake, my beautiful wine, my intoxication. I hope you cannot sleep for sheer love, for sheer lust. I want to smother you front and back, up and down, all over—you're all love and pleasure—until I see you writhing under my hands like a fish.' When I flew from the cauldron of the Gulf to the mists of the Lebanese Mountains, she quoted my letter at me. 'Make me writhe under your hand like a fish!' she said. 'I'm all love and pleasure. But please do not stop me from sleeping. Lack of sleep hurts me!' Whereupon, she slept like a log! Agony! How did it sneak in through the secluded coverlets of love and pleasure? In what cell did Mahmud imagine he was at that particular moment? I hope he is sleeping like a log too. But let's turn back to affairs of the heart. Maha is coming on Friday. Till then, Jacqueline will also have been writhing under my hands like a fish. It is difficult to rid oneself of suffering, just like getting rid of torture. Everywhere I turn, I can see people writhing like fish, whether they are in love or not, in agony or not.

I came to myself in time to hear Emilia commenting that the sea was very rough for June.

"The passengers are all retiring to their cabins," Isam said. "How's your stomach, Wadi?"

"Still in place, I think."

"I feel as if the sea has begun to betray me."

"Just like everything else in life?" Emilia commented.

"What about you?" I asked.

"I'll resist," she replied.

"Resistance won't do you any good," Isam said. "Come on, let's lie down on one of those deck chairs."

"Abandon hope all ye who enter here!" No! On board a ship, it should be written as follows in letters of sun and wind: "Abandon all memories, all ye who enter here!" For voyagers, the sea is a tremendous eraser that can wipe out the most stubborn types of ink, even images etched into the soul like wounds. But unfortunately the sea is not the river of oblivion, however much the travelers might wish it were. That only happens when it turns wild and nasty.

It now began to reveal its ferocious grey aspect and hurled itself up and down like a snake with a thousand heads and tails, attacking the small ship like a giant trying to demolish a fly by shaking his foul body around. For each and every passenger the future became more important than the past. The present moment was a hellish brew of upset stomachs and, in many cases, a futile vomiting, as though to proclaim that they were rid of everything they remembered. A hankering for the moment to come, that was all that remained; a desire to retrieve their lost dignity and find their sea legs again. The raging of the sea is a frightful experience in oblivion, a total involvement in the present moment when everything else has vanished. The stomach is turned into a hateful, querulous presence that sucks all the blood out of the head and imposes a complete stupor on the mind while at the same time keeping it in a state of grim consciousness.

However, some people can overcome a stormy sea. You could see them walking upright—actually they were leaning over—while the ship tossed and turned and the white waves kept up their savage raging and smashed like lava against the sides of the ship. However hard you tried to avoid it, a needle-sharp spray battered your face and then retired, leaving behind streams of water with dark yellow bubbles that seethed their sinister way across the deck. Most of the passengers had by now retired to their narrow little beds to nurse their ailing stomachs as best they could in the agony of the hellish moment. Others lay back in the chairs on deck, hoping that the wind would provide some sort of relief from their miseries. Still others, men and women, kept walking through the surging water as the waves sprayed the deck;

they seemed intent on defying the savage weather which they had not expected from the mild, blue sea which they all loved.

Falih was one of the people who was walking in this wild storm. I saw him as I was lying on a deck chair. His hair was flying in all directions like broken spears. He was walking around the ship on his own, facing the wind at one point and then turning his back on it; buffeting against it at one moment and then resisting its insistent pushing from behind. He was determined not to let it get control of him. He did two or more rounds, and then I stood up and joined him.

"Moving around seems better than being still," I yelled so that he could hear me.

"Of course, man!" he yelled back.

We walked together. When the wind was in our faces, progress was slow; when it was behind us, we found ourselves pushed reluctantly forward.

"This is the way I like the sea!" he said.

"As long as it doesn't keep this up too long."

"Are you going to eat lunch?"

"How's your appetite?"

"Not bad! How about you?"

"I could eat a horse!"

"I don't like seeing these people clinging to the railing. It puts me off."

"You mean, the ones throwing up over the side."

"So, life is not all a matter of dancing at night and arguing by day?"

"The state of man... A single blast of wind is enough to..."

"Did you hear what happened to Mahmud?"

"Did he see the guillotine again?"

"What?"

"I said, did he see the guillotine again?"

"It sounds as though you've seen him."

"Yes, a little while ago. He's still unconscious. I don't think the storm will make his situation any easier."

Just then, I noticed Emilia rushing towards us. I had no idea where she came from. The wind was pushing us backwards and her forwards. It was becoming increasingly difficult to stand. Emilia's long, luxuriant hair looked like a black cloud surrounding her head, and her dress kept flying up around her waist, uncovering her thighs. She came rushing towards us holding on to

the railing and trying at the same time to keep her legs covered.
"Hello, Doctor!" she said.
When she reached us, we continued our vigorous promenade.
"And how are you?" Falih asked.
"The winds are sweeping me away!"
"Terrific!"
"Thank you!"
"What about your stomach?"
"It's resisting."
"Luma's staying in bed."
"Poor girl."
We proceeded on our wind-blown circuit of the deck, meeting
the crest of each wave and relishing the salty taste of the wind.
The ship kept tossing and yawing as it groaned and creaked its
way forward. Emilia was between the two of us and put up a
courageous fight against the elements. The three of us linked
arms and sparred with words that may or may not have had any
meaning. We resisted together.

When it was lunch time, we found very few people in the
dining hall. The expression on some of their faces discouraged
one from looking at them. It is an incredible sensation to be in
completely good health and to possess all your resolve and
appetite, when everyone else around you is suffering in misery!
However, what really amazed me was Doctor Falih, who kept
laughing for all he was worth. He was happy as could be, and so
was Emilia. I had not expected them to be so incredibly happy. It
was as though they were two lovers who had met unexpectedly
in a foreign country, as though the raging storm outside was the
only thing Falih needed as a background for him to spend a
couple of happy hours with mankind.

What about me? I shared their happiness with them. I forgot. I
forgot Maha and Mahmud. I forgot everything except the
incredible storm. I had discovered that I had a stomach that could
crush rocks.

We asked for a bottle of wine with our lunch, and then had
another.

"Where's Isam?" Falih asked by way of challenge. "Where's
Jacqueline, Luma, everybody?"

"They're all flat on their backs!" I replied.

"Terrific, darling!" Emilia said with a hearty laugh.

"Emilia, darling," said Falih, "why don't you throw yourself flat
on your back sometimes!"

127

"What a wonderful idea!" Emilia replied, still laughing. I thought the joke was a little crude, but even so I laughed with them. I had been struck at that moment by a peculiar thought: Could it be possible that Emilia and Falih were old friends? That word 'darling' which they were throwing back and forth at each other had an unmistakable ring of familiarity and freedom to it. It was certainly not the kind of remark exchanged between strangers, even as a little amorous dalliance on a ship being tossed around by a raging sea. In fact, Falih was soon flirting with Emilia quite openly—I don't know if it was the effect of the wine. When we parted, they went off together. I was fairly certain that they went to Emilia's cabin, which she had to herself since Maha had not come on the voyage. But I did not really care. After all, why should I worry about who went to whose cabin in that damned outrageous storm?

Isam Salman

I could not stand the storm. I was not "a good sailor," as the saying goes. I dragged my feet along, worrying in case I threw up before I could reach my cabin and lie down on my bed. Every time I saw a pale face around me, I became intensely aware of what one of my teachers at school used to call "man's misery." I left Wadi to revel in his philosophical thoughts, describing "the hellish moment" as he pleased. I left Emilia, too. The lucky devil! Her cheeks remained as red as roses. There was no room left in my heart to grieve for Mahmud. I was not really interested in him, unlike Wadi, who was bitterly shaken by the incident. Perhaps Wadi did not know what I knew. I could no longer sympathize with people who suffer a fall and then start yelling and screaming about despots, only to become even more tyrannical themselves when the wheel of fortune turns in their favor. Who knows? Mahmud may some day return from his exile victorious. Who will then be at the receiving end of the whip as he sits and watches, unmoved, and how many "Nimr Ajamis" will he set loose in order to spy on his adversaries? Of course, the whole idea was ridiculous. Mahmud was sick, as the captain said. He was living in a state of continuous terror. But in all probability most of it was a figment of his imagination, or perhaps a necessary product of the kind of thoughts that were dogging him. At any rate, the heaving waves and howling wind made me forget him. I was interested only in reaching my cabin safely. In the corridors I almost bumped into Falih, who was on his way up to the deck.

"What's the matter, Isam?" he asked.

"I feel awful," I replied.

"Take care of yourself."

"I'll try..."

No sooner had I opened the door of the cabin and gone inside than the bow of the ship plunged into the waves and the door slammed behind me. I landed on my bed fully dressed. Shawkat was not in the cabin. Those businessmen, I thought, their stomachs must be made of steel. If the sea had been calm, Shawkat would have been lying in his bed reading one of his silly magazines. But whenever the sea roared and heaved, he would take his steel stomach with him and go out to watch the waves. This trip meant nothing to him. He simply wanted it to end with the least amount of effort possible so that he could resume his business activities as if nothing had happened. And Luma? Where is she? In her cabin, no doubt, on the other side of the wall, writhing in bed alone, or is Falih back with her? Why don't I get up and find out? If he's there, I'll pretend I need his help. I'll ask him for some pills for seasickness. Seasickness! All of a sudden the ship heaved and then dropped again, shaking everything in the cabin. I found myself in the little bathroom emptying my insides out and feeling miserable. Luma was in the adjoining cabin. What was she doing at that very moment, I wondered? Even then I loved her, I desired her. I was dying, and still I desired her, even as she tossed about feeling seasick. She was by herself, I was sure. What a joke! The opportunity for us to meet seems to come only when we're both sick! I went back to my bed and listened. If Falih returned, I would hear the door slam. Other doors did slam but they were on the other side of the corridor. When I feel better, I told myself, when the sea stops this foolishness, I shall go to her, just for a moment or two. She will be lying there like a Sumerian queen on her death bed. Shubad. She was a stunning beauty, Shubad. When she died, a hundred beautiful women died with her, all in their lovliest finery. The ship shook and lurched. What a farce! Luma was just a stone's throw away from me, but I could not touch her. Let the gods laugh as long as they please! They had laughed before, when they made my father stab Jawad Hamadi in the heart in a sidewalk coffee-shop in the Karkh district of Baghdad. Twenty years later, the gods sent his niece to hunt me down in a students' dance hall in London, in the streets of Oxford, on the punts that skimmed the waters of the Isis and the Cam, in an abandoned piece of land in Baghdad—to hunt me down and then discard me on the other side of the wall. To the bathroom... ugh... I glimpsed my face in the mirror. It was blue, repugnant; yellow lips and stupid, round eyes.

The door in the next cabin did not slam. There was nothing left in my insides to worry about throwing up. There was hardly any blood left in my head to help me keep my balance. I tried to fall

130

asleep, but it was hopeless. I tried to remember the other passengers, one by one, but it was no good. I could only think of the Frenchman and his dead wife who lay in a coffin near his bed. At least he had something tangible there, even if it was just a coffin, an iron box. I decided to go to Luma's cabin. I stood up, combed my hair, staggered to the sink, and splashed water on my face, trying hard not to look out through the porthole at the spiteful, swaying horizon. One look would have been enough to throw me back on my bed. The howling wind alone was more than I could take. I brushed my teeth, wiped my face with eau-de-cologne and sat on the only chair in the cabin, which kept sliding back and forth between the walls. I gathered up sufficient strength, stood up, and opened the door. It slammed after me, and I walked cautiously towards the adjoining door. I knocked and waited. I knocked again, and again. The door opened, but only a little. Luma looked out through the small aperture.

"Yes?" she said.

"Luma, are you alone?" I whispered.

I pushed the door with the little remaining strength that I had, went in, and closed the door behind me.

Luma was wearing blue pyjamas. It was obvious that she had had to get out of bed to open the door. She was barefoot. Her face was pallid, but it had not lost any of its fascination. On the contrary, the faint pallor of her complexion made it look more beautiful than ever. Her firm, well-rounded breasts showed through her open pyjama top. Surprised, she fastened one or two buttons with her trembling hands and threw herself helplessly on her bed. Her eyes seemed larger than ever. "How could you, Isam?" she said. "I feel...'"

I sat on a chair by her bare feet. "I feel the same way," I interrupted. "Don't worry."

"I haven't been able to get out of bed since morning."

"I was wondering how you felt."

"Please, Falih might come back any moment."

"Luma."

"Please go back to your cabin. I don't want you to see me like this."

"If only you knew how beautiful you look!"

I caressed her bare foot, toe by toe. "Please leave, Isam!" she said with a faint smile. "Wait until the sea calms down."

"That may not be today."

"If it doesn't," she said, "I'll surely die. Please, I've no strength

131

left in me. I'll see you when the sea calms down. Please!"

From the porthole I could see the waves as they receded, gathered force, and then crashed against the ship with tremendous force, spraying their foam against the glass porthole and rocking the ship viciously. Leaning on Luma's bed, I stood up. I took hold of her delicate, translucent fingers. They had given up any attempt at resistance by now and felt lighter than a canary with broken wings. I raised them to my burning lips. They felt ice cold, but smelled fragrant and tasted delicious. I kissed her fingers. She pulled her hand away slowly. "Isam!" she pleaded, then suddenly turned her face towards the wall as if she was gasping for breath. Her right breast sprang out of her pyjama top, as if it too could not resist any longer. A desirable handful, but only for the eyes.

I staggered towards the door. "Until the sea calms down, then," I said. I opened the door and walked out slowly. It shut behind me once again, and I feebly groped my way back to my bed.

From the depths of the relentless storm I could hear an old Iraqi song. The words suddenly came back to me—I never thought that I would remember them—"If you pass over my grave, my love, my bones will quiver." I buried my face in the pillow, stretched my arms out as far as I could, and clutched the sides of my bed. Did I really see Luma, or was it all a dream? Where is your beloved Christ, Wadi? Why doesn't He walk on the waters of this accursed, murderous sea and still its fury with a sign from His right hand?

At last, around four o'clock in the afternoon, the miracle happened. The waves subsided and the storm died down. I tried to remember if we had already sailed through the fabled region of the Mediterranean that sailors spoke about as long ago as Phoenician times, recalling its horrifying eddies. I did not know exactly where we were. I could only remember the notorious Scylla and Charybdis whirlpools which I thought we had passed earlier. The compassionate sea! It roared, fulminated, and lusted like a sex-starved giant, and then died down. It scared us for a few hours in case we took its serenity for granted and then resumed its smiling composure. Soon the sick passengers began to feel better, and the deck once again filled up with people who moved about cautiously, like patients recuperating after a long illness.

I knew full well that every minute brought me closer to the

treacherous brink. In fact, during those first trying days on the ship, I wanted to run headlong towards that brink. I wanted to make a decision, put an end to my agony. I could no longer stand the tantalizing sight of grape clusters that dangled so close to my lips I could almost touch them, then moved out of my reach. And Luma! The woman I saw now was different from the one I had known before; she was taking two steps forward and one step backward on her way to the same brink.

Finally we both closed our eyes, took a step forward and jumped.

When we were about to dock in Naples in full view of Vesuvius, the ship's officers announced a group tour to the island of Capri for the next morning. The ticket was fifteen dollars, payable in advance. After supper everyone talked about the tour. Falih was ecstatic as the ship steered its way between the boats towards port against the background of the twinkling lights on land. I was drinking Cointreau with coffee when Falih slapped my back and asked, "Are you going to Capri tomorrow?"

"No," I replied, "I've been there before."

"Luma insists on going," he told me, "and I've never seen the island before. One must make the pilgrimage, I suppose."

"Have you bought the tickets?" I inquired.

"Of course!" Luma put in. "I've heard about Capri all my life. This is my chance to see it and get it out of my system."

Emilia had just arrived, accompanied by Wadi. She too seemed happy.

"Are you going to Capri?" I asked her.

"I've just bought my ticket," she replied. "I shall see Capri for the third time for the sake of all these distinguished guests."

"The Blue Grotto," I said, "is a miracle of rock and water. The house of Axel Muntheh, the hero of war and peace, the art collector, the man who finally rejected the world from the heights of his enchanted palace...the ruins of the Emperor Tiberius... In which century did he live? Who can forget all those marvels? Ladies and gentlemen, now you see on your left..."

"Come with us and be our guide," Luma said. "You seem to know so much about the place."

"Capri is for lovers," Wadi said. "For newly-weds, for old people who are afraid thay may die without seeing it. Isam surely is not one of those?"

"What a hypocrite you are!" said Luma. "You were one of the first people to buy a ticket. To which category do you belong? The lovers or the old and dying?"

"The lovers, of course," Wadi replied as he pulled Emilia closer to him.

Emilia in her turn put her arm around his waist and laughed. "Let's take advantage of the situation before Jacqueline comes... What say you, Doctor?" Emilia asked.

"It's a great idea," Falih answered. "Lovers should swap their mates.

All he had to do himself was look for Jacqueline and the game would be perfect. I would then take Luma in my arms. "These are the rules of the game," I would say to her. "Please play by them, and no cheating!"

I spotted Jacqueline. "Hurry up, Jacqueline," I shouted over Wadi's shoulder, "before it's too late!"

She ran towards us, her boyish hair falling over her eyes. "Have you people got a place for me?" she asked innocently.

"Your place is right here, next to the doctor," Emilia answered cunningly. "Come on," Emilia insisted, pushing her gently towards Falih.

Luma moved back two steps and bowed gracefully, leaving a space for Jacqueline next to Falih. "There you are!" she said.

Falih reached out with his hand and pulled Jacqueline towards him, without trying to hide his excitement. "Let's spite Wadi and Emilia," he said. "Right Emilia?"

At that moment Falih looked very handsome to me. It was not surprising that Luma had actually fallen in love with him. Emilia was looking at him as she had never done before. Her arm was around Wadi's waist, but her eyes were fixed on Falih's lips as he laughed wholeheartedly for the first time.

"And Luma," inquired Jacqueline, "who is she going to be with?"

"With me, with me, my darling!" I shouted. I felt Luma chide me with her silent Sumerian eyes. I grabbed her naked arm for the first time in ages and pulled her towards me. "Say yes, say yes!" I insisted.

"Yes, yes, yes!" she responded.

Falih called a waiter and ordered whiskey for everyone.

The passengers, meanwhile, were clustered by the railings watching the ship's final docking maneuvers. Everybody was shouting at the top of his voice, the sailors, the men on the wharf, everyone. How marvelous arrival was! With our phoney partners we rushed towards the railing in order to be a part of the general

134

joy and clamor that permeated the scene from every direction. I wished I could hold Luma tightly in my arms, within my heart, within my veins, where her blood and mine would flow together in one vibrant, frightening torrent. But the game was soon over. The ice cubes rattled in our glasses. We had all toasted the happy city, the Italians, and all mankind. But the night was full of lies, all kinds of lies. It separated us, and soon the ship was empty. All the passengers went to the city to try their luck, to rid themselves of their frustrations. Luma and her husband disappeared, and Wadi and I walked aimlessly in the streets of Naples.

Late the next morning I awoke to the sound of all kinds of din and clatter. The cranes were busy loading and unloading crates and bales, while the wharf teemed with porters, passengers, and large trucks. The loading and unloading of the cargo was being carried out to the accompaniment of shouts from the men who supervised the operation. Italian words added a musical aura to the scene. Yet the ship seemed all but deserted. Most of the passengers had left, either for Capri or for a stroll in Naples. The sun was high in the sky, and the hot humid air made me feel sticky. None of my friends were to be found on deck. It was as though the ship had changed its identity. Only a few deck-hands and porters were left.

Then with an abruptness no less intense than my realization on the first day of the cruise that Luma and her husband were among the passengers, I spotted Luma coming down the stairs that led to the main parlor. She walked towards me with firm and confident steps and told me she had been waiting for me to come out of my cabin.

In a flash I realized everything.

I rushed towards her, towards her gorgeous, candid eyes. She stretched out her hands and lodged them in mine like a precious gift.

"You didn't go to Capri then?" I asked her.

"No," she said, "I didn't feel well all night, and so I couldn't wake up early enough to go on the boat with the others."

"And Falih?"

"He went with the group," she replied. "He said he did not want to miss the opportunity of seeing the island." She looked out through one of the portholes that overlooked the noisy dock. "I was afraid I wouldn't find you," she said with a smile.

"And I was afraid you'd left for the Blue Grotto," I said. "I was also afraid you wouldn't go!"

"I'd have been furious if you'd left the ship after I'd gone to all this trouble."

She stared into my eyes. Was she able, I wondered, to see in them all the contradictions, yearnings, and bitterness that raged inside me? "I can't believe it," I whispered into her ear, as I usually did when I did not want anybody around to hear, "I never dreamt you would..."

"Isam," she interrupted me in a loud and cheerful voice, "time's very short."

I realized there was no one around. "We have a whole day," I said.

"Less than that," she said.

"When will they return from Capri?"

"Sunset at the latest."

"A few hours, then," I said. "Our kingdoms for just a few hours."

We leaped up the stairs to the deck. There, by the railing under the bright sun, in the midst of porters and sailors, and in full view of Vesuvius, which was slowly discharging clouds of black smoke, I took her in my arms. Our lips met in a violent kiss. I could feel her teeth, her tongue and her body—fresh, slender, firm, soft—while between kisses she whispered, "Enough, enough, Isam, not here. Let's go down to Naples."

Her scent filled my nostrils, chest, and head. I buried my mouth in her hair and devoured her neck and lips. She was laughing, as though, like me, she could not believe we were doing what we were doing; as though, like me, she had died of thirst a long time ago. She slipped away from my arms delicately and enticingly. She caught my hand, pulled me behind her, and sped towards the gangway. As we went down the rickety steps, I forgot everything, except that I wanted to keep holding her hand, almost as if she were a bird trying to escape while its legs were caught in a trap. Soon we were running on the sidewalk, hardly able to avoid the crates and the ropes that littered the dock.

"Luma, why did you get married?" I asked her suddenly.

She started. "Don't spoil our day," she said. "Never ask me that question again!"

"But..."

She stopped abruptly. "If you insist on asking me," she said, "I'll go back to the ship or jump in the sea."

I took her in my arms and kissed her again. It was stupid of me to ask such questions or try to find out the truth. It was stupid to knock my head against a brick wall.

We walked into a strange world that was totally indifferent to us. The streets and buildings in the old port section, the charm of which had once captivated me as a tourist, were now devoid of any meaning except that they held us as two strangers, refugees. All meaning was enclosed in the hand I was holding. "How would you like to live here forever?" I asked her.

"If only we could!"

"Shall we go to the Castle?"

"Which castle?" she inquired.

"Castel Nuovo. I can't remember the details of its history, but it's full of love, betrayal, and tragedy. Everything here is founded on love, betrayal, and tragedy!"

"Just like our life," she said.

"Yes, just like our life."

"Do you remember Nelson and Emma Hamilton? He defeated Napoleon, but the poor ambassador's wife conquered him, here, in this marvelous city. Will my end by like hers?"

"With a difference," I said. "I didn't defeat Napoleon, and you're not going to die from alcholism."

"In a women's prison... Do you remember me at Oxford?"

"Your little room at St. Anne's College? The gas heater that you kept feeding with shillings in order to keep the gas on?"

"And the tea?"

"And your ferocious resistance...?"

"Poor Isam. Did I resist you that much? In those days I had convinced myself that I didn't know what wrong was and that I couldn't distinguish between right and wrong, good and evil. My resistance was tantamount to good as I understood good to be at that time."

"I said it was evil."

"Let me confess! You were absolutely right. I thought I'd return to Baghdad and wait for you. Penelope and Ulysses, you know..."

"Ha, ha, you've never even knitted me a sweater!"

"Don't you see? No sooner had I finished my studies than everything changed: right and wrong, good and evil. And when I returned to Baghdad..."

"Everything there had changed, too," I said.

"Yes, but...love, betrayal, and tragedy...I knew them all, I knew them all."

"And there I was in London, counting the days and the weeks and waiting for you to return. I wanted to finish my studies. I was under the illusion that I could put up with anything for your sake, anything, including death."

"Don't exaggerate, Isam. Death's an easy romantic concept when you're a student living in an atmosphere which is constantly stirred by movement, discovery, and sex. When I went back to Baghdad after ten years of intermittent absence, I found that everything had changed. Even you had become part of that new experience. For me, death was a difficult, horrifying concept, and you could do nothing to rescue me."

We were walking on the sidewalks weaving our way between pedestrians towards a destination we neither knew nor cared to know. My head teemed with thousands of things to say, all those words that I had told myself dozens of times and probably told her before on numerous occasions. But I was afraid that in those few moments of happiness we would revert to the very point at which we had finally separated, and so resume a quarrel whose agonies we both seemed mysteriously to enjoy. This was exactly what she did. She was skillful at analyzing the paradoxical position in which she found herself with me: any way out, nevertheless, was an insult to the mind and one more pain to be endured. And Luma—Luma, who always kept a safe distance from people and looked down on everything around her—took great delight in returning to me and taking me back to the same old vicious circle, employing a new style every single time.

"You have made yourself both the hostage and the ransom. Aren't you satisfied?" I asked.

She stopped walking. Gazing into my eyes, she began to feel my face with her long, slender fingers, as though she were a blind woman who could see by touch.

"For the last time," she said, "I got married, and it's all over."

"All over?"

"And you, like an idiot, are still in love with me."

"Because I'm like you," I said. "When other people make mistakes, I pay the price. And people always make mistakes."

"What do you expect from me? I got lost between right and wrong, good and evil, and I'm still lost."

How lovely it is to be a stranger in a strange city with the person you love. I kissed Luma quickly on the nose as we walked. "Ever since you went to Oxford," I said, "you've become an expert at deceiving yourself, like all philosophers."

"During my first weeks at Oxford," she said, "the boats on the Isis looked very inviting, but I didn't go for a ride in one. Later on when I did, I felt guilty. Thereafter, I sought every opportunity I could to take a boat ride down the river. I wonder, did I enjoy feeling guilty? When I had almost got my degree, the three years I'd spent at Oxford seemed like a hundred. I'd matured and become very wise.... I tried to find out why the boats had scared me at first. Was it because I couldn't swim well and was afraid of drowning in the green waters? No. Was it because the boats were always filled with tall, blond young men and women with bare legs—which we consider a scandal to be avoided? I don't know. Or, was it that on their river journey the boats smoothly glided into the thick willow trees which almost blocked out the sun's rays? You see, that all smacks of adventure, and adventure is another scandal! But I've been a rebel ever since I was a teenager, ever since I started thinking on my own. Of course, there was always the little voice that came to me from the deep recesses of my consciousness: 'You weren't born for this sort of thing, Luma! Remember the women's lot at home...' I could see them all... trailing behind. The poor women's skin gets chapped and cracked, their breasts sag more each day, and their hands turn into battered wood. The rich women grow wider, fatter, and more fleshy. I, on the other hand, was in a different world: professors smoking pipes, drinking sherry, asking questions, always debating, never convinced. Students getting hoarse arguing about strange, lost causes, spending their evenings flirting, drinking, climbing college walls... Books, theories, politics, Whitehead, Averroes, Aquinas, music, fog, freezing weather, colds, plays, museums, songs and dancing that hurt the feet. We discussed the Palestine question and participated in angry demonstrations. Do you remember when my nose was as big as a pear after I was hit by a policeman? I used to visit you in London on Sunday mornings, as though I were on some mystical journey. You used to drive to Oxford to see me, and we'd talk about the college buildings, their dates and architects. We discussed your Marxist views about the relationship between building materials and architectural styles from Phidias to Christopher Wren, from Le Corbusier to Basil Spence. See how well your student remembers her lessons? You used to take me to Stratford, and we went dancing even in Birmingham. I used to tell myself that someday I'd go to Baghdad and become a lecturer at a college where the students would be more interested in jobs than in education. I'd have a car as long as a train, and my father would pay for it. I'd drive it up and down Rashid and Sadun Streets. I'd build a new house in the Mansur quarter. It would have marble stones from the quarries of Carrara, wall-sized windows, and a small pool paved with blue mosaics, which would be called a swimming pool, although the only swimmers would be mosquitoes on hot summer nights..."

"Don't you see?" I said. "I never figured in your plans, even in those days. I was simply an accidental stranger that came and went."

With a laugh she stopped me and gazed at me yet again with her huge Sumerian eyes. "I've always been in love with the strange and the accidental," she said.

We had by then reached a sidewalk café, full of black tables and red chairs. We sat at a table in the shade. "I had no plans at all," I said. "I did have a few thoughts, and you figured prominently in all of them. The streets of London were filled with memories of you, all of London, not just Bloomsbury. One of our professors used to take us to the older parts of the city to study the buildings. We would comment on the windows, doors, tiles, wood, and iron. Dozens of beautiful girls passed by, but in every window and every door I saw only you."

"Don't lie!" she interrupted me. "You often went out with English girls, just like that Italian divorcee on the ship whom I see you with all the time. Then you'd go back to your room and write your passionate nonsense to me! No matter! Why not? For me, you were always the strange and the accidental. I told myself I'd wait for you in Baghdad, but actually I was afraid to make you part of my plans. It was as though you were a being from outer space, a Martian. You and Baghdad were a contradiction. I had that feeling especially during my last few weeks at Oxford. 'Will I see him again?' I kept asking myself. 'And what if I broke off with him and refused to see him again? What would I have proved?'"

"You would have proved that 'blood is thicker than water!' No doubt you used to say something along these lines: 'A quarter of a century ago, a man called Saadi Salman killed a man called Jawad Hamadi—my paternal uncle—and now the son of my uncle's murderer wants me to love him'...'Blood is thicker than water.'"

"What do you mean? My blood has turned to water, Isam, brackish water at that. This is what I used to say: 'A man was so consumed by anger over a piece of land in some remote area of

140

southern Iraq that he killed another man. Why should I be punished simply because the victim was my uncle, who was killed before I was even born? And what has Isam to do with what his father did?"

I squirmed in my chair. I did not know what this evil, sadistic woman wanted from me. At that moment I hated her as much as I hated my father, my past, my present, and my life. I wished I could fall upon her body and devour it, out of spite, out of lust.

We ordered two espressos. "At any rate," I said, "you punished both me and yourself and then thought it was all over. Right?"

"You probably think I victimized you," she said. "I was the victim, the real martyr, but you didn't know it."

"Luma," I said, "I reject your metaphysical interpretations."

"Metaphysical interpretations? But that's what I did to myself."

In moments of anger or misery, Luma's face reminded me of the way my mother looked when I was a child. My mother used to wear a black scarf round her face, which emphasized her beautiful features. I have never forgotten her face even when it became wrinkled and shriveled. She had a lovely dark face with a high nose and large, round shining eyes that became even larger and rounder when she talked to me about my father. She used to describe him as one would describe a legendary hero, and I used to picture him as looking like my uncle, who used to take care of us; Uncle Dawud was rather old. He still wore an Arab headdress over his hoary head, as he had done in his youth when he and my father and the rest of the family farmed an ungenerous piece of land in southern Iraq. They struggled with the saline soil, brought in water through canals, and build rusty water-wheels which they tried to replace with English pumps. It was because of this land and his attachment to it that my father killed Jawad Hamadi in Baghdad. The tragedy was that they were cousins and belonged to the same tribe. They were both descended from one ancestor who early in the nineteenth century had become famous for his violent temper and arrogance. His numerous disputes with the Ottoman rulers added to his daunting reputation for aggressiveness and increased the size of his land and the number of peasants who worked for him. Ghadban Ibn Khayyun—even his name spelled terror. Yet soon the family got fragmented. Some settled in Baghdad and became rich, while others, like my family, were hardly able to make ends meet and were torn between living on the land or slowly emigrating to Baghdad. In the twenties the Iraqi government started to implement its land reclamation plans and to go into all the intricate details of land ownership. That is when the trouble began: the two sides of the family quarreled. All this happened years before I was born. The bitter strife went on and on; it was like a running sore that no one could heal, while the whole body was being slowly poisoned by it. Then, in one of those fits of anger for which my father was well-known, he did what he did. The elders of the family used to say that my father's violent temper reminded them of their first grandfather, but the murder took place at a time when the law, the police, and the courts had little sympathy for anyone who disturbed the peace. In reality, if the Tribal Law had been applied in my father's case, he would have gotten away with little more than a few years' imprisonment, which would have been reduced later to two or three years. But the family of Jawad Hamadi was able to take the case to court in Baghdad, and my father was tried *in absentia* according to the Baghdad penal code. He was sentenced to death *in absentia*, but the police simply failed to lay their hands on my father. At first he escaped to southern Iraq. Then, as they were still after him, he escaped across the Shatt al-Arab to Muhammara in Iran where some of our relatives and friends lived. When we received letters from him, my elder brother would read them to my mother, and she would weep and wail for hours. I used to watch her sway under the burden of her grief and anguish, sitting on the ground reciting monodies in a low voice while the tears glistened on her dark face and flowed down her cheeks in streams full of all the pains and sorrows of mankind. My brother and I tried in vain to console her, but nothing we said could lighten her burden.

One day when I was five or six years old, I saw him. He was asleep on the floor next to me. I opened my eyes, and there was an enormous, tall man sleeping on a rug next to my mattress. His face was shaven. He had a thick black moustache that almost completely covered his mouth. His thick hair concealed his forehead and ears. I recognized him at once. "Daddy!" I yelled and fell on him, embraced him, and kissed him. He woke up, wrapped his strong arms around me and kissed me on the face and head as he laughed loudly and rolled with me on the cold floor. His body was warm and strong; he smelled like soil after the first rain. My mother came in carrying freshly baked loaves of bread. She laughed and cried and poured tea into sparkling glasses decorated with gold circles. My brothers, Ghazi and Kamil, joined us. They had just come back from the market with meat, vegetables and fruits.... My father had returned to Baghdad disguised in Western clothes, risking arrest and death. He stole away in the middle of the night through the streets of Karkh so that I would see him, and his legend would then assume a concrete form in my mind. And just as he came, so he left. He brought money for my mother, a hundred or two hundred dinars, which he had amassed through hard work and with some assistance from his debtors, who had got together to help him get back on his feet. He only stayed with us for four days, but they were just like a wedding celebration. We opened the door to no one except Uncle Dawud.

On the morning of the fifth day I opened my eyes, but the enormous, tall man was gone. It was as though a wind from Paradise had blown over our house and then gone, leaving us to its cold crumbling bricks. Like a rose covered with dew my mother had bloomed, and then, like a rose without dew, she languished and withered. I watched the long days of waiting tear her to shreds. She kept hoping for her husband's return on some auspicious night. She lived in hope that one day the walls would crack open; he would step in laughing and nestle his head in her arms. But my father never returned, not even as a ghost. Little by little he vanished until eventually we lost all news of him. Some people said that he had emigrated to India, to the Arabian Gulf, or the mountains of Bakhtiyar. There were rumors that he had fallen in love with an Iranian woman and that her tribe had kidnapped him and made him marry her. Others said that he had died, that he was killed. In moments of anger and frustration my mother wished that he was dead, that he would be killed, because he did not come back to us, and because what he had done made it impossible for him to come back. Around the house his legend was fraught with contradictions. I admired him, remembered him with pride, with sadness, and with disappointment. My memory of him got colored by tedium, even hatred. He did not return. We never heard a single word from him and so we gave up. Once I was ten years old, it became difficult for us to keep wondering what had happened to him, whether he had willingly deserted us or whether he had been stabbed to death: none of the options was very pleasant.

My mother no longer mentioned the only man she loved. She carried herself upright and resolved never to allow the tragedy to ruin us. "We must educate the children," she would say. "It's important to save the land, to rescue what's left of it." She became an equal partner with my uncles, who lent us their support even when the court confiscated a portion of our land to compensate the descendants of Jawad Hamadi. In time we were able to pay back all the money we borrowed for land development. When the Kut Dam was built on the Tigris, we introduced the cultivation of rice on a small scale. We were now able to defy the poor seasons with a degree of optimism. My mother carried herself tall again and held her chin high.

When I grew older, I thought of settling down and becoming a farmer in southern Iraq, but my mother would not hear of it. "You must be joking!" she told me. "You'll go away and study all those things you've read in books, even if we have to sell all our land. We're not rich, but our will is strong...We shall scorn our enemies as we have always done. Don't forget, I too am a descendant of Ghadban Ibn Khayyun."

In a way, Luma was also a descendant of Ghadban Ibn Khayyun. Perhaps therein lay the secret of the similarity between her and my mother, or indeed the reason why I felt attracted to her the moment I spotted her at one of those rowdy balls that the Chelsea art students give every year in the Albert Hall, at which thousands of students, artists, and rebels drink and dance with abandon, giving vent to all the crazy desires within them. The feud between our two families had erected a huge wall, which kept them completely apart. I did not know then that Kazim, Jawad Hamadi's brother, had a daughter who was now studying in England after spending a few years at a high school in Switzerland. The only thing I knew about the Hamadis was that some of them had become rich, not from land cultivation alone (for they owned fruit orchards in the suburbs of Baghdad and Hilla), but also from business, especially in the fifties when they were large shareholders in a variety of factories and companies. I did not think they either knew us or cared to know anything about us. In fact, when I saw Luma with an Englishman at that ball in London, it never even crossed my mind that she was from Iraq. She was speaking English with native fluency. Had it not been for her rather dark complexion and her name (which I learned on being introduced to her), I would have never guessed that she was related to anyone I knew in Baghdad. She called herself Luma Ghani then, because her father had chosen to call himself Kazim Abd al-Ghani, dropping the surname by which his brother had been known.

But then, after it was too late, after she and I had started to have an affair, which the distance between Oxford and London rendered all the more violent and intense, I found out everything. I had no idea whether she herself knew about our families' history when we began to see each other. She did find out about it later, however. But she did not want to mention the subject, even when we both returned to Baghdad in the summer of 1957, one year before she obtained her degree and two years before I obtained mine.

In Baghdad we met secretly and had to use a thousand different ploys. Luma was afraid that her father would find out about us. For my part, I was not quite ready to confront my brothers with the matter. We returned to England separately and started seeing each other again.

"Metaphysical interpretations?" Luma said. "But that's what I did to myself."

"What you did to yourself," I said, "was metaphysical stupidity. You used it to resist everything I was willing to do to atone a wrong for which neither of us was responsible."

"The land demands blood and pain. Not from any one individual, but from a whole family."

"But why should anyone go on paying for the sins of the family forever? The vicious circle has to be broken somewhere."

"Yes," she said. "But it seems that we couldn't so easily evade the responsibility that was forced upon us."

"That is precisely what I rejected," I said. "Why didn't I leave you when we first discussed the subject? I wanted you to stab me, to avenge yourself, or else to forget it. It is my right to refuse to take upon myself a wrong that was committed by someone else."

"Someone else, Isam? We're all part of that wrong, that sin, that curse—the curse of the land. Who knows how our old ancestor acquired the land a hundred and fifty years ago? How many people did he kill in the process? How many women and children died of hunger and destitution?"

"But you only remembered the subject," I reminded her, "when you were about to graduate. I was desperate. I told you I wanted you to wait for me in Baghdad. I couldn't return in the summer of 1958. I asked you to wait for me, but, as soon as you went back, you forgot everything."

"You can thank the revolution for that!" she said. "What did you do to help me when my father was arrested and my brother fled to Syria? You were having a good time in Piccadilly Circus, Bedford Square, Soho, Queensgate. Waiting, indeed!"

"I was waiting for something to happen, something that would change everything. Suddenly your parents and mine would forget all that happened; or else they would disappear, or you and I would disappear."

"You were waiting for a revolution that would destroy my family, so you could have me!"

"I wrote you dozens of letters after the revolution, but you never answered."

"Because I could sense spite in every word you wrote. I could see your mouth watering for news of killing, torture, and demonstrations. I hated you. Then I stopped opening your letters. I trembled every time I received one. My father was in prison; my brother had disappeared; our money was sequestered. Every time I went to the college where I was teaching, all I could see in the students' eyes was spite and hatred. What could I have done?"

What could Luma have done? What could I? What could anyone? I was finishing my last year in London, while Baghdad was rumbling, boiling and lusting. Things changed overnight. I was eager to return and play a part in the whole thing. I knew it was full of risks. Anyone could be transformed overnight from hero to traitor, or vice versa. Let anyone with the wisdom and cunning of a serpent come forth and take a chance. The risk was exciting. Everyone was intoxicated by the thought of destroying the old order and founding a new one. Everyone wanted to pluck out oppression and plant justice and freedom in its place. Walking a tightrope one had the illusion of power in one's hand, while under one's feet lay a hell with no illusions. Those were the months of 1959, when people screamed in the streets, screamed over the radio, screamed in their prison cells, and screamed in their homes. Who won? Who lost? I argued incessantly with my colleagues in the streets of London, in its restaurants, in student clubs. We shouted at one another in joy, in anger. We listened to the news with painful suspense. We supported, and we denounced. We thought and planned for a new age. We were reckless, full of faith and fire. The news we received was contradictory. All the Iraqi students from extreme leftists to extreme rightists, and the other Arab students as well, were het up, confused, and hopeful. It was then that I felt I was being extravagant in my relationship with Luma: her wealth and (hitherto) influential social status put her right in the enemy camp. That's the way I felt at the time. Even so, I kept writing to her because she was the only person I worried about and wanted to save. No one else mattered to me. I was sure better times would come.

146

Despite their differences, right and left would meet and people would get together and live in an earthly paradise. Luma and I would become a symbol of love that all humanity would share. All past crimes would be forgiven...Under love's spell, how easy it is to commit the foulest crimes or embrace the highest ideals! Yet idealism is made of air, and reality is more powerful than one thinks. Reality confronts you with its austere face day after day, while you cling fast to your idealism like a drowning man clutching at a straw. Eventually the day comes when you find that the easiest thing in life is to give up your idealism; you scoff at your ignorance, feel ashamed of having been gulled, and decide to come to terms with your reality. Yet it seems that those who do so are born that way. Others cannot achieve it. I, for one, scoff at my ignorance every day, and yet I still commit the same foolish mistakes every day. I am forever suffering from a lack of harmony with reality.

"I know you suffered a great deal," I said to her. "We were supposed to sweep people like you out of the path of the revolution. Don't you remember? At the same time, I loved you. Illogically, irrationally. And it certainly wasn't necessary. I knew very well that your pride would crush you."

"Despite your peasant background, Isam," she said, "you're still a bourgeois at heart, like most revolutionaries. That's your problem."

"Bourgeois? Why? Because I wanted to marry you?"

"No, because you rationalized, weighed matters carefully and took your time doing so."

"I knew you would reject me," I said, "no matter what happened. It would either be for sound family reasons or for even sounder political reasons. Didn't you tear up my letters without even reading them?"

"You left me in order to make me the victim. That's what matters."

"But now you're beyond sacrifice and forgiveness," I said. "It's your turn to enjoy the favors of the gods and society! Isn't that important? As for me..."

"You?" she interrupted, "You're free, and you don't even realize it. Your freedom has spoiled you. Don't you see that my marriage has been the end of me!"

"Strange!" I asked ruthlessly, "don't you love your husband?"

"Love him? Of course I do!" she replied quickly, "but he has his problems too. However, I refuse to discuss the subject!"

147

Her expression seemed to turn sullen. Her eyes and lips tightened up. She could not deceive me, even after such a long separation. The incompatibilities that existed between her and her husband were quite clear throughout the voyage. I remembered the first night on the ship when I heard their violent movements on the other side of the wall of my cabin as they made love. Were they actually making love or fighting? Was he wrapping his arms passionately around her naked body, while the bed squeaked under them, or actually giving her a beating?

We were sitting next to each other, our thighs touching. Suddenly, I was overtaken by the desire to inhale her perfume, to play with her hair, to imagine that she and her husband had been fighting that night, not out of intense love but intense hate.

I did not want to meddle in her marital affairs, especially since we had so little time together. Naples was bursting with its own boisterous joy all around us. Besides, how could we ever hope for another day of love? I teased her a little. "How," I asked, "could you allow the husband you love so dearly to go to Capri by himself? He'll be at the mercy of the beautiful Emilia!"

It did not occur to me that my question might touch a sensitive chord. She gave a start as if she had been bitten by a snake. "Emilia?" she asked. "Do you think my husband is having an affair with her?"

"God forbid," I replied.

"Please, Isam," she pleaded. "Maybe you know something I don't. Do you think he's interested in her?"

"Who? Falih?" I asked innocently. "As far as I can see, he's a difficult, unreachable man. I doubt whether he'd be drawn into such things in four or five days of sea travel. At any rate, you know him better than I do."

"He doesn't talk, even when he drinks a lot. I mean, he doesn't discuss his emotions. I don't really know what he likes, although I do have a good idea of what he dislikes."

"Then, you know that he loves you," I said.

"Of course," she replied without hesitation.

"Are you sure?"

"Of course, but he expresses his love in a strange way." She was irritated. "Why do you make me talk about him, anyway?"

"I assure you," I replied, "he doesn't interest me at all."

"Aren't you jealous of him?" she asked, almost coyly.

"I don't know what jealousy is," I answered. "I love you. I desire you. I suffer because of you. I want to run away from

Baghdad in order not to see you. But I'm not jealous of anyone. Not in the least. He doesn't figure in my emotional life. Tell me, though, do you love me?"

All of a sudden she put her trembling fingers on my arm and pressed. Then without uttering a word, she dug her nails into my flesh, driving love into me like screws. She put her mouth on my face and moved her slightly parted lips up, down, all over, until they found mine. Her lips were tender and delicious, scented with the aroma of fresh coffee. We kissed while her nails pierced my flesh.

"Haven't you wondered how it was we came to meet on the ship?" she asked as she slowly moved her lips away.

"A damned coincidence," I replied. "But a sweet one, God's last gift to an ungrateful man."

"A coincidence? Listen to me, then. I must confess everything. A month ago, I met your friend, Ihsan Hikmat, at Dr. Abdallah Faiq's party. That was probably a coincidence. There were twenty or thirty people in the garden. Ihsan came and sat in the empty chair next to mine. Falih was at the other end of the garden talking to some people. At first, I tried to control myself, in case I should sound too eager to ask about you. I asked him about his work, and he told me that he was your partner. I told him that I already knew that and then tried to change the subject slightly. I remarked that architects stood to gain a great deal from the unprecedented amount of building activity going on in Baghdad. He said that was true to a certain extent, but that it was not always easy to get jobs. He said that, as I might be aware, you were only interested in designs of great originality, which people in Baghdad found difficult to accept. He also told me that he was afraid you wanted to go to England and work with an architect whose name I've forgotten. 'Why not?' I asked him.

" 'It's fine with me,' he replied, 'but it seems he doesn't plan to come back.'

" 'When will he leave?' I inquired, without showing much interest.

" 'Just today he made reservations on a Greek ship that will leave Beirut early in June,' he replied.

" 'Then he's traveling by sea,' I said nonchalantly.

" 'Yes,' he replied.

" 'Who travels by sea in this jet age?' I asked without betraying any emotion.

" 'Ask Isam,' he said smiling. 'He likes the sea, it seems. In fact,

149

the ship he chose is a very slow one that docks in almost every Mediterranean port.'

"That was the extent of our conversation. The party was over, and we went back home. I couldn't sleep that night. The sea! Isam and the sea!

"Next morning, when Falih had left for the hospital, I went to Cook's Travel Agency. See how my intuitions are always right? There I expressed interest in traveling on a Greek ship that would leave Beirut in early June and call at as many Mediterranean ports as possible. The travel agent mentioned the names of several ships, the various ports they visited, and the ticket prices. Since I was interested in one particular ship, I asked the travel agent innocently whether there were any Iraqis traveling on these ships. He produced a list of passengers, checked the names and dates, and told me that the *Hercules* and the *Esperia* were both popular among the Iraqis. 'The *Esperia* is excellent,' he said, 'but it's fast. The following people are listed on the *Hercules*.' Your name was third on the list. At first, he read it wrong as Isam Sulayman. 'Isam Salman,' I said, correcting him. He scrutinized his list. 'I'm sorry,' he said, 'that's right. Isam Salman. He's traveling second class.'

"Do you think we would have traveled second class, if it hadn't been for your proletarian tastes?

"I made reservations right away. The only other thing I had to do was to convince Falih of the advantages of traveling by ship: the beauty of the sea, the importance of saving money, and the opportunity to meet people on a summer cruise....'"

At this point, if Luma had told me that she fixed a trap for me on the ship that evening, I couldn't have been more shocked, scared, furious. "Then you arranged everything," I said angrily. "Luma, you're terrible!"

"Did you just ask me if I were in love with you?" she asked shamelessly.

"You're playing games with me. You scare me!" I was very angry. "After all these years, you still scare me. But...you make me laugh too! 'The opportunity to meet people!' What a joke coming from you who always stay out of people's way!"

"Since I was quite prepared to use such a wicked ploy as fixing the whole trip, why shouldn't I pretend that I liked people's company and urge Falih to come along and meet them too?"

"But you've ruined everything. You're the one I'm running away from. Don't you see? I'm running away from many things:

the madness, the flood, anything that has to do with my inner being. For years I dreamed of revolutions. When the revolution finally came, I was in London. I felt that I was the victim of some hidden plot that kept me away from the one thing I was sure would achieve miracles. Yet, when I returned to Baghdad, I couldn't bear the thought that we only managed to talk to each other on the phone once every month or two. How many times did we telephone each other? How many times did we meet and pretend that we were strangers? We shook hands like strangers and talked in clichés like strangers, but the fresh lingering taste of your lips never left mine. And when I finally managed to escape, you pursued me even in my defeat. Luma, you are terrible!"

She dug her nails into my flesh again. "I'm your destiny," she said.

"My destiny? You're like the Eumenides!"

"No!"

"All you need are snakes in your hair!"

"You mean, I'll destroy you!"

"Exactly! My father's a murderer, and apparently he hasn't been punished enough for his crime."

"Now, Isam, which one of us is guilty of metaphysical interpretations?"

"You've ruined all my plans. I imagined the cruise would be leisurely and luxurious, and I'd be able to flirt with all kinds of women. But you've changed all that. Instead it's turned into a road strewn with nails. I'm walking on it with my bare feet and sleeping on it naked."

"You know very well when I make up my mind about something, I become...how did you put it? Fierce?"

"Yes, fierce as a cat in heat."

"That's right! Fierce as a cat in heat."

When we were in England, she always kept her promises, even when they were crazy or unreasonable. She promised once that she would go to Devon with me during the Easter vacation, and she did so despite the fact that a day or twc before we left, her brother had told her about the feud between our two families and warned her about getting involved with me. She kept her promise and did not tell me about what had happened with her brother.

We spent four days on the beaches, in the boarding houses, and the wheat fields of Exeter, Torquay, Dawlish, and Broadhembry. The wheat fields....There Luma lay on her back among the green stalks, near the hill. Where was that hill? Where was that green land? What lovely dawn was it? I remember how we left the boarding house in Broadhembry before sunrise, with a few sandwiches in a small bag. We went down the hill like a couple from primordial times, dancing through the rocks and wild flowers as though we were the only lovers in the whole wide world. Luma was shouting "Rhododendrons, rhododendrons," at the top of her voice. We danced our way to the bottom of the hill, whirling in circles like dervishes, like idiots, singing and spiraling towards the wheat fields, where oceans of green stalks caressed our bodies and closed in upon us. (We promised each other to return some day, when we would roll in the hay.) There she allowed me to bare her breasts and touch her nakedness. We squashed the wheat stalks with our bodies and wondered what the owner of the field would have to say when he saw what had happened to his tender green stalks.

On the train to London that evening she told me something about her conversation with her brother. She was not concerned. "What do you know about rhododendrons?" she asked me. "Do they have a name in Arabic, or are they too tender to grow in our searing sun?"

"I've never heard the word before," I replied.

"How could you have lived in England all this time and never have heard of rhododendrons?" she asked. "They are the white wounds, the clusters of stars that flash behind your eyes when you give way to your passion. Have you ever done that, Isam?"

"What's the use?" I replied. "My father's a murderer."

"Hush!" she whispered. "If it weren't for this respectable married couple in our compartment, I'd kiss you right now. But, after tonight in London, I won't be seeing you for a long time."

"What about tonight in London?" I asked.

"We shall enact the rest of the drama. We shall rise to the climax and then vanish in the clouds."

"You mean London's fog?"

"Alright, London's fog. You'll go back to studying brick, wood, and iron, and I'll write articles about the Cambridge neo-Platonists. Do you know that people in Oxford hardly ever mention Sartre's name? If they do, it's usually in a whisper. Then they completely banish him from their minds."

"In Baghdad," I said, "they speak of no one else."

"Then, I won't talk about him, and I won't see you for a long time. Agreed?"

"Agreed, my fierce cat!"

I took her hand and smothered it with kisses.

"But first, the drama and the climax," she said, as though she had made up her mind to die. "In London, tonight."

That night in London, however, she disappeared. She was afraid, and so she ran away from me and from herself, from both of us. She took the night train to Oxford without any explanation or apology. Perhaps she felt she had already kept one promise and was no longer bound by any further obligations. She never wrote to me from Oxford, although she did answer two of my letters briefly as she was preparing to return to Baghdad. Did your brother scare you, my fierce cat? Were you too ashamed to admit it?

Today in Naples, my fierce cat herself was mad with excitement. But how could we vanish into the clouds? We left the café and steered our way through crowds of noisy people, talking, staring, gesticulating. We looked at store windows and went into one store after another to ask the prices of goods. It felt as though Luma was mine, as though all those years that had passed, all that thirst and longing, had not made any difference; as though time never was and never would be, and the present moment was eternity.

She bought a pair of gold-laced slippers from a small store near Galleria Umberto. At another store I bought her a cameo engraved with the picture of Europa fleeing on a white bull. How marvelous the disguises of Zeus were in his sexual escapades! "Do you know that Europa was a Lebanese from the city of Tyre?" I said. "And, who knows, she might have drunk from the waters of the Euphrates! Why don't I follow suit: put you on my back and carry you away?"

"I would prefer your private yacht."

"I have the *Hercules*," I said. "Aren't you satisfied?"

"Never," she said emphatically. "Let me try these golden slippers."

She stopped in the middle of the street, removed her shoes, and slipped the slippers on. Two young men with long bushy hair passed by, and one of them gave a wolf whistle. "Even your feet exude sex," I said.

"What if Vesuvius erupted now," she wondered out loud, "and destroyed Naples as it once destroyed Pompeii?"

"We'd be buried together," I answered.

"With me in your arms?"

"What a scandal! What would people say?"

"What do I care about people? Tell me, what do people eat in Naples?"

"Pizza Neapolitana."

"Alright, we'll eat pizza, but not with anchovies."

"With mushrooms?"

"Yes, a lot of mushrooms."

"And a bottle of Chianti."

"Of course, what else with pizza? Don't be too clever!"

"Nonsense! I want to be clever. After lunch I'll take you to Pompeii."

"Great. And you'll let me see everything, including the notorious paintings?"

"Of course. What's the use of visiting Pompeii without seeing everything?"

"But they're obscene."

"The lovers' manual!"

"See how God sympathizes with lovers?"

"Yes. He buries them alive in each other's arms to make sure no one will separate them—ever."

"And at the moment of ecstasy!"

"Luma!"

"Everything else is dust..."

"Dust, dust, dust."

"So let's remember Pompeii, always."

We talked about Pompeii again after lunch, but we never got to visit it. Luma wanted to get back to the ship before the others returned from Capri. She felt the trip to Pompeii was impractical. It would have to wait for another time.

"Impractical! That's exactly like you," I said. "You do the impossible, and then you waiver before something trivial and say it's impractical!"

Everything we did was impractical. We ate pizza and drank Chianti on a sidewalk table, then we moved inside and sat in a cool isolated corner. We ordered more wine, then coffee, then tea, hour after hour. We talked and kissed for hours. No one was shocked; no waiter cared. There was joy all over the place. It was after six when I realized we had seen very little of Naples.

"Who wants to see Naples, anyway?" I asked. "Do you want to see Naples?"

"Me? Never," she replied.

We walked through the ever-increasing crowds in the evening rush hour. Suddenly, she stopped me. Her eyes froze. She looked serious and sad. " 'See Naples and die,' " she reflected. "Do we have to die after this?"

"Yes," I said, "but we haven't seen much of Naples."

"What are you doing this evening?"

"I'll run away from the ship."

"With Emilia?" she asked with a faint smile.

"A great idea," I replied.

"I'll kill you," she said.

"Why not?" I said.

We huddled together in the back seat of a small taxi cab and headed towards the ship. After I had kissed her goodbye on the wharf, I felt the evening start to fall apart around me. A feeling of unfulfilled desire left my body pining and exhausted. It was as though I had fallen out of the clouds into a slimy swamp, as though Vesuvius had erupted and buried me alone, empty-armed, among thousands of strange bodies.

I watched Luma's figure as she walked away, as she climbed the gangway to the ship, as she turned around one last time and waved to me. Is this the way all good things come to an end? What sorrows are these that can be neither rationalized nor tamed? It was as though Luma had died, without reason, purpose or necessity.

The little Fiat taxi was waiting for me. I huddled back inside it, and it sped off towards the city again.

Emilia Farnesi

I never imagined things would be this difficult. Falih is so near, yet he might just as well be a thousand miles away. When he is sitting with his friends, he tends to be silent; when he is talking, he tends to be sarcastic and irascible, rigidly adhering to his own mental isolation. The *Hercules* is such a small ship, and yet it is very difficult to get in touch with him. When Maha told me just before we left that she was not coming with me on the voyage, I was delighted for a purely selfish reason. I imagined that Falih would find lots of excuses to sneak into my bed in the early dawn hours. But he only did it twice, and even then I was the one who made the arrangements for him; and it was not during the dawn hours either. Once I dragged him away from Wadi and Mahmud by claiming that I wanted him to examine me; even then, I could only keep him in my cabin for half an hour. The other time, ah yes! That was the day of the big storm! We were both full of wine, and his wife was flat out in bed feeling seasick. After lunch I was able to embrace him in my cabin, while the ship tossed and turned and kept rolling us over like a crafty old woman encouraging us to make love. In deference to his wishes I did not want to arouse any suspicions regarding my relationship with him. My friendship with Isam helped me stay reasonably close to Falih. I spoke to him via other people, using all the cunning and equivocation I could muster. But what I really wanted was to be alone with him. Then I could tell him whatever I liked, not the things that this endless falsehood willed me to say. He was drinking a lot, non-stop. I could not make up my mind whether he was more agitated because of me or because he noticed what was going on between Luma and Isam. But he did not notice anything for days. Men never notice the things that women see. A fleeting glance, a flutter of an eyelid, that is all a woman needs to feel that something is going on in secret between a man and a woman. I was delighted that Luma and Isam were having an affair, and also that Isam was paying attention to me. Paying attention, did I say? I realize he was using me to avoid thinking about the Doctor's wife, but I could use his attentions to arouse the Doctor's jealousy. Then he might eventually give way enough to express openly something of his relationship with me. What a fool I am! When Falih sent me a cable from Baghdad telling me to reserve a cabin on this ship, surely I ought to have realized that he was sentencing me to silence, pain, and dissimulation. We would be going on a sea voyage where all the other passengers would be having fun and flirting for all they were worth. I, on the other hand, would be playing the stranger's role, the friend of a friend, faking laughter with the passengers but definitely not faking the tears when I was on my own in my cabin. Why didn't I think of that at the time?

If only Maha had not lost her temper with Wadi again and decided to stay at her white, disinfected clinic! I would have been able to confide in her, to unload on to her all these repressed emotions that are driving me crazy. Isam provides some consolation; I can't deny that. But he is being crafty with me, and I am doing the same with him. We duel with words, like two adversaries with unloaded pistols. The few kisses we have stolen have not been a big thing for him or for me. We are both responding to this game that is a requisite for his love as well as for mine. Even Wadi Assaf has started to imagine that Isam and I are having a lasting affair—or at least, he thought so during the first days of the voyage. But then, Wadi will stop at nothing, at nobody. He wants to embrace everyone, to love everyone, and then to go laughing into seclusion far away from everyone. He only moves towards his own complicated self. Wadi is plagued by a serious temperament that worries even himself; and so, in the end, he tries to deceive himself with laughter. Just the opposite of Falih. And Maha, mercurial, affectionate, eruptive, dormant, Maha will be the best woman for a man like him, although I worry about even her because of his seemingly uncontrollable moods. Otherwise, how could he leave Maha in Beirut and come on this voyage with that French doll, as though Maha did not even exist? Poor Maha! She faced the thought of separation and was afraid. So she sent him a telegram. I would be afraid to marry a man who can attract men and women with such speed and respond to every person looking for some warmth from his radiant sun. It's very odd that Falih takes issue with him sometimes, as though he too is afraid he may fall under his spell. The precious days passed, and Falih kept arguing with this fellow and that. I got the impression he was parrying me too, at least until this morning, this bright, dreamy morning, when I got into the boat for the trip to Capri. Falih got into the boat on his own. He came straight up to me with incredible openness.

"Let's get off the boat!" he whispered in my ear.

"Why?"

"Luma's not well; she's staying on board. Let's go to Naples, just us."

Why go to Capri with a boatload of passengers who know us, when we could be on our own in Naples' crowded streets? I agreed at once. We both made our excuses to the captain and went down the gangway to the dockside in full view of Wadi, Jacqueline, and the others. The sun was a little way up, and it was not very warm yet.

"Let's get some breakfast in one of the cafés by the sea," Falih suggested. "It feels so nice to have solid earth under one's feet again!"

In the café we sat close to the wide window. The place was not particularly clean; the chairs were shabby and the tables were of colored metal. The few other customers talked loudly in the coarse Naples accent and in other accents that I could not make out. They were not quite the type of people whom a man would travel the seas to meet so early in the morning. Even though I had not seen my native land for more than four years, I only had eyes for Falih at that moment. His big black eyes were flashing beneath his bushy eyebrows, which kept going up and then contracting with every word he said. After such a long, agonizing wait, I clung to his eyes, to his long fingers, which I felt were exploring my body even from afar.

"I thought the voyage was never going to end," I said.

"I was afraid your heroic patience would let you down at the last moment."

As he said that, he was fondling my long hair, which fell down over my shoulders exuding a light perfume which I knew he liked. I wanted him to put my head on his chest while he was talking to me, even in this squalid café. I wanted to listen to those words and to feel them rising from his chest and throat. I wanted to go on like this till evening. All those days had not gone by in vain! The waiting had not been for nothing! I love the sea in any case. So why all the worry, as long as I get a single solitary look from time to time? "But I wish you weren't so bitter, Falih; you look as though you're at a funeral, when everyone else is happy."

Falih laughed. "I've been writing my memoirs," he replied.

"Does that mean you have to frown all the time?"

"I have to be serious at least."

"Only when you're writing. Kiss me!"

He snatched a brief kiss, and bashfully at that. But I took his face between my hands over the plates and cups and gave him a long, luscious kiss. Then we ate the usual Italian pastries and drank some coffee. We asked for more coffee. I felt a warmth coming to me from his ravenous admiring looks, a warmth that increased and intensified. I felt I was beautiful, full of a femininity that could arouse this giant who was so angry at the world. I wanted to feel his manliness, his gruffness. I liked to picture him getting soft and tender and finally dissolving sweetly on my breast.

I looked at my watch. "Falih!" I yelled, "the morning's flown by."

"Emilia!" he replied, "why did you have to look at your watch? If only every morning could pass this quickly. Naples can wait!"

I saw Falih look over to the opposite sidewalk of the street. He gave a sudden start. I looked where he was staring and saw Luma and Isam arm in arm hurrying away towards the city. I was not particularly shocked (in fact, I probably felt a certain malicious and selfish glee). But Falih seemed to lose all his self-control. I was afraid he would get up on the spot and run after them. I held both his hands; they were shaking. His lips had turned pale and his eyes were wandering. He said nothing.

"How can you possibly remain married to her after today?" The words escaped from my mouth in spite of myself. "Let's get married!"

But he didn't hear a thing; he just sat there without saying a word. His eyebrows had come down over his eyes like a black curtain. I started to say something, but he obviously had no desire to look at the street or at me. He collapsed like a massive load too heavy to lift.

"Let's go to a hotel," I suggested. It was all I could think of to say. "We can spend the rest of the day there."

And that is precisely what we did. We went by car to an air-conditioned hotel. We told them our baggage would be arriving from the travel office two or three hours later and then went up to a room on the fifth floor. From the window you could look out on the huge bay gleaming in the sun, and away in the distance to

Mount Vesuvius from which a thin column of smoke was rising. But Falih did not want to look out at anything. In fact, he pulled the curtains, put on the dim light by the bed and then threw himself fully dressed on to the bed face down. I had to be kind to him and not make his misery any worse. So I left him alone, looking like a wounded man dying. All I could hear was an occasional suppressed moan.

I sat beside him for a while, not saying a word and at a loss as to what to do. Even here, I thought to myself, I'm out of luck! If only we were in Beirut. I got up and went over to the bathroom, which was included with the room. It was green and shiny. Why not have a real bath, I asked myself. I turned the water on and left the door open so that Falih could hear some other sound besides my voice. I took my clothes off and threw them through the doorway on to the floor of the main room. I got into the bath, lay on my back, and relaxed. I began to move my outstretched feet and flap my arms so the ripples of water lapped softly against me, caressing my body. I wanted Falih to hear the noises I was making in the water through the open door. If he had just lifted his sad face from the pillow and looked in my direction, he would have seen me playing with the water, naked. But for a long time he did not move, and I gave up all hope. I took the soap and started lathering my body, making sure not to get my hair wet. You don't want to get angry, I kept telling myself. Why get angry? He's in a frightful state. Even my body can't arouse him. It ought to, but he's feeling utterly wretched. I must let him deal with his misery by himself, at his own pace.

Suddenly he moved a little, then turned over onto his back and raised his arms so that he could rest his head on his hands. He still did not look at me; in fact he was staring at the ceiling.

"Emilia," he said, still staring at the ceiling, "are you still in the bath?"

I splashed the water with my hand but did not reply.

"Are you still as beautiful as you always were?"

"Beautiful? Why don't you check for yourself?"

"Later."

"Everything's later! The whole of life is later!"

"Misery is later. Death is later. Emilia, what are you going to do with that youthful body of yours, with no husband and no lover?"

I did not reply. If I had, I would have sworn at him.

"Or is it that you're chasing Isam too?" he continued. "And who else?"

161

His voice sounded quite neutral; there was no anger, jealousy or malice in it. It was almost as though he were a complete stranger to me. Even his prying was not deep enough to require an answer, so I said nothing. I made do with kicking the water and felt a cozy wave enveloping my thighs, coming up over my stomach and surrounding my breasts, which protruded a little above the surface of the water. I repeated the whole maneuver, eager to feel its soft touch once again lapping gently over my body. Falih still refused to look at me.

"If you keep ignoring me," I said, "I shall start chasing the whole lot of them, one by one."

"You'd better be quick about it then. There aren't many days left for the voyage!"

"I've all the time I need. Thank you!"

"I, on the contrary, have so little time left. But even the little I have is so much, so much!"

I slapped the water again nervously. "Your black moods irritate me," I said. "I don't know what's the matter with you."

"You don't know?"

"You made me leave Beirut and come on this voyage all of a sudden. Then you started behaving as though I were a plague to be avoided. There I was hovering around you and your friends like a dog hovering around a group a people eating, waiting for someone to throw it a bone or something. Ugh!"

I moved my arm vigorously in the water, and it splashed all over the floor. I felt as though I were swimming at the Sporting Club in Beirut, and Falih were trying to catch up with me, even though he was not a good swimmer. He kept begging me not to go out too far from the rocks, but I kept pounding the foamy water with my arms and legs. The emerald water gleamed around me, echoing the sounds of the people who were swimming, playing, and sitting on the balconies drinking beer and eating sandwiches. Every time Falih called out to me, I felt that life had started to be good to me after my separation from Michel. Beirut—with all its colors, its stench, and its uproar—had been a pleasant surprise to me. I loved it all, so much so that I began to fear that I might get lost in a labyrinth of sound and movement. My husband seemed to be forever dithering somewhere behind me; it was as though he were a weaker swimmer than I was. So I struck out towards some brilliant horizon, while he vanished into the distance far behind me. I knew he was there, somewhere or other, stumbling around flabbily with no sense of enjoyment.

Then came the day when I found myself alone in the apartment. Michel had gone and would not be coming back. But there were still friends, cafés, the St. George Hotel with the swimming club, and the Sporting Club, everything except Michel. He took refuge in a monastery in the mountains. And I met Doctor Falih Haseeb, a tall stranger with a bushy mustache who looked like a movie actor who had given up acting. He was somewhat shy and said little, but when he did speak, he did not hesitate to state his views frankly, however much it hurt. "That's the way we Iraqis are," he said; "we only say what we mean." One day when I was feeling lonely and abandoned and was afraid I might be left on my own for a long time, my friend, Doctor Maha al-Hajj, invited me to go with her to a large soirée being put on by a medical conference at the St. George. There I met Falih. He seemed lonely too; like me, afraid of being left on his own. What is it about me and doctors? After dinner we went together in my Volkswagen to a discotheque in Rawsha. We enjoyed each other's company; it was all as easy as downing a glass of whiskey in the murky red light which was pulsating with the non-stop noise of recorded music. I found him attentive and fascinating, and felt happy when he leaned over towards me—half-furtively, half-openly—and gave me a kiss. When he told me it was the first time he had done something he couldn't tell his wife, I didn't believe him. How was I supposed to know that his wife was so stunningly beautiful? But I came to believe him later on; I believed everything he told me. I found him innocent in spite of his bitterness. He kept writing short letters from Baghdad, but avoided talking about emotions, although I could detect the way he felt even from his cautious words. He did not promise me anything I could feel sure about, except, that is, the few visits he made to Beirut. He would come for two or three days at a time and see no one but me. I was at a loss as to how to keep our affair a secret in a city whose every secret was known to all. How did I come to agree to go on this voyage, when he had his wife with him? The contradiction and the irony appealed to me, and I was not afraid to challenge the incompatibilities and complications. I was sure he would marry me one day and felt even more confident than ever when he told me that he was studying Italian in his spare time and trying to read Pirandello!

Oh! But how I wish he had come on his own. We could have spent a long vacation in some of the cities I know well, Florence, Milan (my home town), and the beautiful villages dotted along the shore of Lake Como-Bellagio! I used to dream of going with him to the Uffizi Gallery and to St. Mark's Convent. There we could see Michelangelo's statues and Fra Angelico's paintings: the captives emerging from slabs of rock, the saints and the angels; the visions of Paradise by a monk who worshipped in a closet just like a prison cell and painted on the walls in rose and gold the Virgin and Child and the chorus of angels as they sang their hosannas in the spacious heavens. In Milan, we could go to La Scala and see Donizetti's *Lucia di Lamermoor*. "Ah, Edgardo," sings Lucia in the mad scene, "E te amo ancor, Edgardo mio, I still love you, Edgardo, I have always loved you... Ah! non fuggire, for mercy's sake, do not run away, Edgardo," whereupon she stabs herself. Who besides the Italians can sing with such magnificence, such power, such insane bravura? I am a sea in which you swim like a fish...Here lies Emilia in an overflowing bath in the Quirinale Hotel in noisy Naples. But such is the Doctor's misery that he rejects life, water, both the earthly and heavenly Italy, and Lucia who commits suicide at the edge of a marble fountain in the Castle of Lamermoor.

"Do you want me to kill myself for your sake?" I asked suddenly and sat up in the bath.

There was no reply.

"Falih!" I repeated, "do you want me to kill myself for your sake? Can't you see to what depths I've sunk just for you? Does Luma know you're having an affair with me?"

"Luma? Of course not!"

"Then I'll tell her tonight."

He gave a start as if he had been stung, and sat up on the bed. "Don't you dare!" he said. "You do that, and I'll kill you, so help me God!"

"But you saw her for yourself, didn't you?"

"Yes, I saw her!"

"What are you going to do then?"

He looked at me through the open door of the bathroom, looking just like someone who had come round after a trance. "Emilia," he said, "how lovely you are!"

"Thank you, but what are we going to do? Are we going to carry on just as we are on board the ship and then go back to Beirut as though nothing had ever happened?"

"Forgive me, I beg you, please forgive me. Everything will be over soon. Come on, hurry! Get out of the bath. Let's go down to the bar. I'm thirsty. Aren't you?"

"I'm hungry."

"Hungry?"

"Very hungry."

When I stood up and got out of the bath dripping with water, he got off the bed and came towards me. I grabbed the large bath towel to cover up part of my naked body. He looked at me and gave a short laugh and then another one. I laughed too and started to dry myself.

"Why do you like scaring me?" I asked him as I moved over to him.

He was looking at me as though I were a picture, or a statue, or something—anything but a woman. But with a little malice I moved towards him, threw the towel over his head, and dragged him strongly towards me. He fell on me reluctantly, gladly, laughing happily. I grabbed him in my arms, which were glistening with drops of water from the bath.

"You devil!" I said, my lips embedded in his, "I'm hungry, very hungry indeed."

"You're human. You get hungry just like everyone else."

"And what are you supposed to be? Divine?"

"I don't get hungry; I get thirsty. I am endlessly thirsty."

"And what about love? Do you regard it as hunger or thirst?"

"Pure instinct, and a sickly one at that sometimes."

That made me scared, really scared. I felt like someone who has just seen a ghost even though he does not believe in them. I clung to him again, feeling really afraid. I found myself embracing a lifeless corpse. I started fooling myself: maybe it wasn't dead after all. I felt that a fire had been blazing within me, for a couple of moments, but then someone had poured a bucket of water over it and put it out. But still I clung to him in spite of everything; I held on to this stubborn corpse.

"I love even the sickly instinct inside you," I heard myself whispering against his lips.

The rest was silence. Slowly the fire began to rage inside me again, and slowly I felt Falih begin to catch fire and burn on top of me. His lips began to devour my body, greedily, savagely, and the feel of his mustache confirmed the touch of his lips on every quivering limb. I did not utter a single word, nor did he. His agony was fused into the raging fire of which I found myself a part. My panting sank into his chest like that of a thousand women who had lost their minds and had only their bodies left to catch fire and burn.

165

About an hour later, we went downstairs and ate lunch in the hotel restaurant. After lunch, Falih paid the bill and apologized for the fact that we had to leave the same evening. (How many humiliations I've had to suffer for his sake!) It was almost four o'clock. We walked around the streets of Naples. I could feel a slight but delicious tiredness in my joints. We went into San Gennaro Cathedral and joined a group of German and American tourists who were listening to the guides' commentary and looking at the murals and statues. Falih looked like a man walking in his sleep; I was afraid to wake him up. But I sensed he had come to some kind of decision, one which meant everything in the past was no longer important. The future was everything. So much so that I begged him not to stir things up with his wife when we all got back to the ship.

"Of course not!" he replied, as though the whole thing was already settled.

"Shall we complete the voyage?" I asked.

"Of course," he replied, "right to the end."

I was still worried. I did not feel at all happy about the few words he did say, words totally devoid of anger and yet fraught with an unmistakable misery. Our hour of lovemaking that afternoon stayed inside me like a coiled spring, one which might hurl me at any moment in some unknown direction.

We went back to the port at around seven in the evening. I suggested that I stay behind in the city for the sake of appearances (he was so punctilious about such things that it frightened me). I got out of the taxi in the street while he went back to the ship. At that moment, I felt a strange hunger rending my stomach. Some young men gathered round me as they usually do here whenever they spot a girl on her own, but I totally ignored them. I went to a restaurant and drank a lot of wine, alone. Then I had a pile of delicious oysters served on a platter full of crushed ice. It was followed by a marvellous piece of Chateaubriand steak along with some more red wine. I asked for a cup of Espresso coffee and looked around to make sure that I was in a place that deserved all the money I was spending so freely. That's all life is worth: a good meal, a good wine, a city singing, and a loneliness which love cannot cure. Love? I ought to be ashamed of myself. A little death, a little shyness, a little passion. And then a return to the Arabian waves in Rawsha. But there's still the rest of the voyage, the voyage of life and non-life. The little that remains. To infinity.

Isam Salman

Late that night, when I returned to the ship, Falih, Wadi, Fernando, Jacqueline, Mahmud, and others whose names I do not remember were playing cards. Luma, like me, never played cards, although, unlike me, she could sit behind the players and follow the game. I don't understand card games. As far as I'm concerned, they are mysteries that I have no desire to understand. They simply don't appeal to me. I hardly ever sit around people playing cards. Somehow I feel they are doing something impolite, and I shuffle away. Mahmud seemed to be the best player and the most enthusiastic. He was jovial and talkative again after spending a couple of days in isolation under the care of the ship's doctor. Wadi and Falih were different. As they played, they both gave the impression that they hated cards and hardly uttered a word.

I left them alone and went to the deck. I no longer knew how to look at Luma. I was afraid that the slightest glance or the most casual word might expose us. I had returned to the ship feeling completely drained, as though I had been robbed of everything. In the cabin, the walls appeared to collapse upon me from all sides and crush me under their weight. I could smell that characteristic mixture of fresh paint, antiseptic, and harbor stench that sea travelers know so well. I missed my cabin mate, Shawkat Abu Samra, who had disembarked in Naples, where he had business to look after. He used to spend his evenings in the cabin, reading a large assortment of Arabic magazines that he had brought with him from Beirut. Later he would sleep soundly. He left me a box of Syrian candied fruits with a note which read: "To Mr. Isam Salman, a memento of our cruise together in a beautiful summer. Please accept it with my thanks!" No, my dear Shawkat, not with your thanks, but mine. Why didn't you leave me an address so I could return the favor someday? "A memento of our cruise together!" Together? Yes, in the same cabin, mostly when we retired to bed! I was ashamed of myself. I took a candied pear out of the box and tasted it. It had the taste of Luma's lips.

The ship was to spend another day in Naples. If I wanted, I could visit the city again. But how could I enjoy it alone? The sites I wanted to see remained yet another unfulfilled desire. I wanted to revisit some of the places I still remembered from my previous visit: the Church of San Severio, which contains a statue of Christ shrouded in a thin veil that seems to ripple across His face like a wave. It was sculptured by the greatest of eighteenth century Neapolitan artists, Giuseppe San Martino. Despite its age, Naples for me is the creation of the artists and architects of the eighteenth century. It is the product of the Baroque style, in which I was once particularly interested and about which I wrote a long paper when I was a student at the Architectural Association in London. I would have liked to see the Royal Palace of Caserta, designed by Luigi Fanfitelli, who brought Italian Baroque to the peak of its maturity. His Royal Palace was considered an exquisite but sad ending to a period in art that had filled Europe with churches, palaces, statues, and large murals teeming with human figures, horses, and movement. Light and darkness struggled over men and gods in a manner that would have prompted a veritable flood of comments from Wadi Assaf. Then there is the Museum of Capodimonte, where paintings by Paolo Pannini, and more important ones by Francesco Solimena, are exhibited. "Solimena is your namesake!" Luma said jokingly once when I mentioned his name to her. Solimena, the great artist who lived half of his long life—90 years—in the seventeenth and half in the early eighteenth centuries and whose stylistic and intellectual influence dominated Neapolitan art for scores of years, may have been like me in some ways. His works abound in so much darkness and shadow that light spells danger whenever it appears in his paintings among the multitudes of people and around the high buildings. I do not deny that he had an aristocratic bent, as his subjects clearly demonstrate. And why not? The bourgeoisie in southern Italy was unheard of in those days. People were either rich landowners or poor farmers. In the works of Baroque artists even the poor look well-off. Their clothes are redolent with the smell of the soil, mingled with the scent of love and folly. The further south one goes, the more aristocratic the poor become, so much so that the words 'aristocracy' and 'poverty' lose their meaning. Honor, revenge, and family pride become the central

168

symbols that keep a tyrannical hold on life. It is as though one has gone full circle back to the ancient Arab origins of all this, so marked by rough instinct and stern vigor. That is the way I am. In less than thirty years, I found myself moving from one extreme to the other. At which extreme were the Arabs of Andalusia in the age of Ziryab? Where were they in the age of the Caliphs Harun al-Rahid and al-Mamun? Is there a 'middle way' in civilization? Should not the great pre-Islamic poet Imru al-Qays (assuming that he was not a concoction of someone's rich imagination) be placed at one of the peaks of civilization where maturity and violence exchanged roles and complemented each other? His poetry, his love songs, his night, and his horse were all towering examples of the maturity and violence of his life, feelings, and attitudes. But let us return to Francesco Solimena. Tomorrow, I promised myself, I would look for his giant paintings. I would go armed with insights from the poetry of Imru al-Qays and thoughts from Baghdad. In spite of the tragedies involved, they never seemed to achieve their full potential; things were continually bursting into the open and yet they never fully crystalized. I would bring with me part of my bleeding love, my tribal roots, and my modern love of Phidias. I would confront their dark, clamorous, and integrated world with my own clamorous, unintegrated darknesses and with my escape. I would be carrying in my heart the Castle of Ukhaydir from the edges of the desert into the cities of concrete and steel.

I bit into another sugared pear to make sure I was not deceiving myself. Yes, I could savor the taste of Luma's lips: sugar, desire, and thirst. I wonder what she told her husband when he returned from Capri? I can see her now, sitting behind him with a book in her hands, peaceful and relaxed. What lie had she made up? Had he believed her? Or had she simply feigned innocence? "I'll tell you the truth," she had said, "I swear to God! I spent the day with Isam, and we talked about old times. There's no need to worry. I preserved your honor."

I imagined him giving her a kiss filled with the breeze of the cliffs of Capri, then handing her a set of Santa Lucia bells as a present and saying, "You're wonderful! Come on, let's have dinner. But don't be too hard on the poor fellow! OK?

"OK," she had promised as she fixed his tie with her slender fingers. Then she had rung the little bells and chuckled at their attractive sound. Finally she had put the last touches to her face and lips, sprayed a little Nina Ricci behind her ears, and pulled him by the hand towards the dining room. "Did you enjoy your lunch without me today?" she had asked. He had replied that he had lunched with Wadi, Jacqueline, and Emilia and that they had talked about her throughout the meal.

Emilia? Where was Emilia? I could not find her in the lounge, which was full of passengers just relaxing after returning from burning sensation in my gullet. It was ten o'clock or even later of coins in front of them. Luma was in her usual place, reading. The moment I entered, she lifted her head and gave me a suggestive look that lasted only a second or two but left behind it a painful vacuum; then she latched her eyes to her book. I hoped she would follow me outside, but she remained where she was. I almost went over to her to ask where Emilia was, but then I turned around and walked away.

I looked for Emilia all over the ship. I went to the bar, ordered a double shot of Remy Martin, and took two sips that left a burning sensation in my gullett. It was ten o'clock or even later when I left my empty glass for a stroll on the deck. I spotted Emilia coming out of the lounge and walked straight towards her.

"Where were you?" I asked.

"Where were you?" she responded.

"In Naples."

"I know. You didn't go to the island."

"How was the Blue Grotto?"

"Same as you've always known it."

"On whom did you concentrate your attentions? Wadi or the Doctor?"

"Are you getting jealous?"

"Of course."

"How many museums did you visit alone?"

"Will you come along with me now?" I asked without answering her question.

"Now? Where to?"

"Naples! It's a big city."

"Are you crazy?"

"People say its night life is really wild."

"Only for men!"

"Don't you like walking around cities at night?"

"Is that a challenge?"

Her face shone and lit up the night around me. She was very pretty and sad, a real female—a mixture of woman and vixen. I put my hands on her shoulders and stared in her large almond-shaped eyes.

"What?" she asked, parting her lips slightly. "Are you going to kiss me here?"

Her breath smelled of perfume and alcohol. She put her arms around my neck and pressed her lips to mine.

We descended the stairs to the main lobby and left our passports with one of the ship's officials (as we usually did every time we disembarked). We were given a disembarkation card and left the ship. We got into the first taxicab we could find and instructed the driver to take us to a night club. He drove around, giving us a ride, like all taxi drivers. All the while, Emilia and I were kissing each other passionately. She was a completely different woman from the one I had known for so many days on the ship. She was burning with desire, but it was the sort of desire that was devoid of any joy. At one point, I could sense large tears trickling down her cheeks.

More sorrow? I was tired of the sorrows of humanity. What could she possibly tell me that I had not already suffered and grieved for even more than she did? At present, however, I sympathized with her. What did this beautiful woman want from life when her stay in Lebanon had only given her a makeshift home and a self-deceptive peace of mind?

In the night club the dancers kicked up their legs and shook their buttocks. One girl after another stripped to the beat of drums and guitars.

"What will you and Luma do?" Emilia asked out of the blue.

"What do you mean? Luma and I?" I asked, pretending to be totally ignorant.

"Don't you realize the whole thing's as clear as day?"

"Emilia, please, that's dangerous talk!"

"Haven't you noticed something strange about me?"

"You mean your constant liveliness? Your casual flirtations?"

"No, my attachment to Falih, for example."

"Not really! The more we drink, you and I, the more we tax our imaginations!"

"Imaginations! Do you really believe I went to Capri today? Or Falih?"

She was drunk. I was afraid she would blow matters out of all proportion, matters that on the next day would seem mere frivolities so typical of sea cruises.

"Luma didn't board the boat for Capri," she continued, "so Falih and I seized the opportunity and went into the city. Perhaps you don't realize that Falih is in a dreadful state of mind; he's suffering that grim, black melancholia characteristic of people on the verge of madness. And, when one is as intelligent and as educated as Falih is, the matter becomes pretty dangerous."

"Emilia," I said, "I hope the Doctor has not behaved like other men, and tried to take —"

"Don't be silly! You know him better than I do. Do you realize we've known each other for ages?"

"What!"

"And that we had a secret agreement to come on this cruise, despite the fact that his wife was to accompany him?"

I hit my forehead with my palm in complete shock. She was lying! Impossible! Or was she...? Yet why should she lie? Did not Luma do the same thing, exactly the same thing? I wondered if Luma knew about all this and if Falih knew that Luma had chosen the time and the ship? How much did each one know about the other's plans?

I did not think aloud for fear that Emilia would discover things I did not want her to know. Women's intuitions may be accurate, but they remain in doubt as long as they are not corroborated by real facts.

"Does Luma know anything about this?" I asked her.

"Of course not," she answered without hesitation.

"But what's the point, Emilia? Falih lives in Baghdad and you in Beirut..."

"What's the point of your relationship with Luma? She's married and you..."

"Please!" I interrupted her, "All there is between Luma and me is an old friendship that goes back to our college days. In addition, we're relatives from the same tribe. That's all there is to it. Nothing else!"

Emilia laughed loudly. "Poor Isam!" she said, trying to control her laughter, "you're afraid of confessing the truth!"

"There's nothing to confess and so nothing to fear," I replied, continuing the lie.

"OK, OK, I've confessed to you. That gives you the right to ask what the point of all this is. Vanity. Nothing else, just deadly vanity."

"The strange thing is that I thought you were in love with me, if only a little bit!"

"And I too thought you were in love with me, if only a little bit!" she said, mimicking my own words.

"And the truth?"

"I enjoy your company, your flirtations; I enjoy feeling your body next to mine."

I held her hand and squeezed it. "Me too," I said. Her hand was cold and trembling. I could not make her change the subject. "I love Falih," she said. "He tortures me, and I love him. I live for the few days I see him every time he comes from Baghdad burdened with worries."

"How could you accept his invitation under these circumstances? He doesn't seem to pay much attention to you. Maybe he doesn't want Luma to know. Maybe, but...there's a limit to everything."

"We spent the day together," she said, oblivious to my rambling thoughts.

"Ha,ha! Marvelous!" I exclaimed.

"The same way you spent it with Luma! Ha, ha!"

"And then?" I asked.

"Nothing. You and I will return safely to our bases. Tell me, do you find me beautiful, desirable?"

I stared at her and did not answer. Apart from saying "Yes," there was nothing left to be said except more lies. The guitar players sang loudly and enticingly, twisting their bodies as they screeched and screamed.

"Will you dance?" I asked.

"Yes," she replied.

We joined the other couples on the floor, amidst the deafening music. There was no need for words any longer.

It was about two a.m. when we returned to the ship. There was hardly anyone on board. We parted company by the lounge, and Emilia went to her cabin. I took one quick look at the empty room, the gambling table and the scattered ashtrays filled with cigarette butts, and then walked towards my cabin.

It is useless to say that the only voice ringing in my head all night was Luma's. It is useless to say that, every time I kissed Emilia I could picture Luma in my arms. As I walked in the hallway, tired, bored, and nervous, I yearned to see Luma standing by the door of her cabin waiting for me. I was fumbling about in the kind of repugnance that follows disappointment, the kind of choking sensation a dying man suffers.

When I heard my name whispered from behind, I thought I was imagining things. I stopped for a moment but did not turn around. My neck felt as if it had received a dagger's thrust. Luma

173

was standing by the door of her cabin. She walked hurriedly towards the exit, and I followed her nervously. The feeling of intense thirst came back to me.

"Did you go out with that Italian woman?" She confronted me with the question.

"Haven't you gone to bed yet?" I asked. "You're still wearing your day clothes."

"How, how could you?" she asked trying to stifle her indignation. "I can see you're drunk too. You went drinking with that silly woman."

"What else did you expect me to do," I asked, "when you left me hanging in mid-air, not knowing what to do?"

"At the very least, I expected you not to parade your infidelity in front of me. I must go back to the cabin."

"Would you have preferred me to urge you to be unfaithful?" She came right up to me; I thought she was going to slap me in the face. Instead, she suddenly put her fingers on my throat.

"I wish I could strangle you!" she said as she tightened her grip.

"Strangle me!" I said defiantly. Our lips joined in a long, thirsty kiss.

She relaxed her grip. In place of her initial harshness there was now a kind of dry, sweet, delectable tenderness. She nibbled at my lips, gently, ever so gently. But then she dug her teeth into my lower lip and pressed and pressed. She let go to give me a taste of her tongue and again bit me mercilessly until I yelled in pain. I disengaged myself and felt my lips with my fingers; they were bleeding.

Luma threw herself into my arms. I planted my bloody lips on hers while she panted and moaned. Then without uttering a word, she slipped out of my arms like a cat and rushed away as though to return to her cabin. I stood riveted to the spot, licking my lips, feeling them with my fingers.

Suddenly she stopped and ran back. "Wait for me," she whispered. "I'll be back in a minute." She ran off, and I was left waiting.

I did not have to wait long. She returned before I was able to regain my senses. She had a light coat on, despite the fact that the night was chilly. "He sleeps heavily at the beginning of the night," she said, referring to Falih.

"Is the night still young?" I asked.

"Don't be silly," she replied, "there are two more hours till dawn."

174

I grabbed her arm and led her towards a huge crane; its machinery and hawsers made it look like a huge sleeping monster. All around us tiny, flickering lights from all the ships riding at anchor were reflected in the black waters. She nestled her head on my shoulder.

"My lips are still bloody!" I said.

"Let me have them. You kept me waiting for almost two hours!"

"Luma," I said in total resignation, "nothing is left but madness."

"And in two more hours life will regain its senses and its boredom."

"Listen," I said as I pulled her back, "my cabin is empty tonight."

"Your cabin!" she hesitated.

"Yes. There's only a thin wall between my cabin and yours. Shawkat left the ship yesterday. They'll probably be assigning a new passenger to my cabin tomorrow."

"But, Isam, how..." She did not finish what she was saying.

We walked quickly to the cabin, almost as though we were afraid that dawn would beat us to it, or that night would give us away and hasten the dawn before its time. Holding my hand, she followed me silently. Like thieves we entered the cabin, which was pitch dark apart from a glimmer of light from the porthole. She stood in the middle of the small, cramped cabin, her arms hanging lifeless at her sides. I could just see her head bent over her chest. The faint flashes of harbor light that came in through the porthole left her features indistinct; two dark pits were all I could see of her eyes.

"Is that really you?" I asked.

"This is the ultimate stupidity," she mumbled.

I helped her take off her coat and threw it on the narrow bed. "Do you know why he drinks constantly?" she asked.

For a moment I did not know who she meant. "Who?" I inquired.

"Falih," she replied. "He drinks because he's afraid to be alone with me. He can only stand it when he's dead drunk."

"Every night?"

"Yes, every night, every night...This famous surgeon!"

"Let's forget all that now."

"Forget it? While he's on the other side of the wall looking like a dead man?"

175

'If you hadn't waited tonight for me, I would have died too."
"How? Of desire, lust? Go ahead, Isam, you can laugh if you
wish. You've won! But please, rescue me. Kick me out now.
Before the stupidity is complete."

"I'm the most stupid of all. And that luscious neck of yours, the
talk of the ship, how can I let go of it?"

My lips devoured her perfumed neck and bit into all the bare
flesh around it. How was I supposed to know that, all those years,
her body, like mine, had yearned for this ultimate moment. And
how can two stingy hours before dawn, in a foreign sea and
among foreigners, slake so much thirst, satisfy so much hunger?

"Tomorrow, you won't have any lips left," she said. "You won't
be able to kiss or talk to anyone."

Every folly, I told myself, however excessive it may seem, will
always lead to an even worse one. Did Falih, I wonder, hear us on
the other side of the wall as we rolled off the narrow bed on to the
wooden floor? Did he wonder what all the noise and movement
was about? What if he woke up early to take a stroll on deck and
found the sheets on the other bed untouched?

Eventually, Luma walked out carefully and closed the door
behind her.

I lay on my bed and was about to fall asleep. Suddenly the
door burst open, and Luma rushed in.

"Isam! Come over quickly," she screamed in a choking voice.

"What?" I asked.

"Right away, please!" she pleaded.

She was sobbing. I imagined that Falih had been waiting for
her and had found out about everything. I jumped up, quickly
grabbed my dressing gown, and ran after her to her cabin. The
light in the cabin was so strong it hurt my eyes.

Falih lay there motionless under the bed covers with only his
face and arms showing. He looked shrouded, like San Martino's
Christ, which I had not been able to see the day before. His eyes
were open; they looked appalling, like two glass balls. His skin
had a yellow waxen hue with a touch of blue to it. His lips were
closed and showed a faint smile, frightening and malicious. His
hands clutched the sheet that covered him.

Luma collapsed on the only chair by the bed. She uttered a
horrible cry as she buried her face in her hands. "All this time
since midnight," she said, "I thought he was asleep!"

Luma was in such a state of shock that there was no way she
could know when Falih had committed suicide. Was it before or

after two a.m.? Most probably before, when the card game was over and the players had gone to bed. Luma had told him she could not sleep and was going to the library to read so as not to disturb him. He raised no objections, and the reason was now all too clear: he had made up his mind to do something he had been planning for quite a while. On the little table he had left the evidence of his suicide with all the attention to detail of a surgeon readying himself for an operation. There was a short note in Arabic for Luma addressed to "My wife Luma," and another in English for "the Captain of the *Hercules*." Both were unsealed, and I read them. To his wife he wrote: "Read the papers in the little file. Goodbye, my lovely one. Don't be too harsh on me and forgive me as I have forgiven you." He wrote to the Captain that he had taken his life with his own hands and had been planning it for a long time. He signed the note in both English and Arabic and wrote out his name and titles clearly. Next to the two notes there was a small pill bottle; it was empty. There was also a sealed envelope addressed in English to "Mrs. Emilia Farnesi Asad, Passenger on the *Hercules*."

As soon as Luma saw this envelope, she almost fainted. She turned pale, and her jaw dropped. I carried her to the chair, sat her down, and placed her shoulders against its back. After some time, her pale lips moved slightly. "So he was having an affair with her..." She articulated the words with difficulty. I did not say anything.

It was dawn. From the porthole the sky appeared like a blue canvas, bright and cool. We could hear the voices and movements of the crew on deck.

"Let's leave everything as it is and tell the Captain," I said.

My head felt heavy and solid as a rock. I found it difficult to think. My mouth was as dry as sand. After the initial shock, I had an uncontrollable fit of shivering that lasted for a few moments, and then I sat on the other bed, like an idiot, trying to clear my mind. Was I responsible for Falih's suicide? Did he know? Had he any proof against me in that small file? We both stood up. Luma took her note and read it again. "The small file?" she wondered. "That's where he kept his private papers and a prescription pad. He had been involved in a long study on tumours."

The file was on the table too. Luma opened it hesitantly and with great care, as though she were opening a wasps' nest. She pulled out a paper and read the first few lines, then stopped and handed it to me. "No, no!" she said. "I can't do it. Here, you read it."

"Me?" I hesitated.

"Yes, please."

"But it's bound to be very personal!"

"Who else should read it, if you don't? It may well involve you as much as it does me."

"Shouldn't we inform the Captain about the death first?"

"What? Before we've read the papers?"

The smell of death filled the little cabin. Even after we had closed Falih's eyes, the sardonic smile on his face made us feel we were about to fall into a spiteful trap of his own devising.

I took the papers, knowing full well that I could not understand much of what was in them. They were written legibly, unlike the handwriting of most doctors. There were only a few of them, as though they had been extracted from a larger collection. Some lines were crossed out, and that made it clear that, despite his frankness, he had deliberately erased some details. One page was in English. The memoirs of a suicide! A black document that only a doctor endowed with Falih's sensitivity and intelligence— and his misery as well—could have produced; one, I thought, which lent a special significance to its author's death and provided the kind of argument that was futile to refute or even discuss.

Something else caught my eye, even during those blind moments. The papers had been torn off a prescription pad. Each one had printed at the top the doctor's name in Arabic and English and his phone number. Next to the word 'date,' the date had been written and then erased for some reason, so that it was impossible to make it out. Yet there was plenty of evidence to make it quite clear which parts had been written before the cruise and which during it.

The following is what was found in the file of Doctor Falih Abd al-Wahid Haseeb: (Three lines were crossed out with heavy ink and could not be read. Then:)

"Like craving a wine never tasted before, in a country that I never visited before, in a country that I visit for the first time.

"The rain in Beirut came pouring down! It looked as though the sea had inundated the city, or else the surrounding mountains were pelting the city with seas of their own. And the noise...rain, thunder, and wind, it was all a new language I had learned overnight. And that dreadful craving set fires in me. Was this really me, I wondered, naked and heedless of the cold? All around me, the world thundered and roared as I examined her eyes, lips, or breasts like some precious work of art that I wanted to take with me and keep hidden from curious eyes.

"And the rain fell incessantly. I was away from home with a stranger who brought me out of myself and took me through uncharted forests, caves, and waterfalls to shores of dark suns and twisting roads strewn with remnants of moons that I could take back with me to Baghdad, rich like Sindbad.

"Dark suns? Why did I say dark?

" '...or not to be.'

"How is that possible? But it is, and still more, while dust clouds envelop the city in hacking coughs. Heavy, vicious rain follows, mud falling on mud made of people. Nothing but pure malice, without identity or purpose.

" 'To be...'

"Is that possible? Yes, and more, when the sun explodes like a huge shell in the middle of the skies, strafing the clouds with shrapnel that falls on the city from end to end, filling the parks, the roads and the guts, and igniting fire in men, trees, and animals.

" '...or not to be.'

"Luma, Emilia, Abu al-Khasib, Beirut, Brummana.

"Today I operated on a seventeen-year-old girl. She died. Yesterday I operated on an old man more than seventy years old. He lived. He will live.

"Dust clouds engulf the city. The sick in the hospital fill up all the hallways and balconies. This evening, when I entered my clinic, I stumbled over a woman who was lying on her back behind the door moaning. It was then that I remembered the dead and the stench of death in the streets of Baghdad four years earlier.

Are not fearful poisons set up in the soul by a swift concentration of all her energies, her enjoyments, or ideas; as modern chemistry, in its caprice, repeats the action of creation by some gas or other? Do not many men perish under the shock of the sudden expansion of some moral acid within them? *

"Life and death. That may well be a doctor's job, and especially a surgeon's: to interfere in the affairs of Nature and of God. But it is assumed that God does not like to harm man. So it

* From Balzac, *The Wild Ass's Skin.*

must be the evil powers of Nature that lie in wait ready to pounce on man.

"To excise a caecum, a fibrous tumor, or a part of an ulcerous stomach, these are all logical procedures for a doctor, a case of one plus one equals two. The important thing is to find the one and know how to add another one to it so as to end up with two. Life and death. One plus one. Of course, a little zero might ruin the whole equation. Zeroes! Those non-things, they are the dark power, the germ, the virus, the devil. Greetings to the high priests of Sumer and Thebes! They treated patients by exorcising devils and genies. Zeroes, non-things, genies, they are the means of our subsistence. Through them we search for love, the soul, and feelings of the beyond. The logical procedures with which I saved a thousand patients from pain and death were unable to save me. I was plagued by zeroes. I searched for love, but found none. Emilia. She was a mid-summer's night's dream in Lebanon. She was toyed with in her sleep by a wicked buffoon who dropped into her eyes the distillation of illusion. When she woke up, she saw me and thought I was a Greek god challenging her Italian femininity, a Greek god from the banks of the Arabian Euphrates, from the remote regions of the desert. And the desert is the mother of all illusion. Its laws are constantly violated by zeroes. Some distance from Baghdad, there are the remnants of an ancient ziggurat, which looks far bigger from a distance than from nearby. Amid the ruins of the early Arabs I saw from a great distance a young man climbing one of the dilapidated walls. He looked enormous, as though he were being magnified on a cinemascope screen. Yet when he came down and walked towards me, he grew smaller and smaller until I could hardly see him. That is how Emilia perceived me. From afar I looked bigger and clearer to her than when I was near. Maybe I viewed her in the same way. Tell me, you brutal dispenser of pleasures, why have I been doomed to travel the seas before I could feel my heart quiver and my sexual passion rage? Luma, why did you marry me? Why did you come so close to me, so close that I could hardly see you?

"It was Kafka's habit in his *Memoirs* to describe an experience in one way, then again in another way, then again a third way, and so on for a fourth, or a fifth time in some cases. He may have been trying to find that better description which he believed he could not achieve with just one try, so he kept trying again. But each time he would start differently, abbreviating some details in the previous version and expanding others, and so on. Each attempt was thus dependent on the previous one and improved on it. It's like looking at a huge object and walking around it. From every angle you see certain things you saw the last time and many others that you did not notice before. This is the closest thing to a kaleidoscope of words and ideas. Every time it is turned, a new shape appears, or a new idea. The ingredients are the same, but their relations and proportions change. And truth changes according to the very same process. How many facets does truth have then? How many facets are there for each of my experiences? The people I see every day, whom I associate with, love, hate, neglect, influence, reject, ignore, etc., etc., how many times can I make a new kind of truth out of every relationship I have with them? Which of them is the most "right", the most correct, the most truthful?

"To L:
"I find it incredibly difficult to write, especially about things which concern me rather than other people. My profession trained me to care for others, for other people's bodies and souls, but it never taught me how to apply the same methods to myself. I can advise patients in the clinic, write prescriptions, and suggest cures. I can prepare myself to perform an operation with a clear mind, like a carpenter fixing a chair or a mechanic replacing one automobile part with another. But, when I face myself, I can't think clearly, or write a prescription for my illness. It's very hard for me to write to you when I'm fully aware of this impotence of mine. So forgive me for these confused lines which you may or may not see. (I'm afraid that in the end I may change my mind and tear these papers up.) I'm afraid of what you will think of me because I loved you, even though it was the kind of love that is the closest thing to impotence. No matter now. Your love kept me busy, gave me pleasure and at times tortured me.

"Letters written by suicides usually tell the truth. They may even be too truthful and reveal everything in microscopic detail. Everything emerges enlarged, in motion, spiralling. The images are real enough, but they are enlarged a million times. Yet how could they be 'real' when they have lost their relative connections with reality? Maybe, after all, the letters of suicides do not tell the truth. They are simply inflations of minute thoughts which, when enlarged, lose their meaning because they are isolated from hundreds of other thoughts.

"As you know, I always refused to read newspapers, listen to the radio, or watch television. It was not that I wanted to sever my relations with the realities all around me, but rather that I wanted to concentrate on my personal experience of things, of human relations. I wanted to concentrate on my own ideas, on the dicta of long studied books concerned with perpetuity. I wasn't interested in ephemeral notions which seemed to infest the here and now like flies on garbage. I wanted to remain pure and clean, because I used to shiver every time I saw Mr. Hyde's savage features emerge from Dr. Jekyll's face. You, Luma, the philosopher, were a perfect unity. The beauty of your face and body was in harmony with the excellence of your mind. I sought in you a refuge for my double vision and my distraction, but you thwarted me. You were a wall I could not penetrate.

"Did I try to camouflage my impotence with drunkenness, only to find myself caught in a vicious circle where the more impotent I became, the more drunk I got, and the more drunk, the more impotent? But I don't like to link the two. My craving for alcohol has nothing to do with my impotence, although it does provide me with a narcotic that helps me forget much of what I want to forget. My craving for alcohol is part of a profound, tacit longing to hurt and disparage myself.

"Imagine my feelings when my grandfather died a madman in Istanbul. He died in a mental asylum with his hands tied behind his back because he had become a danger to himself and others. Wasn't I justified in drinking to excess? But I would have done it in any case, even if my grandfather had conquered Georgia and Dagestan in his youth....He left us a library of ancient Arabic and Turkish manuscripts. The British Museum made copies of some of them, and many people tried to purchase them. My father rightfully bragged about them, but I preferred to be involved in surgery. Every time I finished an operation, I hurried back home for a drink. Don't you think that my hands are steadier than those of any artist who has never had a taste of alcohol?

"I was not terribly keen to attend the medical conference in Beirut, but I went anyway. And the four winds crashed open all the gates of the universe.

"During the first session I met many doctors, most of whose names I have forgotten. But there was one young woman doctor whom I saw at every meeting. At a dinner party she introduced me to a friend of hers, Emilia, whom I found extremely sexy. At first, however, it was the young doctor who lowered my resistance with her Lebanese dialect that reminded me of songs from the mountains, and the fullness of her supple body and her small hands were enticing too. She discussed medical problems with a warmth and intelligence that one does not expect from a beautiful woman. The dinner party and Emilia were my downfall. I told myself that here was a woman whom I really wanted, something which I have never said before. Our behavior at the party lacked decorum to say the least. We left without saying goodbye to anyone. (Emilia said she would apologize to her friend the next day.)

"We got into her car and drove through the streets of Beirut from end to end. Then we walked for hours on Rawsha right by the roaring sea. On dark nights the violent, challenging, seductive sound of the waves is especially thrilling. There was a cold wind and rain. We went to a discotheque that was close by. I had never seen one before. It was dark inside except for a flashing red light that synchronized with the rhythms of blaring jazz music. It was like going into a mechanical womb, a return to the murky chambers of birth. We sat in a remote corner. I could hardly see my own two feet. A few young men and women were dancing, but we did not. We just drank. I kissed her many times. That night I could not sleep, and the following three nights were no better. A new man was born inside me; a dead man was resurrected. Beirut, the city of life and resurrection! I felt I had never been uprooted from the lands I owned in Abu al-Khasib. I no longer cared who picked the ripe dates of my lands so long as the irrigation water from Shatt al-Arab was brought to it. It was life that mattered. Emilia!

"I had to be discreet for a year or two. When I left Beirut, I went back to Abu al-Khasib. All that poverty! When would it ever end? Who would put an end to it?

"In Baghdad, two letters from her.

"There were moments when I felt we should remain in a state of stagnation, despite all the evils that were ravaging the country. I felt I would suffocate in such a brackish swamp. Everything I heard and saw ate into my heart like poison. I felt I was burning inside. For a man can behave like fire, can be eaten up from the inside, day after day. The mind gets hungry, and then the flesh, and so both mind and flesh search for an illusive fire to consume and be burned in, day after day, night after night. My mind would then address itself to things I could not define, to the most terrible, fugitive desires. I never thought about revealing any of this to you, because you did not care; at least, I never thought you cared, and I still do not....Feeling hurts; it stung me and it still does. Who, what, will soothe it? Like fire, the sting keeps on renewing itself, but for how long? The skin can apparently tolerate an unlimited number of stings, as many as it has pores. That's the way I have lived and still live the clamor of the skin— silently. Silence is killing me. I shall go to Beirut.

"Your dance last night was my death sentence. It helped me reach my final decision. I could have killed you yesterday. I don't know how I put up with it, how I listened to my better judgment and decided not to do it. Maybe I wanted to save you the blame and concentrate all on myself. You must live, no matter what happens. I'm finished. I'm waiting for the cruise to end because I don't want to create a fuss on the ship among scores of people who don't know me and whom I don't know. I don't want anyone to gloat over me. I've had enough. And I don't want anyone to gloat over you either. Let my little tragedy be ours alone. I shall send a letter to my brother in Baghdad placing all the blame on me, and I shall ask him to take good care of you. There's no need for you to show these papers to him or to any other member of the family. They are yours and mine, ours only. Yet, if some day you find that your conscience can no longer tolerate such a heavy secret, then... I leave it to your judgment.

"My dear Luma, as I have just been saying, we are in the age of worms. Worms, worms, worms, worms. Worms are in everything. People scramble about; they squabble and swarm all over each other like worms. They eat away at one another like worms, live like worms, die like worms. Beauty has no meaning, and I remain as unconvinced by talk of love as I always have been. Mere chemical secretions, instinctive frenzies, gyrations round and round the self: that is all we are.

"At this moment you're in the bar. I'm writing these words quickly before you come back because I don't want to confront you with them. I'm tired; I want to sleep, but I can't. The worm is in my heart and in everyone else's too. When? When will I be finished? What will you say about me? 'He never loved anything, not even himself.' Not so! At times I loved my work. Sometimes I loved you too. And I loved this other woman. But the worm has defeated me. What will happen to Emilia in the future?

"Even if I wanted to put my hand in the flame of a burning candle, I couldn't do it. And yet the thought of death no longer scares me. But pain, pain is something I can no longer face every day. The deep wound in my soul is bleeding and festering. I can't stand it any more.

"Jealousy? Perhaps.

"Yet what I feel is something more horrible than jealousy, more pervasive, more profound. It's something related to darkness as it was known and understood in centuries of old. The sun would set, and a terrible blackness would descend everywhere; the streets would empty of people, and everyone would go to sleep; the little oil lamps could not ward off the genies and demons, and the barking of dogs and jackals filled the air all around.

"That's the way I feel. Life is dark. The days are as dark as death. The ship is like a prison cell. The sea is an abominable monster. The sun is dark, and it's here in my heart, in my bowels, black and rigid, scoffing at everything, at you even, at our friends, even at Wadi Assaf. Is it jealousy? No. It's darkness. And the barking noise fills the four corners of the earth.

"In Baghdad, I consulted some of my colleagues about my depression. I kept it a secret from you. None of them could bring himself to tell me frankly that I was schizophrenic. They speculated about the cause and beat about the bush. I used to dismiss the entire subject with a laugh. My sober moments were terrible because they let me see the more fearsome aspects of my own self. I had to drink or die.

"Why on earth did he do it, people will ask. He was a successful surgeon, his wife was beautiful (and so was his mistress, they may add); he made lots of money and was in his mid-thirties. So what demon can have tempted him to commit suicide? Anyone would think the whole thing boils down to wife and money; as though life can be bribed into modifying its internal laws to accommodate man's destiny. Wadi talked to me about a crisis in history, a return to the land. Mahmud spoke of revolutions still on the drawing board. I spent my entire life searching for crises and revolutions such as these. Yet my humanity was always rejectionist, because it was maimed, disfigured, crushed from within and without. I reject the age of murder, the age of frustration. I reject despair. And now at last I reject hope. I wanted to rise above human beings, their concerns, their wretchedness and their cruelty, but I have failed. Something is making me digress along a path that I cannot comprehend, something elusive, which is felt by all the senses and yet manages to double-cross them all. It's like time, which we can feel but cannot grasp or preserve. It envelops us, keeps us company, flirts with us, and overpowers us until we reach our final limit: dust. Everything besides dust is a lie. I am trying to put all this down in written form, but words only confuse the issue. What began as a torrent of blood congeals into a black spittle which tells me that I am deluded. I can deal with a single disappointment; to put an end to my life because of a disappointment would be despicable. Something in the blood runs deeper, it is more profound, more tyrannical and more insistent. This is the real crisis, and this is how I eradicate it.

"In an age of tyranny, to accept life in silence is to be a tyrant yourself. And if all roads lead to the mill of tyranny, where can you turn?

"To L:
"These are my last words. I did not go to Capri. Instead, I went with Emilia to Naples. In the restaurant where we were having breakfast, I saw you with Isam, as I had expected. When you pretended to be sick and said that you did not want to go to Capri, I knew why. But you too, without realizing it, gave me one last chance to be with Emilia. I saw you both disappear into the crowded streets. There's nothing left now except a little darkness. Don't judge Emilia too harshly. If there's any room left for remembrance, I shall always remember the woman who loved me during my hour of weakness and during my fall.

"I would have liked to go to Amalfi and Sorrento with you. Maybe tomorrow. But the hour has come, and it's stupid to procrastinate any further. It's strange, but this is the first time I can honestly say I feel good. Just a few pills, and it's all over.

"Worms, worms."

Wadi Assaf

Maha could not have been coming to Naples on a worse day. I thought it would be a day of rejoicing, one that all our friends on the ship would share with us. But from the very beginning it turned out to be a day of mourning. Even the sun looked weighed down by shock and foreboding.

I will not pretend that I could not sleep the previous night in anticipation of her arrival. I left the card game and wished Falih and the others good night, and then went to bed, although I did talk to Fernando about our trip to Capri. I had a good sleep till morning. As a result of my long experience with the complexities of life, I am able to put pressing problems right out of my mind until the moment when I have to face them. Then I can face them with a clear mind and cool nerves. For the duration of this voyage, I had intended to blot Maha from my mind so completely that the mention of her name would evoke nothing at all. Then, if she came later, I could view everything in a fresh light. Deep down, I felt sure this woman was the one I would come back to, whatever I did and wherever I went. If at the start of the voyage I had pictured myself discarding her like an old overcoat, at least the overcoat was mine. I realized I would only feel warm again when I went back and put it on again. So why didn't I give up Jacqueline? Because I had no need to; in fact, I needed her on the voyage, for getting off at the various ports we visited, for walking round the sites we toured with guidebooks under our arms. Through Jacqueline—and through Isam, and the others, in fact through all the passengers on the ship—I was cleansing my soul of the sin I had committed against Maha, or rather the sin that we had both committed. Then, if we met in Naples—assuming that she did not send another telegram to cancel the first one—I would come back to her a renewed lover, one who had wiped the previous pages clean and come back virgin pure.

Was I fooling myself? I don't think so. I wanted Maha to be one of the rocks of Jerusalem, a rock on which I could build my city. Needless to say, I did not talk to her in such symbolic terms—occasionally they're too obscure even for me. However, the memory of Fayiz was still as fresh as ever in my mind, as though he had never been killed. The land we both loved as we wandered back and forth, day and night, through the streets of Jerusalem and the surrounding villages still represented everything we both loved and everything I still love. In all of this, past and present were closely intertwined, each one of them alive and pointing to the other. And after I had been away for so many years, Maha was gradually taking her place in this involved mesh of everything I hold dear. When I was angry with her, I felt like someone trying to pluck his feet out of his own soil. I wanted to get away from all the things that weighed me down and exhausted me through love, dreams, craving—and frustration. With Maha I came to realize how a man can kill the person he loves.

The few occasions when Maha and I quarreled were all false starts, just like this one. Each time we had to start again, to go back to the rock. The sea is foreign to me, however much I love it. However much I enjoy wandering among islands, I can find no haven there. I have to go back to the land. Ulysses was a much better sailor and voyager than any of us. Yet even he, like us, would escape so that he could eventually reach somewhere where he could plant his feet firmly on land and say, "This is my soil." And, when he most needed rest after the toils and travails of his voyage, did not Calypso the enchantress give him the choice of remaining with her on the island forever as a deity or returning to his homeland as a mortal man? Yet he refused immortality and chose to return home. Maha will doubtless come to see that too. Let Jacqueline or any other woman, for that matter, be another Calypso. In the end, mortality with your land is better, more enjoyable, and more profound. As soon as Maha can see that, there will be no more disagreements between her and the things I love. The two halves will become one again as they should. I will take her to my own land and then I will plough them both.

Poor Falih. Judging by what I have learned today and what I already knew from our conversations in the past few days, I can only view his tragedy in the framework of this very same issue of land with which he too felt at odds. He came to feel that they were chopping away at his roots with axes, chopping insistently, brutally, ferociously. So he got angry, he yelled, and he resisted.

Eventually he saw himself as a trunk that had been cut up and left on the land of his fathers and forebears. Maybe I can only say this because I now know about his suicide. Yet perhaps he was just too strong and stubborn to have his roots torn up, however hard the axes came down on him. Could his suicide have actually been a victory over the people who were brandishing their axes in his face? Whatever the case may be, I felt a tremendous sense of loss at his suicide, even though we had spent such a short time together. Life today seemed as though it had lost a wonderful part of its essence. I felt that too, as I waited for Maha to arrive from Rome.

I was very worried about Luma. Even so, her composure amazed me as she responded to the questions that the detectives who rushed to the ship were asking about her husband. She was at her most beautiful: austere, melancholy, and silent. Her brown complexion was dangerously radiant, and her big eyes looked like two seas of gloom drowning anyone who looked at her. Even then I sensed that she was challenging anyone who looked at her to say, 'As soon as I look away from you, I'll forget you.' But like an actress who had forgotten her part and was left standing on the stage, she had nothing to give: all she had left was her face and figure. She was like a rose without any scent (they say the most beautiful roses have no scent at all); like a marble palace with its doors and windows wide open, but all you could see through them was an empty void adorned with the frost of a long, icy winter. Was that what Falih had discovered in her? Had he failed to find the warmth he yearned for whenever he found himself totally naked in the midst of those raging blizzards filled with the howling of wolves and dogs?

But Isam saw something else in her. He was running away from her and rushing towards her at one and the same time. He had been caught in vicious circles for many years; he too was running away from his land, without which he would have been nothing. I wonder if his affair with Luma had anything to do with Falih's suicide? Very little, that's for sure; Falih's papers show that clearly enough. I was really stunned when I recalled what Mahmud had said just a few days earlier: that he could smell the whiff of suicide in what the Doctor was saying. Even if he was right, I still don't think he had specified the real reason.

Emilia was the only one who was really weeping. Her eyes and nose were red from uninterrupted crying.

"Wadi," she told me, "you'll never know how much I loved

him. You'll never know. Only Maha knew. She's arriving today just in time to see me die..."

"Why didn't you tell me from the start?"

"How could I when you're one of them too?"

"One of whom?"

"Oh, one of those who'll never agree..."

"What about Maha? Does she really know?"

"Everything, for over two years. She's the one who introduced us and then left me to it. She used to tell me all about you every time you came to see her from Kuwait, and I talked to her about Falih when he came to see me from Baghdad."

"But, Emilia, was there...anything between them, I mean Falih and Maha?"

"No, I don't think so. Otherwise, I wouldn't have risked starting an affair with him. I don't think he'd seen her before that conference or saw her afterwards either..."

I laughed at the incongruity of it all, at the irony of this total stranger actually being someone who had a connection of some kind or other with my life without my even knowing about it. Does Isam have some previous connection too which I don't know about? What is it that has brought us together on this ship?

"So you'd made previous arrangements with Falih then?" I asked Emilia.

"Arrangements? What for?"

"For coming on the voyage, even though he was coming with his wife?"

"Of course. We planned the whole thing together."

"But you told me you'd made your plans with Maha."

"Yes, that was after Falih had told me the name of the ship we would be traveling on."

"Terrific! So my coming on this voyage was all due to arrangements made by Maha via arrangements made by you via arrangements made by Falih! Fantastic! That's the way things happen by chance on these wonderful sea voyages! I wonder if Falih really chose this ship himself?"

"Luma had fixed things that way!" Emilia replied, smiling through her tears.

"Oh no!" I shouted. "That's just too much!"

"I can see it all now," she continued. "Luma decided to travel on this ship because she knew Isam had reserved a place for himself!"

She was fooling herself, apparently relishing the thought of

190

some kind of conspiracy against Falih. I knew all about the affair which Luma and Isam were having, of course, but it still amazed me to see Emilia tracing the fact that we were all on board the ship to a specific moment in time when an Iraqi architect named Isam Salman had decided that he wanted to spend several days at sea far away from his own country on his way to a distant exile! But Emilia meant what she said. The tears kept streaming silently down her face; from time to time she would take a Kleenex out of her handbag to wipe her cheeks and blow her nose.

"When's Maha arriving?" she asked me as she cried.

"I hope she won't be too long," I replied. "I feel a tremendous sense of loss."

"What about Jacqueline?"

"I think she's gone into Naples."

Just then, she took a letter out of her bag. "Do you know about this?" she asked. "It's a letter from Falih. He left it for me before he committed suicide."

Isam had told me about it when he showed me the file of papers which Falih had left behind to justify his suicide. I had seen Isam for just a few minutes before he became tied up with the captain, other ship officials, and the detectives. He now had to help the woman who had become his responsibility. I got the impression that his lower lip was swollen and cut. When I asked him about it, he responded that he would tell me about it one day. I was well aware, of course, that he had not exactly spent an innocent night; those wounds were really love bites that had eventually shown up on his body. One thing about such wounds, however, is that they require more than one body to dig into.

"Is there anything in the letter," I asked Emilia, "to reveal secrets or details which might help the detectives?"

"What do you think?" she said with a loud sob, the letter shaking in her hand. "It's just a few lines in which he says 'farewell' and 'I love you'..."

Mahmud walked past us, with Yusuf and the Egyptian girl behind him. He looked sad and upset.

"Didn't I tell you he'd commit suicide?" he said, anticipating me.

"What really matters is why he did it," I replied.

"Didn't he leave any papers or a will or something..."

"Certainly. I read through them quickly."

"What were the reasons, then?"

"Very complicated."

191

"It seems to me that by his suicide a complete segment of society is removed from the stage of our life."

"You're right," I replied angrily. "It's that group of intellectuals who dare to defy the sword of tyranny. And it's rapidly disappearing."

"No, no," he said, "that's not what I mean. Our world's in the middle of a tremendous upheaval, and this is just one of its symptoms. But do you know what the passengers are saying? That last night in the bow of the ship he saw his wife in the arms of another man. So he committed suicide."

"Rubbish. Just look at the way Emilia can't stop crying."

He shook his head looking utterly depressed. "If only you knew, Wadi!" he said. "If it weren't for Emilia, I wouldn't even be on board this ship today."

"You too, Mahmud! Impossible!"

But he did not understand what I was alluding to. He did not realize that he too had been led on this sea voyage by the wishes of a young man whom he had never heard of.

"And what did I get out of it?" he asked. "She ignored me and turned her attentions to Isam. And now here she is weeping over the Doctor...the Doctor! Aren't things incredible?"

"Didn't you tell me you'd given her up some time age?"

"I tried, I tried," he replied miserably. "I'm bad luck personified. Even my Egyptian girlfriend has left me for Yusuf."

Just then, he looked round. "Yusuf, Iffat!!" he yelled.

They came up to us.

"I'm Cyrano," Mahmud said. "All I need is the long nose! Do you know Cyrano de Bergerac, Iffat? Or was he way before your time?"

Iffat gave a laugh. "But Yusuf's the one who writes poetry," she said.

"He writes free verse and uses my back as a cover to look at you while I'm reciting rhymed verse! I've just about got you interested and then...Come on, confess, Yusuf! That's the way it always is for me with women, Wadi..."

"And politics too?" I asked.

He opened his eyes wide behind those thick spectacles glinting in the morning sun and raised a hairy hand with its long index finger.

"Politics is another matter," he said.

"What about Nimr Ajami, for example? I notice you aren't talking about him. What happened to him?"

192

"The swine escaped. They smuggled him off the ship. As soon as we reached port, they got him off. I looked for the so-called Greek sailor throughout the ship, but couldn't find him."

"Is that so? That easily?"

"Things are more complicated than you imagine," he responded in a low voice, as though he did not want Iffat and the others to hear. "No matter, no matter! Our voyage is only just beginning."

It was not difficult for me to decide that Mahmud was still slightly 'out of it' as a result of his psychological trauma, even though he made a good show of being fully recovered. His thick lower lip was quivering a little as he tried to manufacture a smile. He turned towards the brown-complexioned girl with the circular, green earrings.

"What rubbish has Yusuf been pouring into your ears this morning?" he asked.

"Rubbish?" Iffat replied, allowing a ringing laugh to emerge from between her pearly white teeth. "He told me I was the queen of women! But he's a big pessimist: he doesn't believe that contact between people is possible."

"Don't disgrace me," Yusuf shouted, trying to stop her, "I'm at your mercy!" He turned towards me. "Every time I recite a line of poetry, this girl has it memorized," he said, grabbing her by the arm.

She wriggled out of his grasp coquettishly. "Do you think I'm studying acting for nothing?" she said. "As I said, this lover-boy here does not believe that genuine contact is possible..."

"Don Juan trying to escape from Hell?" I said.

"On the contrary," replied Mahmud. "He's trying to stay right there. In any case, it's rubbish. Unless poetry deals with the struggle..."

"As you wish, sir," said Yusuf. "My next poem will be exactly as you wish."

During all this, Iffat made it clear that she would love to recite Yusuf's poem. "Listen to the words he dedicated to me this morning," she said.

"I know what he's going to say," Mahmud butted in. " 'The laughter of the Nile upon your lips digs tunnels of passion in his mountain heart...' or something like that."

"No, darling," Iffat said. "Listen. This is the way he woos me:

Can we ever come really close?
Can we say that what we share
Is love, with souls intermingled like wine?

Mere Fable!
Stars we are, each one swimming in its firmament.
What each sees of the other
Is but a gleam flashing forever from afar.
Drawing close without contact.
Mouth on mouth is just
One gleam to another
From sphere to sphere across the skies
And contact can only be
An anomaly·in the cosmic law:
A collision leading the two stars
To their destruction..."

For several seconds, there was absolute silence, a silence of participation in the anomaly in the cosmic law. All around us could be heard the noises of the ship, the repetitive lapping of the waves, shouts from afar perhaps directed at us from other worlds. I continued to look at the dockside through the railings, waiting for that gleam which I could distinguish from all others: Maha. Maha, where are you? But did the cosmic law, I wonder, bring Falih to a collision? With whom did he collide? Himself? And did Isam send a beam from his own galaxy to Luma, only to discover that contact was an illusion? Or was it that the anomaly in the cosmic law embraced him too?

I felt we were fooling around. They had come to take Falih to the autopsy room in one of the city hospitals. They took him away oh a stretcher wrapped up in a white sheet, went down the gangway with great care, and put him into a waiting ambulance. A large number of men and women had gathered around and were asking each other questions; they looked shocked and distressed by what they saw. Emilia kept pacing back and forth by herself near one of the lifeboats. The minutes ticked by, heavy and oppressive. Eventually, Iffat took Yusuf and Mahmud away towards the gangway. Stars we are...each one swimming.... The ship was almost empty of passengers, while the sea glistened brilliantly under the hot sun.

There she was, Maha! She was wearing a white dress with a white handbag to match, no doubt asking one of the sailors on the dockside which was the right ship. "Maha, Maha!!" I yelled at the top of my voice, and waved. She heard me and then saw me. I sped down the rickety gangway.

How wonderful you feel in my arms, cool even in this heat, like a glass of water from a mountain spring. How lovely your lips, your cheeks, your hair, your body, which is so full where it wants to be. Maha! What's the color of your eyes? Let me be sure. Black? Hazel? Honey? No. These are reflections from the sea. "Wadi, what's the matter with you? Have you gone crazy? Take me up on board the ship. I've been dreaming about it all night. Is it white? Clean? Two funnels? Do you dance all night? And you talk...you keep talking, that's for sure, Wadi, or can't you find anyone to listen to you?"

I spoke, I driveled, I bickered, I advised, argued, assured, denied, remembered, requested, provoked, babbled...the sea unlocked my tongue like some hallucinatory drug...

We had barely reached the top of the gangway when Maha shouted, "Emilia!" They hugged each other and kissed each other on the cheek. "What's this, Emilia?" Maha asked. "Have you been crying?"

"He's dead, Maha, dead! He committed suicide." Emilia gave a sob and then burst into tears again.

"Who?"

"The one man, Maha, who meant everything in the world to me."

It was wrong of us to spring this sad news on Maha. After all, she had not really been involved at all; apart, that is, from the fact that, one day, more than two years earlier, she had met a doctor who had liked her. However, it had been her friend Emilia, just deserted by her husband, who had obviously felt more inclined to respond to him. I really wanted to take Maha far away from all this, but her sympathy for Emilia was much greater than I had expected. Her eyes filled with tears immediately.

"And here I was trying to imagine you all spending such happy evenings together at sea...Wadi, have you been taking good care of Emilia?"

"Has anyone not been?"

"But you haven't seen Luma," said Emilia.

"Should I?" Maha answered.

I longed to go into Naples. However, I had decided to wait till Isam and Luma finished with the detectives investigating Falih's death. The interrogation had been going on for a long time in the Captain's cabin. They might need help.

Just then, Emilia took out of her handbag the letter that Falih had left for her. "I need your advice, Maha," she said, "now, while the problem's still fresh." She handed Maha the letter.

Maha read it quickly. At this point, I discovered that she was more beautiful than all the other women on the ship: more fun, more sympathetic; her voice was kinder, and her movements more graceful. A wave of love and pride engulfed me. Her hands! How long and slender her fingers were and how beautiful. On the little finger of her right hand she was wearing the carnelian ring I had bought her during one of my visits to Bahrain.

Maha looked up. "What about the check?" she asked. Emilia nodded her head and took a check out of the envelope that had contained the letter.

"Ten thousand Lebanese pounds, drawn on the Arab Bank in Beirut," she said.

I could not help laughing. "Is that what's bothering you?" I asked.

"Yes, it scares me. Why did he leave me ten thousand pounds? Shouldn't I tear the check up?"

"That depends on what the letter says."

"Read it, please."

I noticed that it was a full page long. "No, my dear," I replied, "you should think it over with Maha, not me."

Maha gave Emilia the letter back. "The important thing is not to tear up the check when you're feeling as you are at the moment. When a man who loves you as Doctor Falih Haseeb did commits suicide, minor things such as this lose their significance."

"But should I tell Luma? Should I give her back the check?"

"Listen, Emilia," I said, "after everything you've put up with, you've every right to keep something like this from Luma. If you tell her, you'll make her even more miserable. I don't think she'll be happy whatever you tell her, whether you keep the check or tear it up. In either case, you'll just make her and yourself feel even worse. Put the check back in your bag and forget the whole thing."

Emilia was not totally convinced, but she did slip the check into her handbag.

I took Maha's hand. "Now, come on and I'll show you the ship you refused to travel on. Come with us, Emilia."

"No, I'm going to wait here. You two have a lot to talk about. You don't need my problems."

Maha insisted that Emilia come with us, but she would not budge. So Maha and I went on our little tour of the ship.

"Tell me everything," she said. "First of all, were you faithful to me?"

"In my own way," I replied and gave her a kiss on the cheek as we were walking. "So didn't you go to your conference in Rome? Did you stay in Beirut?"

"Here you are playing around among the Mediterranean islands, and you expect me to broil in the Beirut heat and stew in my own anger in the clinic? After I sent you the telegram, I went to Rome and attended the conference. It's not over yet, not till tomorrow."

"Maha, Maha, another conference? Whom did you meet? Which doctor did you seduce this time, how many doctors in fact...?"

"Ha ha! Guess! I was just longing for the moment when your ship arrived. Do you know? Every time I found myself with a lot of people, I felt a huge chasm opening up inside me. Only your face, your voice, and your endless words would fill it up."

"You're talking as though you're beginning to love me."

"Beginning? You unbeliever, you traitor! This little fingernail of yours is worth all the conferences in the world."

"We'll go to Jerusalem then and settle there?"

"Can there be any other city for me when you're there?"

"Go on, go on! I've started loving your voice too..."

About an hour later, we met Isam and Luma face to face. They looked weary and exhausted. I was delighted to see them greet Maha so warmly; in fact, they seemed to come to life once again in the incandescence of this meeting. Everything was over now: the authorities were convinced that Falih had committed suicide, although they were still waiting for a final report from the police doctor in the city.

"So our journey ends here, right in the middle," Isam said.

"On the contrary," I replied, "it's just beginning."

I noticed Isam and Luma exchanging glances.

"I insisted to Isam that he continue his journey to London," Luma said. "He has a job waiting for him there. But he's adamant about staying with me until I return Falih's body to Baghdad by plane."

"That's only natural," I said.

"And I was the one who wanted to escape?" Isam muttered.

"This is where your myth has come to an end, Isam," I said. "It's gone up in smoke. The cordon around you has been broken. All you have to do is step over the rubble and proceed to the place where your freedom is to be found."

"In Baghdad, you mean?"

"Yes, in Baghdad. You won't find it anywhere else. It's not in that misty, illusory, enticing 'there' in Europe or anywhere else. There's the lapse into inanity; there's the real defeat. Do you realize, Luma, that Isam claimed he was running away from you? What I say is that he was running away from his city and his land. He'll never find his freedom anywhere else. Are you listening, Isam? It's in the alleys of your country, in its orchards, its deserts. Your freedom requires that you refuse to run away, face up to things, accept whatever pains you; that you know that pain, that anger, and the whole slow, agonizing progress. Your freedom involves your being an architect in your own country, however much it aggravates you and contrives to hurt you."

Maha poked me in the ribs. "Is the sermon over now?" she asked with a laugh. "Did he spend all this time preaching to everyone on the ship, Luma?"

"Actually," Luma replied, "we enticed him to talk because we love the sound of his voice. Even Falih. Just two days ago, he told me he had been wrong about Wadi. 'He's as innocent as a child,' Falih said, 'and loves like a child, too. He talks out of love, whereas I only talk out of...'"

But before she could say that ugly word, I interrupted her. "Not out of hate. Certainly not. Out of anger. Falih was the greatest lover in the world, but an angry one. Lovers always suffer a tragic end."

Luma burst into tears, the first time she had done so that morning. Her wailing was loud and painful. We sat her down on a chair. She carried on sobbing in a way which I had not seen for ages, in fact not since I had watched my mother mourning my father, tearing her hair as she sobbed. Maha may well have felt alarmed to find herself unexpectedly dragged into other people's grief, but in any case she sat down beside Luma. Isam took me to one side. He looked so worn out; the strain showed in the muscles in his face.

"I'm going back to Baghdad with Luma, of course," he said, "but I can see no solution to my own problem. Can you? As far as I'm concerned, Falih's suicide was in vain. It neither moves things forwards nor backwards. He wasn't a rival, even in his marriage to Luma. For us to marry was impossible from the very beginning. Don't you see? The basic obstacles are still there."

I was so furious, I felt the blood rushing to my head. "Haven't you had enough of your tribal nonsense?" I snarled, grabbing him by both arms and shaking him hard. "When are you going to be willing to face the storm in order to get what you want?"

"Just tell that to the woman weeping over there," Isam replied. He leaned his whole weight on the railing, looking as though he would collapse from sheer exhaustion.

That evening, the four of us disembarked shortly before the ship sailed. Emilia preferred to remain on board. In spite of all our attempts at tact, we discovered it was difficult to bring Luma and Emilia together during those particular hours that were so miserable for both of them. That is why I could hardly believe my eyes when they fell on each other in tears when it came time to say farewell.

"Do you hate me, Luma?" Emilia asked.

Luma shook her head sadly. "No, Emilia," she replied. "I hope you were able to inject a little sweetness into his bitter life."

Then they embraced once again. We all did the same.

"I'll write to you from Baghdad," said Isam.

I kissed Fernando on both cheeks, and we agreed to meet in Beirut. He told me he would play me a special tune he was composing, one which had just started playing itself over and over again inside his head. He told me he would put it into Arabic; after all, he said, all Spaniards, Lorca included, are Arabs....

Then we said farewell to the many people who in the interim had returned to the ship. But Jacqueline had disappeared; I could not find her anywhere. We waved from the dockside at the people standing by the railings. I gave a start when I saw the glint of Mahmud's glasses a short distance behind Emilia. And there was Jacqueline's youthful face; she was giving us a gentle, cautious wave.

We got into the taxi. "Hotel Quirinale," said Maha confidently to the driver. "Emilia recommended it to me!" she said, turning towards me.

We decided to stay in Naples for a few days while Luma fulfilled her difficult responsibilities. We took rooms on the fifth floor of the Hotel Quirinale—in separate rooms, of course. Two or three hours later, we all gathered again for dinner. As we were going down in the elevator from the fifth floor to the dining room, Maha told me that Emilia had admitted spending the previous day with Falih in this very hotel, in fact, on the same floor. That was why she was so glad to send us all to it!

That made me laugh, but then so did many things because they were very sad. I remembered Falih and his rebellion against people's meanness, lies, oppression, and cruelty. I thought of him, glass in hand, as he quivered with rage at all the treachery he had seen in people, and as he opened the small tube and swallowed the pills with a curse of protest. How many people would read his memoirs? How many people would ever know the other side of him? That he loved Emilia, that he did not hate Luma?

At dinner our conversation ranged far and wide. I kept trying desperately to bring the talk back to the other side of things, the side which Falih knew, the side which I wanted us—Maha and me, Isam and Luma—to know. In the storm there is rapture for the body; in agony, victory for the soul; in facing the enemy, the pride of rejection. Only on this basis can I be happy with anything. To be able to say "no" is a right that I will cling to with my very fingernails, my very teeth, even if it makes me bleed. To say "yes," that is a revelation I'll cling to with my fingernails and teeth too. Deep down inside me, when I reach down with my fingers—however difficult it may be—through all the layers of my experience, black and painful, there still lurks that innocent, simple, loving, heedless youth, Fayiz' twin, aged fifteen, sitting on the threshold of the old building eating a small pretzel with thyme and sketching people's eyes, overflowing with the fountainheads of life itself.

Just then, Isam looked at his watch. "It's midnight," he exclaimed. "They'll have just finished dancing on the ship."